Court of Snakes

This Desert Cage

Court of Snakes: This Desert Cage

Text copyright © 2022 by Tycho Dwelis

Originally published as Crowning Justice

ISBN-13: 978-1-948740-05-0

LCCN: 2022906468

To my supporters who are so constantly uplifting. Thank you for keeping a sinking ship afloat while we paddle through life.

Contents

Roadkill
Terran

The Slums, January of the First Year

A puddle flowed out across the river rock cobblestone, catching on the lips of the uneven masonry, the red, coagulate ooze staining the gray as it passed. Someone's nasally, violent laughter chortled among the discordant murmur of the crowd passing by, feet on stone, wheels in puddles. Terran's eyes trailed from the sky, which he had hoped would swallow him up, down to the dead man that lay in the street. The pickpocket, who had made off with some poor sap's coin purse, had run straight into a mammoth, the beast that was commonly ridden by the rich in the city of Segeno. Because they were enormous creatures, with dark, gray, leathery hides and large lower tusks, the mammoth crushed the pickpocket flat. It plowed over him right in the middle of the road, blood smeared onto uneven cobblestone, and trumpeted out in indignation, not even stopping to acknowledge what it had crushed. The driver didn't even take a second glance.

Mammoths terrified Terran. Ancient humans caged away

7

the beasts in places called "zoos" to keep them away from common folk. After the Great War, humans released the beasts and trained them as transportation animals for the exorbitantly wealthy. The pictures in ancient texts portrayed them as playful and intelligent, but all Terran saw were sharp tusks and monstrous feet.

The packed streets flooded with people walking on their day-to-day commute and many of the citizens that passed by did not stop to assess the condition of the pickpocket, whose life had ended instantaneously. Terran could not comprehend their apathy and, if circumstances were different, he would have shouted out and chastised them all for their lack of empathy.

A man behind him donned in white robes and shining, silver armor, doubled over with laughter and leaned on a nearby stall for support. "D-Did you," he snorted, "did you *see* that?"

He strolled out into the road, glancing both ways cautiously before he did so as to not suffer the fate of the pickpocket and searched the dead man's body. Still, no one noticed or cared and some even dodged around the dead man like he carried the plague. Terran scanned the crowd for guards. They should have been there, preventing this crime, finding out who the thief was, and who the victim's family was in order to deliver the news of his death. Terran spotted not a single shining, metal helmet among the cloth hats and bare heads, and a stone dropped in his stomach.

He kept his distance from the dead body, standing in the alleyway where they had just been chasing the thief. The stranger took the coin purse from the thief's mangled hand and tossed it in the air, catching it again. "*See?*" he quipped. "Told you we'd get back all our money."

"Erik?" a man behind Terran asked.

"Yes, Your Majesty?" the man in white replied.

"What did you see?"

"A *moron* get what's coming to him splattered face first into the pave—"

"I saw the unfortunate loss of human life," his partner spat, his armor glinting in the sunlight as he shifted, his lips cold and pressed into a thin line. "What did you *see*?"

The first man, rat-like in the face and pale in complexion, straightened up and coughed, putting his arms behind his back in stiff respect. "Nothing, sir."

"Head back to base. I'll have words with you later."

Like a child receiving a scolding, the man in white ducked away and out of sight. Terran shuddered as someone put a hand on his shoulder. The person behind him pulled a playing card out of his pocket, and bumped Terran on the arm to get his attention. Terran glanced over at him, a sour taste in his mouth. Death made him sick. The card the man held in his hand, edges worn from common handling, had a beautiful diamond design on the back of its grungy, mud and blood-stained surface, and the diamond shifted and moved in the light.

The man flipped the card over to show the other side and revealed a beautiful woman etched into the front who held two scales, on which rested an assortment of objects: gold, jewels, bones, and a feather. In her other hand, she held a sharp, pointed sword. Terran gazed into the card, trying to understand the joke.

The card went back into the stranger's pocket, and he inhaled, as if burdened by an unseen weight, and muttered, "You

9

see? Blind, perfect Justice."

When Terran thought it was time to move on, the man began searching the rest of the pickpocket's body. He retrieved another bag and stuck it in his pouch, his eyes shifting from side to side to check if anyone cared. "And," he murmured as soon as he was close enough to Terran to be heard, "we made a little cash."

He moved back into the alleyway and motioned for Terran to follow him. The buildings of the district that they moved through were different from what Terran had known his entire life, and every turn brought new sights. He had grown up with the security of a sturdy house and clean streets, glittering palaces and the comfort of roof over head. Here, the dilapidated buildings fell lopsided, holes in shingled roofs and cracks in walls. Pools of rainwater formed in the streets to create muddy obstacles that passersby had to avoid. If one wasn't paying attention, they would end up ankle deep in mud.

To accommodate for the large number of people that lived in this district, buildings smashed up against one another like sardines in a can and, in some cases, extensions of buildings shot up off of the tops of other structures, like some sort of growth. Everything smelled like sewage: the people, the streets, the air. A woman dumped her trash out of her window and onto the street below, and Terran gagged as the rotted food splashed into the mud. He hoped what he was stepping in was not other people's excrement.

"Discounted goods!" a man with a voice like sandpaper called. "Just got it out of the garbage yesterday! Only a day old!"

Where Terran had lived, there had been drainage systems

on the streets to prevent the sewage from bubbling to the surface. His roof never had holes to let the rain in. The cold drafts of the night could never penetrate his bedroom walls due to perfect insulation. In fact, he could not remember a time that he had ever been uncomfortable in his own home. In all honesty, he could not remember even knowing that this part of the city *looked* like this. The Atsa district was foreign to him and even the cobblestone beneath his feet betrayed him. The sky clouded over as they moved through the back, unseen ways of the city. He looked up to check the weather, and a figure in white flitted across the rooftops and out of sight.

Terran followed a man that he barely knew. He called himself The King. At least... that was what everyone around him called him. Before the pickpocket had stolen The King's money, The King had found Terran on a street corner begging for a few coins. After living the life of the rich, Terran had no idea what poorness meant, but when his stomach grumbled the first day, ached the second day, and then screamed out the third, he began to understand.

Terran had been trying to purchase some bread, and the nausea that crept up on him made it hard for him to even raise his hands above his head. The harsh life of the street hit him in full force, having been run out of his home by the guards that he had once called to for protection. He had been too terrified to enter the palace again, petrified by what he had seen. As the days drew on, people thought of him more as a street rat than as the future leader of Segeno.

By the fourth day, he sat there with his hands out in the

Atsa district and people passed him without even a second glance. A pair of street guards had approached him, long rifles in their hands and scowls on their faces. They had ordered him to come with them, and when Terran asked if they were going to take him home, they had snickered at him – spite he had never heard from a guard. They had always treated him with the utmost respect before. The disrespect made him angry, so violently angry, but he could do nothing with a starving stomach and trembling arms.

The guard had jabbed at him with his rifle and Terran was about to flee when he felt the presence of someone behind him. A man in bold colors stood there, and he grinned widely at the guards like someone who had heard a funny joke, a partner in white behind him, fists up.

"Hey there, fellas," he chortled. "What's going on here?"

"None of your business, citizen. Turn away," the guard curtly replied.

"I don't know, my friend. It seems that you two are unjustly cornering this poor, lost street urchin. Isn't it illegal to arrest underage persons, Erik?"

"That it is, Your Majesty," the man in white replied.

"We said to *leave*, citizen," the guard sneered through a metal-plated helmet. "Leave or we will have to take action."

The man in colored robes snickered, his hand on his hip. "You dare to challenge The King?"

The stranger drew a card and flipped it for them to see, a cheeky grin plastered across his face. He knew something the guards did not. Terran squinted in the noontime sun to get a better look at the card but could not see and he was so weak he

12

could not pull his head up. The King pulled a scarf he wore around his neck over his eyes as a blindfold, holding the card in his mouth while he did so. The guards were almost fed up with the stranger's antics when The King slammed the card onto the back of his bare hand, skin touching paper. It vanished in a puff of smoke and fire, as if by magick, and he drew two swords that rested at his hips. He spun the swords in his hands and shifted his feet in preparation for battle.

"Let's play."

The two guards primed their weapons, typical metal rifles carried by the city guard, and rooted their feet, unwilling to back down. Terran twisted around to face the stranger when he felt a strange humming in the ground. When he locked eyes with The King, his jaw dropped.

Bullets flew. Six sharp pieces of metal sliced through air and blocked the shots, deflecting the rounds into the adobe walls of the surrounding buildings. The King stood there, two swords in hand, blockaded by six others floating on their own accord. It was as if he had a magnetic field around his body and when he moved, the swords flowed with him. He attacked the guards, the swords maneuvering themselves with the strength of ten men. His opponents didn't stand a chance. When they both lay dead in the street, The King told Terran to come with him, the swords disappearing into a burst of light. Terran followed out of fear. They wandered the Atsa district for a while and The King doled out small bags of gold to citizens. The residents of Segeno addressed the stranger as "The King" or "Your Majesty" and bowed humbly after receiving the gift.

When they now passed groups of people that Terran's parents had told him to stay away from, the kinds that steal and murder, the criminals would bow to The King. The gesture held either quiet gratitude or adulation that Terran could not fathom. To add to Terran's uncertainty, the Atsa district was like nothing he had ever seen. He did not know what the people here did to survive, but where The King was taking him, passersby began to look worse and worse in dress and stature. Women and children turned to old men, and old men turned to young men with butcher knives and harsh expressions. Inconsequential drops of rain began to fall, a rarity in Segeno, and The King led Terran down a small flight of stairs, hidden on the side of the street and deep underneath the cobblestone. The stairs led to an underground room, tucked out of sight from the majority of the city.

The room was filled with men and women of all kinds and origins; some Terran recognized in the kind of dress his parents wore, others in rags. At the back of the large room stood a bar, and all around the chamber tables and chairs were scattered where some of the patrons sat. It appeared to be a tavern, but Terran doubted everything he saw. Most bowed to The King as they passed, a sign to Terran that they were allied with him in some way, and others eyed Terran with glances of distrust and disgust. The King took Terran to a small back room that was opened with a key The King had concealed in his sleeve. After Terran stepped through the threshold, the door fell closed behind him with a thud.

The back room was stuffed to the brim with objects of varied size and origin, the room too small to hold all its contents in an orderly fashion. Odd baubles and papers scattered in all corners of the room when the door closed, the draft knocking things about, and books that had no room on shelves formed makeshift tables on the floor. Bags, blueprints, plans, and letters were tossed on the floor and stuffed in books. A small bed, donned with silken sheets of bright violet and made with four sturdy wooden posts, stood at the left side of the room; a bed made only for one.

Violet, heavy-looking fabric hug from the posts, forming a tapestry that covered the stone walls, but was pulled back from the edge of the bed to make it accessible. An ornately carved wooden desk hid in the back of the room, masked almost in its entirety by all the clutter, and behind it sat a large, upholstered chair, worn around the edges from use. Drapes hung from the ceiling like fallen cobwebs, most in violet or gold, but one tapestry that drooped directly behind the desk had an image sewn on it that Terran had seen earlier: the woman with the scales. Terran strained to read the spines of the books to figure out exactly what this "king" wanted with him, but he found that most were in languages he could not read or, furthermore, had never seen. The King sat in the chair at the desk and motioned for Terran to sit in the opposite chair of the same fashion. Terran settled guardedly as The King pulled a deck of cards from his pocket, shuffling them as he began to speak. He asked, "So, I stumbled upon a street rat, did I?"

Terran said nothing as he watched the shuffling of the cards, which was smooth and easy in The King's hands. His pride would not allow him to speak. The King was ornately dressed, but that did not mean that he was one of Terran's origins. Those who were born of nobility in Segeno, like Terran, wore only white and blue; blue to mark loyalty and wisdom, and white for purity.

They were fair of hair and of skin to match the white of their surroundings, to show their clean blood, and, only occasionally, one would find a noble with dark hair.

The King had hair like fire, red with flecks of blond that glinted in the dim light, a chiseled face that exhibited the harsh life he had lived. His robes were woven from blue and purple fabric, but included flecks of gold, colors not native to any district. The cloak he wore swept the floor and it was only when he had entered the tavern that he had removed his hood. He looked like he had spent a good amount of coin on his clothing, but nevertheless, he was not one that Terran recognized from the district that he was born into, not royalty, and Terran refused to speak.

"I hear from some guys in town that you are the son of Theresa and Cedric, the Sovereign and her husband, am I right? Part of the Embassy, yeah? Rich folk?"

Pressing his thin lips together, Terran held his tongue and weighed his options. The man was exactly right, but he would not admit it. If the guards were out to kill him, Terran could trust no one. He had rarely left the palace before these last few days, but people knew his face. His face was on some forms of currency, and it was almost impossible to mistake the future ruler of Segeno. Unfortunately for him, he could hide from no one. This did not mean, however, that he would lower himself to this thug's standards and converse with the rabble.

"You would do well to answer me. Opposition won't help you, and if you think your status will prevent you from having to do what I say, you are *horribly* wrong. My word is law on the street. The Embassy wouldn't like to admit it, but I run this town, and anyone who says no to me, well..."

The King drew another card. It depicted a man rowing a boat, a man that was no more than bones, paddling across a wide river to take people to the opposite shore. The river was filled with screaming souls, and the bottom of the card read "Death."

"Yes. My parents are Theresa and Cedric," Terran barked. "What does it matter to you? You already knew that, and I know you're not stupid. Just cut to the chase."

"I saved your *life*." The King snapped, leaned back in his chair, and placed his feet onto the cluttered desk. "Those guards would have torn you apart. I don't know what they plan to do with you, whether kill you or toss you into the wastes to die, but right now I'm the only thing standing between them and you. The least you could do is show me a little respect."

"Just tell me what you want."

"Stop being a brat, and I will."

"I'm not a brat."

"Whatever you say, kid," The King chuckled as he pushed a book aside so he could rest his arm on the table. He leaned forward and Terran flinched. "So, tell me. What would make you take to the streets, hm? If you live such a wonderful life, all flowers and presents and whatnot, what would cause you to wander all the way down here to this little hole of a district?"

Terran recalled the last day or so and his eyes welled up at the thought. He ran, ran from men with guns and clothes splattered with blood. He turned down as many streets as he could to lose them. Days passed. Then there was a pickpocket and finally The King.

"I think my parents were murdered."

"Oh, boo hoo," The King sneered and slammed the cards on the table, causing a few sheets of paper to drift to the floor, as if they were a startled flock of birds. "And I suppose your entire life is over, then? Dozens of citizens of Segeno lose their parents to guard violence, poverty, and starvation every year. You ran? Instead of facing your problems like you should have, you turned and bolted?"

Terran swallowed and licked his lips, contemplating the statement. He had not thought of it as running. In fact, he had not thought of what he was doing, but he wished that he had stood his ground and fought. In the circumstances, what choice did he have? The Elite Guard had thrown him out onto the street and the Embassy put a good amount of the city's budget toward making them the best. Terran had never fought anything in his whole life, and he knew he did not stand a chance.

"Do you know how often I save rats like you?" The King mused.

"No."

"I don't *ever* save rats like you."

Terran's eyes met with The King's for just a moment. They were cold and gray, filled with years of hate, and wrinkles at the corners of his eyes indicated decades of stress. Terran scoffed, "Well, maybe I should get down on the ground and kiss your boots. If you don't like me, then why help me?"

"Because there's something in it for me," The King replied. He stood, took a knife that was sticking into the table out of it, and played with its sharp tip. "*You* are going to help me."

"Says *who*?"

"Says *me*," The King snarled, taking his blade and pressing it against Terran's throat, nearly cutting the skin. He was too close, his hot breath disturbing the blond hair on Terran's head. "You're going to help me take down the Embassy."

Terran shook his head and spat, "That's impossible. And why would you want that? They are the order of this city. Without them, there would be nothing."

The King's boisterous, wholehearted laughter was louder than Terran had expected, and it made him jump. "Do you *honestly* think that?"

"I won't do it."

"And *why* not?" The King asked, pulling the knife away, and went over to the only window that was in the room. The glass reflected colored light as a candle danced behind its stained panes. It led to nothing, seeing as the room was underground. The color of the glass gave an illusion of a sunset, and The King watched the light flicker, continuing, "You're not a part of their group anymore."

"Once in the Embassy, forever in the Embassy."

"Your parents are dead. That makes you nameless and alone. They threw you out into the street and are looking to *kill* you. Trust me. I saw the whole thing. You have no *choice*. Or, would you rather me turn you out, too, so the Embassy guards can pick you off like vultures and you can spend your last few days alive begging for a slice of bread? Before they take you back to the palace and have you executed?"

Terran fell silent again. He did not trust The King in the slightest and he certainly did not want to destroy everything his parents stood for, but what choice did he have? Starving to death did not sound at all desirable and an execution sounded even worse.

"I'll feed you, clothe you, give you shelter, help you survive. In return, you tell me all the Embassy's secrets."

Terran closed his eyes and waited for his heart to decide. He remembered his mother's face the last time he had spoken with her. She had been embroidering a hand towel by the window and had asked him what he wanted to do for his birthday that year. Her smile reflected her genuine love for him, and the realization sunk in again. He was alone. He bit his lip and swallowed like there was glass in his throat.

"Fine."

Treachery
Parisa

The Palace, January of the First Year

"My Lord, we... we lost him today."

"You *what?*" A man cloaked in white rose from a large, alabaster throne and glared at a guard who shook in his own armor. He moved not from his throne, but stood rigidly, as if ready to take flight at a moment's notice. Light filtered through the blue stained glass of the throne room and hit the man's face in peacock colors as the fabric of his robes settled at his feet. His words had bounced around the stone room and now that the echo had settled, the guard gained the courage to speak again.

"In the Atsa district," the guard choked. He nervously tugged at the blue tunic underneath his silvered armor. "We were attacked."

"You're telling me that little *brat* took out *two* of my Elite Guards?"

"N-No, sir. We suspect it was The King."

The man at the throne sunk slowly into his chair, faded

eyelashes guarding his ocean eyes from fleeting light. "My entire army is a joke."

"You don't understand, sir!" Another guard stepped forward into the light from the windows. Someone next to him, a man in scarred armor with a marred face, scoffed and folded his hands behind his back. The guard continued, "It was a bloodbath. He has outmaneuvered us at every turn while we've been trying to apprehend him. He's skilled and—"

"And you all are trained to be Elites! I do not spend thirty percent of the city's budget to train you all for this kind of result. Train your men. Train them hard and do *better.*" The man in white waved a hand at him, disgust on his face. "Get out of my sight."

As the guards left, followed by the man in marred armor, a cough echoed about the room.

"Commander Crevan."

Commander Crevan, whose battered armor caught the light of dim electric lamps that flanked the doorway, turned slowly as his subordinates left the room. He clicked the metal heels of his boots together and bowed stiffly, practiced and precise. "Yes, my Sovereign?"

"Put all guards on high alert," the Sovereign continued. He wove his fingers through the light coming into the window as he spoke, his tight lips a reflection of his disappointment. "If anyone even *thinks* they see the little twit, tell them to fire at will. Attack, even if he seems unarmed. Attack even if it's *not* him! Just kill the damn kid. He threatens my whole operation. If they're right, and he's working with The King now... you will need to be cautious. Do *not* underestimate him."

"Yes, sir."

With another tap of his boots, Commander Crevan dismissed himself and the grand glass doors to the throne room closed with a soft click. After all was quiet for a moment, the Sovereign sighed and sunk into his chair, stress weighing heavy on his shoulders. He pushed his fingers to the bridge of his nose and did not look up when the muted tap of footsteps approached him.

"Daddy?"

A loud sigh left the Sovereign's lips. It was a sigh of impatience. "Yes, darling?"

"Will everything be fine after you get rid of him? The boy?"

"Everything will be perfect. He is the last heir to the throne, so while he is in exile or dead, I can keep my place and you will be next in line."

His daughter nodded, her resolute, blue eyes tracing her father's face for answers. With a huff, she sat down in a pile of frills and skirts to continue to play with a doll. The doll's porcelain feet tapped against the marble as she danced across the floor.

"Don't you have something else to do?" her father asked.

"Oh, I—"

"And aren't you a little old for dolls, now? You just turned thirteen."

"I'm... I'm sorry, Daddy."

The Sovereign looked at her as if he was picking apart every facet of her face with judgement. "All will be well. Once Terran La'Hall is dead, everything... will be well."

"Then you'll spend time with me?"

"Yes," he huffed, sarcasm heavy on his words. "I'll play with you. Go bother Esmond. I don't have time for you."

The girl frowned. Master Esmond meant lessons, and lessons meant Economics. She twirled her blond hair, the only thing her father liked about her, in one of her fingers. She stood, bowed politely to the Sovereign, and made her way to the palace elevator. A boy just older than her pulled the lever after she informed him of her destination, and the compartment went whirring up toward the higher levels of the palace. Her frilly white dress rustled against the scratchy, sheer tights that covered her legs as she twirled it impatiently. Once the elevator doors opened and she had stepped free, out of sight and out of mind, she smiled at her little doll, a small doll with skin lighter than hers and a face that had a small black tear on its cheek. "Did you hear, Theophilia? He finally said he'll spend time with me."

Economics
Terran

Naa'a, January of the First Year

"See them, Terran?" The King perched with him on the edge of a rooftop, balanced perfectly on the corner of the adobe roof in the Naa'a district. His slender finger pointed down into the street below at the nobles that were walking leisurely throughout the city. Terran's stomach turned as he thought of how little it would take to send The King tumbling off the edge of the building and into the street below. The three-story fall would no doubt result in his death. The King had made Terran climb up the side of the building rather than using the stairs like *regular* people. Terran had never climbed anything in his life; not a tree, not a fence. Nothing. The wooden support beams from inside the houses jutted out the sides of the dried stucco and those the two had used to get up onto the roof, one ledge at a time. The climb had been torture, but now that they were at the top, the view, at least, was extremely rewarding.

The Naa'a district was one of the most beautiful portions

of the city because it had the funds to be. Each district contained approximately a thousand citizens, all from the far-flung corners of the region, the last survivors of the area. The city of Segeno was a symbol of hope to those who had nothing. One glorious mother of pearl spire jutted up from the desert, glistening in the sun, and wanderers from other settlements would see the Segeno Embassy Palace before anything else. A beacon of hope in a desolate world.

The palace rose from the heart of the city like a great crystal, tall and geometric, and the apex of it pierced the sky like a dagger. Blue, translucent windows reflected the burning sun. The surrounding, white adobe buildings clustered around the courtyard of the palace like matchsticks in a box. The palace was one of the only buildings in the city that had glass, salvaged from a great pyramid from the ancient times (or so it was said), and the Embassy researchers were hard at work building a new factory to turn sand into the substance again based on ancient manuscripts.

Much knowledge was lost during the Great War. The humans that survived had lived underground in safe havens to protect themselves from the stars that fell from the sky like meteors, blasting away everything the world had. The wastes that surrounded Segeno were one of the only things that left the city untouched; humans had not lived in the desert in the ancient times, so there had been no need to send stars there. Humans took as many knowledgeable books as they could with them into the havens, but they were unable to save everything. Scientists with valuable knowledge perished from starvation or disease in the underground, leaving those who survived to fight for mankind. That knowledge was enough, and Segeno had then been built from

26

the ground up with the finest ancient technology that the world had left. The Naa'a district was the pinnacle of modern technology, hope for the future, and a beacon for those wandering lost.

The Naa'a district was walled in, a large, silver gate keeping the working class out, and housed the richest citizens. The houses of those related to the members of the Embassy, the rulers of Segeno, butted up against the palace courtyard and allowed easy access to council sessions. Far below the edge of The King's boots and the corner of the roof, patrons wandered the streets. A few rode mammoths, descendants of once great creatures that used to be hunted for their ivory and trained for entertainment, and the beasts' blue-gray hide complemented the colors of the Naa'a district. The white of the stone path and the flowers that grew in planters matched perfectly with the clothes of the citizens. Everything was always beautiful and clean, bright and pure, as blue as a cloudless sky and as white as sandstone.

As Terran looked over the edge of the roof, his stomach turning and flipping out of fear of the fall, his eye caught the toe of his shoe. He looked down at his own clothing, a scowl on his face. A few weeks ago, they had been a perfect white, washed by a maid he had never spoken to. Now, they were a patchy cream in some places, brown in others. Even his fingernails were dirty. He was ashamed of the way he looked and missed the comforts of Embassy life.

The King watched the people below like a hawk, part of his gaze scrutinizing, some of it judgmental, and the rest contemplative. Terran tried to pick apart the subtlest movement of his master's eyebrows, the twitch of the corners of his mouth.

The King's face was very hard to read. "You were one of them," he muttered. "Tell me what they're doing."

"Some of them are just chatting, some of them are going to see others or run errands."

The King gasped sarcastically, "Some of them run *errands* by *themselves*? The *thought*!"

"Stop it. We're not all lazy and entitled."

"You sound like a brat."

"I am *not* a brat!"

"You're young enough to be a brat. How old are you?"

"I just turned fifteen."

"Right. Fifteen and already caught up in the lie."

"What do you mean, *lie*?"

"Don't kid yourself," The King replied. "You know what I mean."

"No, I—"

"What did you want to do when you grew up? You're a year from being a man. What was the plan?"

"Take over Mother's position as leader of the Embassy, but—"

"But now your mother's *dead*, isn't she?" he gasped sarcastically again. "Oh, too soon?"

Terran looked down over the edge of the roof, anger and irritation filling his heart. Who did this man think he was? Terran had half a mind to not let this stranger make light of what he had lost. But, then again, Terran had never fought anyone in his life. And what if he fell off the roof? He did not dare to come as close to the edge as The King.

"Look at all of these people," The King ordered.

Terran's eyes dropped to gaze at the ground. He crouched down, his legs stiff from the climb, but he did not look. If The King was going to be awful, he could be awful, too. The King paused for just a moment, but when Terran did not do as he was asked, he grabbed Terran's chin and pulled, forcing him to look over the edge of the roof. "*Look,*" he barked. "They don't care about you. They went right from a funeral to a coronation. Do you think they care where the crown goes? They just care about the money in their fat wallets. You could run right up to any of them, to one of your friends from school, maybe, tell them what happened, and they'd *still* turn you over to the guard."

"They wouldn't *do* that. I have *friends* that care about me. I've been trying to get back, but—"

"You know, there's an order going around the guard that states you are to be made dead on sight. Word of that hasn't hit the city yet. It never will. All your buddies probably think they're looking for you to help you."

"The guards are honest. They wouldn't—"

"They would. The guards keep well enough to themselves unless... persuaded. The man in power now wants you dead. Your parents died three weeks ago and he's already trying to make sure your bloodline stops. No you, no perpetuation of the policies your parents put in place. That's capitalist economics for you."

"No, it's just murder."

"Not quite. Not when you live in a place where killing the person on top entitles you to their funds. I want you to forget everything you know, everything you thought you knew.

Everything you wished to know about the Embassy. Forget it."

"That's my *family*. My *home*."

"Your family is dead and gone. Those people in there are certainly *not* your family."

"You don't even come close to family."

"No, you're right. I'm not your family. But you're going to have to listen to me if we want to make it through this."

"*We* are not a team."

"If you won't listen to me, listen to this."

The King pulled out the Justice card, the same card he had revealed after the pickpocket's death. The woman with the scales was blindfolded, Terran noticed now. He scoffed as he gazed out over the city again. The King spoke in cryptic phrases and riddles, and Terran did not appreciate it. "What's *that* supposed to mean?" he sneered.

"This is what I live by."

"Justice?"

"Justice," The King affirmed as he released Terran's face from his grip. "It's all we have. Those who roll in money, money they suck from people less fortunate, they need to face their faults. They may seem innocent, I know... your judgement is clouded. Nothing proves more faithful than Justice. She pulls those in the right from the ashes and tosses those in the wrong into the fire."

"That doesn't sound like justice. Justice is being fair, being guided by truth and reason. Your justice sounds like vengeance."

"You don't know *anything*," The King barked as he yanked Terran closer to himself by the collar, "about Justice. *You* come from a place where "justice" is snuffing people out when they oppose you. I am ruled only by fate and the cards, so whatever the universe has in store for me, I follow. You're ignorant now, but I'm going to change that. You're not a lost cause... yet."

"I'm *not* a lost cause."

The King stood and jumped from the building he stood on to the building adjacent to it, as swift as a swallow. "Come on," he called. "Follow me."

Terran stood at the edge of the roof and shook as he looked below into the street. From where he stood, he could see straight out into the Black Rock Desert and all the way to the mountains beyond the walls of Segeno. The view was glorious, but Terran was not going to jump. If he missed, he'd die. After living in the lap of luxury (although he wouldn't like to admit it), he was not sure what The King was asking of him. "I can't jump that!" he called back.

The King held up a card, pulling blindly from his pouch. "This is the Chariot," he explained. "It signifies just going with the flow. Just let your feet do all the work. They'll catch you."

Terran took a few steps back, swallowed, and ran. He charged to the edge of the flat roof, jumping with all his might to reach the other building. The gap was ten feet, at least. He was certain he was going to die. His feet hit the very edge of the roof and his weight rocked backwards like a pendulum. He swung his arms frantically, attempting to catch himself, and The King reached out to clasp his hand, pulling him back up onto the roof.

"Good job, kid," he said.

"Don't *ever* ask me to do that again," Terran gasped.

"Don't count on it. I'm going to teach you what it means to

31

be a part of fate, to be one with all the facets of the world. In order to do that, you need to become one with your surroundings. You know why that pickpocket was killed?"

Terran shook his head and guessed, "Because he was careless?"

"That, and..." The King looked over the edge of the building. "He took to the streets. *Never* take to the streets during a chase. The guards will cut you down faster than you can blink. Archers and gunmen are positioned all over the rooftops, especially in this district. Look."

The King pointed to a building not too far off and Terran could barely see the glint of armor in the sunlight. The gunman was well hidden amongst the white of the rooftops and was yards away.

"Not only that, but you get caught in crowds of people. They won't move for you. You would have to move them, which either requires a really big axe," he chuckled, "or the ability to run through steel. Up here, there's nothing standing in your way, which means the guards won't have enough time to aim at you. You only want to walk down below if you're hiding."

"This is stupid. I should be able to walk where I please."

"Not if you want to live. The guards will find you down there."

"They're going to find us up *here*. I don't see how this benefits us at—"

The King whistled and a man cloaked in all white jumped up onto the building from a place that had been in Terran's direct line of sight. Terran had not even seen him, he was so well camouflaged. "You don't have to be wearing all white in this district to be hidden," The King explained. "I mean, look at me. I'm basically a walking kaleidoscope of color and they still won't dare shoot at me. If you're fast enough, you can do whatever you want. The rooftops aren't just good for escape after a steal, either. They—"

"So, you just lead a band of thieves?"

The King frowned and dismissed the other man, who jumped back down to his hiding spot. "I lead a revolution," he retorted. "Now listen. They also provide a great way to assess situations. What do you notice about being up here?"

"I have a great view," Terran muttered sarcastically.

"Exactly," The King smiled. Terran's face scrunched in irritation at the correct answer. His master continued, "You can see whatever you want up here; everything that goes on down below. I will be training you every day to run these rooftops, in this district and in the Atsa. You'll have to keep up with me or else you'll get left behind. Let's go back to base."

"I don't *want* to run. I just want to go ho—"

Before Terran could finish his sentence, The King was gone, and he was left alone. He huffed an aggravated sigh, dug his toes into the rooftops, and ran.

ILLUSION
Parisa

The Palace, January of the First Year

"All right, Lady Parisa, tell me again what the definition of the word economics is?"

Parisa twirled Theophilia across her desk. In her mind's eye, Theophilia glided across the glistening marble floor of a grand palace from long, long ago, showered in the glittering, golden light from thousands of crystal chandeliers. In her daydream, a bird tapped at the glass window of the ballroom... and then Master Esmond rapped his ruler on her desk. The explosion of sound shot around the quiet study and Parisa nearly jumped out of her skin.

"Lady Parisa?" her teacher demanded again.

"Excuse me?" Parisa peered up at him as though she had not been listening.

Master Esmond growled in frustration, a soft vexation that was lessened by concern. "Can't you pay attention just *once*?" he asked. "I am *trying* to give a lesson in economics."

"But I don't *want* to study economics."

"Your father will be frenetic if you don't pass your examinations this week. He's perplexed and worried that you don't show any talent in academics. He just wants to see you succeed."

"No talent in academics? So, that makes me... what? Worthless?"

Parisa had heard the line before. Her father believed that a woman's place was inside, surrounded by books, away from everyone and everything. Women were good for spouting off random facts about Segeno history and providing entertainment at parties, nothing more. Too dull, and you were useless for those two things. Too smart, and you were a heretic. If Parisa was a failure in academics, she was effectively worthless. He never said it directly, but the logic followed.

"I didn't say that. He—"

"If he presumes that, maybe he should tell me himself."

"You know he doesn't want to offend you. He cares about you."

"Does he?"

"I believe he does."

"If I fail all my exams, really be the worst, he can stuff me somewhere and forget about me. That way I can be out of his hair."

"I wouldn't stand for it, dear," Master Esmond replied. "*I* want you to succeed."

"And *I* want to have a little fun again."

"You will," he affirmed. "We just need to keep your mind from wandering off."

"That's the only fun I have all *day*."

Master Esmond exhaled thoughtfully and kneeled next to

35

Parisa's desk. "Where did your imagination take you today?"

Parisa gazed out the window. The cloudless sky hovered blue and flawless all the way to the mountains that broke the horizon many, many miles away. "I imagined that Theophilia was a part of a grand circus," she said, "and that she performed an act in which she danced in a *huge* ballroom with a handsome harlequin."

Master Esmond straightened his stiff uniform and sighed with a lack of patience, "You are to be the next heir to the Embassy throne. You must be knowledgeable and well rounded, not partaking in the circus... at least, not at the moment. There will be time for that. I promise. Now, can you define economics for me?"

Parisa replied, "Economics is the scientific study of the distribution and production of goods."

"Good. So, you *have* been paying attention."

Master Esmond pulled up a chair and sat next to Parisa at the desk. Parisa watched his face as he looked over his notes. There were so many things she loved about Master Esmond, like the way he was far too tall, his long legs making him clumsy and too fast when walking, or the way his dark hair fell out of the pins that held it in place behind his head. Parisa most of all loved his eyes, dark and contemplative. The sun caught in his hair at that moment, glimmering off gray strands that were new and only becoming more numerous. His face was not hardened by the stress of nobility like the leaders of the other districts, and his expressions were always soft and caring. She loved seeing his face more than she liked looking at her own father.

"If you read a chapter of your lessons, I'll let you go outside with Theophilia and we can take our World History lessons under the trees in the greenhouse today," he offered.

Parisa's eyes lit up, she ripped her Economics book from her bag, and began devouring the words.

"We can only go outside," Master Esmond added as he wandered to the front of the classroom, "if you pass the quiz, so read carefully. Don't rush through it."

"But—"

"Read."

Coals
Terran

The Tavern, March of the First Year

"So, Terran, tell me of your parents."

"Why do you want to know?" Terran gasped and then held his breath as his bare skin brushed flame. He balanced on top of a few stacks of books on his elbows in a solid plank position, but underneath him, The King had placed a tray of smoldering coals. He had no doubt his arms would hold him now; he had been training hard. He could lift his body weight with ease up and down buildings after two months of rigorous instruction, so a plank was no problem. At least, it would not have been a problem if the wobbly, precarious piles of books and scalding, hot coals had been removed from the equation. Sweat dripped down his nose, hissing as it hit the embers below, and The King set a cup of tea onto his back. The small office filled with heat as Terran balanced and it became hard to breathe.

"I'm just curious, is all," The King muttered, ignoring Terran's strained breathing and speech. "I only knew them from the political side, which was… a disaster. Your mother had the potential to fix this city, she was a good person, but she lacked foresight. Now, everything is falling apart, and it's only been months since she passed."

Terran took as deep of a breath as he could while trying to not shift the hot cup of tea. "I never saw my mother," he grunted. "She was working always, but when I did see her, we used to have the grandest times. She would take me out and we would go on adventures in the courtyards. We would pretend that there were horrible beasts to face, and my grandfathers would visit, and—"

"Child's play," The King snapped, took the tea again, and slid a card from his coat pocket. A small, nearly invisible pocket concealed the cards on the inside of The King's coat, far to the back and under the arm where no one would find them. Terran jerked his head to the side to look at the card that had been drawn. An illustration of a man walking off a cliff followed by a dog graced its surface. The sun shone behind him, and he seemed so happy that he was unaware of the cliff he was about to walk off. "You were a Fool."

"I was a fool for loving my parents?"

"You were a fool for wearing blinders. You all were. But you won't understand any of that, yet. Tell me about your father."

"He was always there for me. When I fell, he picked me up."

"So, you never learned to stand for yourself?"

"No, I—"

"The world is a harsh, cruel place. Their babying has left you weak and unprepared."

"I'm only fiftee—"

"Nearly a man in a year. I was on the street fending for myself at your age, and many of the kids in Atsa fare *far* worse. I knew how to get a meal, I knew how to come up with a day's labor, and I *never* sat on street corners and begged."

Terran raised an eyebrow at him and huffed, "Never?"

"Maybe once."

Terran breathed out, and the coals flared, shooting hot air into his face. He asked, "Why am I doing this again?"

"So you know what it feels like to be trapped," The King replied and replaced the tea. "Heat above you. Heat below you. No escape. What do you do?"

"I... well, I *have* to stay here until you let me u—"

"You wait it out and think. Hone your mind. I'm not like your father. I won't be here to catch you when you fall, and you need to learn to think yourself out of tough situations."

"I don't see a way out of this, seeing as you won't let me get down, so waiting and thinking won't get me anywhere," Terran inhaled and looked toward the door. "Can we at least open the—"

"No."

"But we're going to suffocate from all this—"

"No. Three more minutes."

Despite all the nonsense that The King put him through daily, Terran had learned to enjoy his home in the tavern, as sudden as the transition was. The King was not as rude and ruthless as Terran had originally perceived. Terran had watched his guard fall on occasion, and when The King was alone, or drunk, or sleepy, he would make quiet, funny jokes or ask Terran if he needed a glass of water while studying. The cruelty was an act, Terran suspected, to keep him in line, but Terran saw through it. Training, on the other hand, was brutal. Though strict at times, The King was a wonderful teacher. Terran had never gotten so much exercise in his life, and the books in The King's study held knowledge that Terran had not even thought existed. The little back office now had a path in the books and clutter to the door that led to the room next to it, where Terran now slept.

It was a humble room, compared to his bedroom back in the Embassy Palace, but it was homey. The King furnished it with whatever Terran liked and it was a home away from home. He would rather be reading on his new bed than balancing above hot coals. Terran raised his head to protest the sweltering temperatures again when the door to the office slammed open. A messenger burst in, her hair tousled by the wind and her pale cheeks flushed from the cold.

If there was anything that The King hated the most, it was being interrupted without an announcement, and his messengers, during states of emergency, tended to forget the rules. The hot air blew out of the room as soon as the door opened and Terran gasped a sigh of relief as cool air filled his lungs.

"This better be important, Bridget," The King barked.

"Your Majesty!" the messenger huffed, out of breath, and she clung to the doorframe for support. "Trouble... in the Dza'ya district."

The Dza'ya district was the worst out of all the city districts, and, from what Terran had heard, filled with the most criminals and had the highest mortality rate in all Segeno. Terran was still grappling with conflicting information. At the Embassy Palace, he was told that the people of Dza'ya made their own trouble. Crime in the district was awful because the citizens had no self-control and attacked each other daily, and everyone born in the Dza'ya district were regarded as predisposed to a variety of mental maladies: alcoholism, addiction, gambling, and violence. From what Terran had heard around the tavern, there were other problems going on. The crime rate was high because the people were starving, and they stole to survive. Terran assumed that the mental plights that plagued Dza'ya were primarily caused by misery, but he wasn't sure. He didn't know what to believe. He had never been there himself, however, so he could not say for sure.

The King stood, his long cloak sweeping the floor, took his teacup, and motioned for Terran to stand. The boy moved off the books, away from the flame, and stood. The King poured a bucket of water onto the coals, set down his tea, and motioned for Terran to follow. "Come on," he said. "We're going."

Steam billowed in heaps and plumes as the coals began to lose their heat and Terran scrambled to pull his tunic back on. His body felt sticky from sweat, and the shirt clung to his skin on the way down. He hopped into his shoes, balancing on a single foot, and gripped the desk for support.

"Me?" Terran asked as he pulled his now rag-tag Embassy jacket over his shoulders. "You never let me come with you."

"You're going to watch me fix this problem."

The King glided through the tavern, dodging the scattered chairs, tables, and people, and out the door. Terran followed, jogging to keep up. Once outside, The King ran up a wall and dodged away, lost from his sight. Terran gazed skyward, anticipation forcing his stomach to backflip, and he raced up the wall. His feet had hardened to the gravel of the roads and the adobe of the rooftops, his hands had formed calluses with which he could grip most surfaces, and he followed swiftly and without trouble. Soon the pair of them shifted across rooftops which degraded from plaster to thatch, and as soon as the rooftops became too unstable to run on, they took to the streets. Shifting in and out of crowds made them invisible, just heads among many, and soon they got to a stone building that was climbable. The King began to make his way up to the top to get a better view of the situation, and Terran, once he caught up, took a moment to catch his breath.

The Dza'ya district lay before them like a growth. When he was first turned out of the Embassy, Terran had been appalled by the Atsa district, which held the middle class. The lowest class was three times as big as the middle class, and it showed. The buildings were tightly packed together, a near sea of thatch, the roads were made solely of dirt, the people were hardly clothed, what they wore mere rags, and sickness seemed to be everywhere. Terran's eyes followed a few women taking buckets of water from a dirty well and imagined the grit of the unfiltered sand passing over his tongue. The thought made him grimace and his skin prickle. He frowned at the state of everything and looked to The King, pain and confusion in his heart. He simply could not believe what he was seeing.

He was going to ask a question, but The King put a hand up and pointed to a nearby area that Terran assumed to be a market. He spotted a wooden table which acted as a stall for a merchant, completely toppled, goods scattered in the mud and trampled on by passersby.

"I told you! I said I'd give you the money on Thursday!"

A woman dove to the ground to protect her goods next to the upended table, which looked to have been covered in various cheeses at one point. She raised her arm above her head to protect her face. An Elite Embassy guard stood there with a wooden shaft above his head, ready to strike again. He looked no older than twenty, but the harshness in his eyes soured his face. Terran used to look up to Elites. They were the highest class of the Embassy Guard and treated with the utmost respect. He had never seen one act like this.

"Thursday, please!" the woman cried out. "Just spare my stall! Without my wares, I can't pay you!"

"You were supposed to have it *yesterday!*" The guard swatted at her hard, hitting her on the thigh. Her dark skin immediately bruised on impact. She yelled out, and he threw the switch into her lap. He crouched down beside her, and The King leapt off their tower into the mud below. Terran followed, and they moved to a nearby corner, tucked away in an alley, straining their ears to hear. The Elite grabbed the woman's face and tilted his head toward her, his silver helmet covering his dark hair and blue eyes. He said, "You have no idea how hard this is for me. Do you know how *boring* it is to come to this hellhole of a district on a *tax* complaint? Everybody in the city pays taxes, miss. You must be stupid to not know how to pay yours on time. I hate you damn whiney sandmaggots. You make the rest of us from Dza'ya look bad."

"Terran," The King whispered, held up his pack of cards, and looked him directly in the eyes. "I told you everything wasn't all poppies and roses in Segeno. You just didn't open your eyes to see the injustice, and it's hard when your parents, your school, everyone shields you from everything. The guards are *ruthless*, and we are the only ones who can stop them. These cards," he said and flipped through a few, "these are more than cards. They are seekers of truth and justice, balance and vengeance."

He shuffled them a few times and pulled a card from the top. Terran watched the Elite guard drag the woman into another nearby alleyway. They were running out of time. The card The King had pulled showed a young woman holding a moon in each hand, both different phases, and below her crouched a man in a cloak, next to candles. The King winked at Terran and said, "They hold a power the Embassy wouldn't begin to understand."

The King took the card and pressed it to the top of his left hand. It began to smoke as if it caught fire. The smell of burning flesh wafted into Terran's nose and he covered it with his arm as the card burned, gagging at the stench. When the card reduced to ash, a burn mark bubbled into existence on The King's skin in the shape of a crescent moon.

"Watch and learn. Don't move from this spot."

In a blink of an eye, The King vanished before Terran. Where he had been standing there was only open air. Terran moved his hands through the space to see if it was a trick, but there was nothing, and The King's body had dissipated. A scream erupted from the alleyway, and Terran dashed across the street, despite The King's previous instruction to stay put.

When he slid into the alleyway, he had to backpedal in the mud to avoid getting in the middle of something he didn't understand. He slapped his own hand over his mouth to prevent himself from crying out in shock. The woman leaned back against the wall of one building, crouched against the ground, a large black bruise forming on her face from where the Elite guard had hit her again. The guard struggled against something that hung around his neck as if being choked, but there was no one there. "You think you can *bully* the innocent?" The King's voice boomed out of thin air. "You're being tricked. You learned too late. You will strangle the life out of these people no longer. You will soon learn... your entire corrupt society will learn."

With a thump, the guard fell to the ground, dead or unconscious, Terran did not know, and Terran's stomach tightened as he watched the man, purple-faced, slump over. The King flickered back into view, like a flame being lit, and the woman, who had started to stand, fell to her knees. "Oh, Your Majesty!" she cried out in a stupor. "I-I, my God... I—"

"Keep out of trouble," he said, searched the guard, and took his coin purse, handing it to the woman. "Use this to pay your tax. Keep safe."

The King grabbed Terran by the elbow and they disappeared into the crowd again as people returned to their day-to-day business as if nothing had happened.

"What was *that?*" Terran demanded. "You were there one second and gone the next! How did you do that? Was it a trick?"

"You'll learn in time."

"You can't *do* that to somebody. You can't just show up

surrounded by floating swords and go *invisible* and tell me— "

"Actually, I can."

"If I'm going to trust you, I need to know."

The King clapped him on the shoulder. "You'll learn in time."

"What happened? Why would that Elite *do* that to that poor woman?"

"She was late on her tax payments. He probably got an order from the tax collector to come make sure she paid and harass her if she didn't."

"That's not... that's not fair. They're supposed to protect people."

"They do. They protect the rich and the high-born."

"They're supposed to protect *everybody*."

"Terran, there's a lot you don't know about how deep this problem goes. Therefore, I need your help. I've been trying to pick apart this corruption for years but haven't been able to get far enough under their skin."

"You... you didn't have to kill him."

"Who said I killed him?" The King raised an eyebrow and turned a corner.

"What... what was that? I... I don't understand."

"Justice."

Fairytales
Parisa

The Palace, March of the First Year

"Now, recite to me the Embassy constitution preamble."

Parisa inhaled deeply and set her tea down onto the table, replying, "The Embassy is one and united under the almighty and all-powerful ruler, the Sovereign. It is true that the Sovereign's one and only intention is to rule the people justly and strictly. It is against the people and the Embassy constitution to perform any sort of treachery or crimes against the members of the Embassy, for the Embassy is all of us. United we stand, united we fall."

"Good," Master Esmond affirmed and sipped his tea. "In terms of responsibility in the Embassy, what does the Embassy constitution mean to you?"

"Well, Papa is the Sovereign now, so I suppose I have to help him uphold the constitution and support him in any way that I can. Try to make the Embassy Council a better and more effective unit."

"Yes, and when you become the Sovereign, you'll have to

uphold the same. Your primary objective will be to rule over our society; they'd be lost without you. A great and ancient leader and writer, Machiavelli, said that you will only be successful as a ruler if you utilize the strength of your ministers. If the men and women at your side fear and respect you, they will not rebel against you."

"That sounds... mean."

"People abuse empathy, Lady Parisa."

"*You* all are the ones who do the heavy lifting," Parisa argued. "You and the other district leaders. The Sovereign, even though they have the final say, doesn't *really* do anything."

"But, without the Sovereign's guidance, we'd have no authority. The Sovereign presides over all of us and guides our decisions. As the ancient leaders dictated, your father has the final say in the matter. Ultimate control."

"I guess I don't think it's fair that all of us up top, just a small, select group, get to make the decisions of the people below without their input."

"Well, Lady Parisa, that is something that you may consider changing when you become the Sovereign. You could also suggest it to your father."

"As if he would listen to me."

"He might."

"He won't. I know he won't."

"Doesn't hurt you to try, but I won't argue with you. You're done with lessons for today."

"Really?" Parisa grinned and set Theophilia up onto the table. The day had flown by and she could hardly believe it was already over.

"Yes. You're learning. Your articulation and speech are improving, and you'll soon be through your etiquette course. Tomorrow we will work on handwriting and music. We'll prove to your father that you're quite the academic yet."

The light from the setting sun filtered in through a small window tinted a soft yellow, an unusual color for the Embassy, and sunlight hit the floor of Esmond's room the color of autumn gold. Parisa did not prefer to study in her own quarters, and Master Esmond's study and living space, which took up an entire floor of the Embassy Palace, was a much more comfortable work environment. Something about the blue and white came off as cold and calculated, and the warmth of the golden rays and Esmond's smile made it easier for Parisa to focus.

He filled every space he could with candles that smelled of sage and the warm yellow light of their tiny flames welcomed Parisa like stars. Her father thought it foolish that he kept candles when they had perfectly good electricity, but she knew Esmond burned them for the calm. His study was organized and clean, books on shelves, and though it was a small room, Esmond crammed a desk for Parisa into the space regardless.

On the wall hung a large map of the Dza'ya district, over which Esmond presided, and pins and strings connected points of interest with trade routes. Scraps of parchment with chicken-scratch notes scrawled on the surface drooped next to the map, tacked on the wall. As the leader of the Dza'ya district, Esmond's job consisted primarily of ensuring that his district thrived and that all functioned as it should. How his district interacted with other districts also fell under Esmond's jurisdiction.

The Embassy Council was comprised of the rich elite in Segeno, those who were either born into royalty or married into it. It contained six members, those the Sovereign elected. Two members each were assigned to the districts of Segeno, but now their numbers dwindled. Esmond now acted as the only representative for Dza'ya, two representatives held responsibility for Atsa, and no representatives stood for Naa'a. Parisa's father had not elected any new council members because he said he could not find those worthy enough for the job, but it impacted the way Segeno was run. It was Parisa's father who organized relationships between the districts, uniting the city as a whole.

Parisa had learned all of this in her studies but studying bothered her. In honesty, the whole thing made her nervous. Only months ago, she had been living in the Naa'a district, not allowed to live with her father in the palace, even though he was on the Council. She instead was raised by her caretaker, Nolan, alone in a huge, empty house. She enjoyed her time sparingly with her father, ready to be wed to a young suitor who was the son of a rich merchant. Now, here she sat, preparing to be the next leader of Segeno. The responsibility crashed down on her like a sandstorm, blinding and absolute. She did not want it. After the first week of studies, she hoped her bullheadedness and her unwillingness to study would convince her father that she was pruned for nothing but a posh, easy life, but it had not. He pushed her harder and harder, almost to the point where she thought she might break. She began to get a headache now and *needed* a break. She scrutinized Master Esmond with blue, guiltless eyes, and asked, "Esmond?"

"Yes?" Esmond murmured as he flipped through a book he

had lost his place in. He seemed surprised that she was still there and had expected her to run off when he had said she was done learning for the day.

"Why... why does Papa want to make me miserable? Did I do something wrong?"

Esmond closed the book he was going to read and gazed at her, seemingly wanting to avoid the subject. He pushed up a pair of silver-rimmed spectacles and sighed, "He doesn't want to make you miserable, Parisa. He's the Sovereign of Segeno now. He's busy and has no more time to coddle you, I'm afraid. That's all."

"I... I know that – I just... Father seems too busy to even look at me, now. I'm practically invisible."

"You're not invisible, my dear. He's overwhelmed, is all. You're very important to him, and he loves you."

"Do you know how long it's been since he told me he loved me? A year, I think. I lost track. I almost miss living in Naa'a, away from all of this mess."

"The old Sovereign was found guilty of treason and executed. Her son, who would have been next in line, has run off into the desert, probably to die. Guilty by association, most likely. It would not surprise me if he was in on the plans, though... incredibly disappointing. I didn't take Theresa for a master of extortion. She told me often that she never wanted to rule like her grandfather, but... it looks like that was a lie. She probably indoctrinated her son, poor thing."

"Without an heir, then, that made my father next in line."

"Exactly. Would you look at that? I *knew* some of the facts

I was teaching stuck in that mess of a brain of yours. Now, go off and play."

"Do..." Parisa paused. She felt scared to ask the next question, as if she already knew the answer. "Do you know if Father has time to read me a story today?"

"No, Lady Parisa. His Majesty is out today, following a suspected lead on the old Sovereign's son. He's hoping to recover the body so we can hold a proper royal burial. I would be glad to read to you, however. Would I suffice?"

Parisa sighed. Perhaps she should just stop asking to see her father. It just simply wasn't worth it anymore. After a moment of pondering, she thought on the idea of Esmond's steady voice reading the words of one of her favorite books, and she smiled at her teacher. "I suppose you'll do."

Master Esmond had been her friend for years, where her father had failed, long before he ever became Sovereign. Her father had always been less than attentive, but Esmond had made up for it, standing in as more than a teacher. She knew she was far too old to be read to, being thirteen, but she didn't care. It was one of her favorite things in the whole world, and the sound of Esmond's voice flowed as smooth as cream. He always knew when to ask if she felt sad and could tickle a laugh out of her, even on her darkest days.

Together, they grabbed a book from the shelf and wandered down toward the greenhouse. Theophilia gripped tightly in one hand and a handful of her skirt in another, she skipped down the hall, happy as a swallow. He hummed as they strolled, and she realized how much he meant to her.

"Thank you for spending time with me," Parisa mumbled. "It gets... pretty lonely up in my room by myself."

"It's the least I could do, Lady Parisa."

Parisa reached for Esmond's hand, but when she missed and bumped his wrist, he yelped out in pain and cradled the joint.

"Sorry, my dear," he apologized. "I bruised my wrist the other day and it hasn't healed quite yet."

"Did you fall?"

"Excuse me?"

"The bruise."

He sighed, his breath heavy with a burden she could not possibly understand. "Yes, I did, Parisa. I fell very hard."

"Was no one there to catch you?"

"No one was there to catch me."

"Did... someone push you?"

Esmond's step faltered for just a moment, his foot hovering in the air over the sandstone path that led out into the greenhouse. "No, no one pushed me. I was lost in old memories and I made a misstep. That's all."

"Memories of your wife?"

"She..." He stopped before the tree, gazing at something that wasn't there. "She wouldn't push me. If anything, she probably tried to catch me as I fell. I did feel a little bit of grace as I hit the bottom of the stairs."

Parisa remembered the day that her teacher had received the news that his wife had died. He had been devastated and had interrupted lessons for weeks after with sudden outbursts of anger and sadness. Parisa had never met Esmond's wife, but had seen her in passing, a lovely lady with flaxen hair and a gaze of steel. Parisa took his hand.

"I think you need a fairytale, too."

Esmond glanced at the book he held in his other hand. "Yes, I do believe I do. It's high time I read this one again. I do love it."

Parisa sat at the foot of the blossoming crabapple, petals coating the grass beneath its delicate trunk, but, before Esmond could get a chance to sit, a guard rushed forward, huffing and puffing in his heavy armor. "Master Esmond!" he blurted. "We found a guard strangled in an alleyway near the market in Dza'ya, sir."

Esmond sighed and handed Parisa the book. "I'll be back shortly. I promise."

As her teacher shuffled away, she looked to her doll.

"I suppose that soon he'll run out of time for me too," she mused. "Right, Theophilia?"

Old Magick
Terran

The Tavern, June of the First Year

"Take the cards," The King compelled, and relinquished to Terran, who was seated in his usual chair, the deck of cards that were always hidden away in The King's secret coat pocket. He shoved them into Terran's hands and gazed at him, like a sailor looking for land on the horizon. "What do you feel?"

Terran glanced at the ever-shifting deck and wondered what his teacher meant. "They're just paper to me. I—"

"You're not *trying.*"

"I don't understand what you *expect* of me. All this paper card mumbo jumbo doesn't make a lick of—"

"It's *not* mumbo jumbo, Terran. I haven't been running around the city for years doing silly parlor tricks on the side of the road for a few coins. This is *real,* and this is *dangerous,*" The King barked, stood, and seized a piece of old cloth that hung from one of the posts of the bed. He moved behind Terran and blindfolded him, continuing, "Now. *Focus.*"

Terran took a deep breath and struggled to understand why The King would put him through such a horrible, boring, pointless exercise. The cloth smelled of mildew, dust, and old blood, and Terran suspected the whole endeavor would result in nothing but—

Suddenly, his chest constricted as though he had hit water from a great height, solid as concrete. A bright light exploded into his field of vision, even though he was blindfolded, and a rush of images darted across the forefront of his mind. His brain cultivated images more vivid than he ever dreamt possible and the realness of it all was nauseating as he lurched to a stop, now standing in a room he knew.

Time travel, Terran reasoned, was impossible. No one could go back to reverse or prevent the events of the past, so how was it possible for him to stand in a room he had not entered in months? The last time he had visited that room, his mother had asked him what he wanted for his birthday. Terran took a moment to look around, trying to understand the illusion he had fallen into, when he stopped at a sound. Two people conversed on the balcony in the place that looked like his home. Terran could not be sure of anything. Everything was blurred and distorted, like in a dream.

The couple whispered soft, tender words to each other, love nested into their eyes, but Terran could not hear what they said, words distorted by the watery essence of it all. He could tell by the softness of their mouths that they were words of compassion. Something clicked behind him. He spun to watch an Elite guard emerge from the doorway and draw a rifle, the emblazoned symbol of the Embassy on his chest. His finger twitched on the trigger.

Bang!

The throne room. Streets of Naa'a. The Embassy. Blood. Bullets. A letter signed with red ink sopped up from the floor. The royal seal. Hands around his throat. Terran stared straight into the face of Lord Talbot, someone who had worked closely with Terran's mother, and Talbot had his hands tightly around Terran's throat.

CLASH! Terran scattered the cards about the room as if they had burned his skin and ripped off the blindfold. He found that his forehead dripped with sweat and that his hands quaked unbearably as he returned to reality, seated in The King's study. He glared at The King with accusing eyes and shoved the blindfold onto the desk. "What was *that*?" he demanded.

"They showed you clarity, your purpose," The King explained and raised a hand. The cards fluttered up off the ground of their own accord and placed themselves, one at a time, into the palm of his hand. Terran scanned the room, attempting to discover the source of the trick.

"My purpose?" he retorted.

The King reclined again in his own chair, feet up on the table, and shuffled the cards. "You have no family, no home," he said. "So what did you expect? You were just going to help me with the Embassy, but then what, hm? Where would you go after?"

"I-I don't know, I—"

"Would you want to rule?"

"No," Terran replied. "I don't think I would."

"What did you see?"

58

Terran looked down at his shoes, which had once been white, and realized that soon his feet would outgrow them. What was he even doing with his life? Everything had come crashing down so quickly. "I saw someone dressed in Elite armor kill my parents."

"And you're surprised?" The King asked, stood, and moved to the window, antsy and agitated. "I showed you the corruption. You've seen it again and again among the guards around the city."

"There was another man... a man I barely recognize from my childhood. He was... *strangling* me."

The King glanced over his shoulder at Terran. "He very well could have been the reason the guards turned you out," he said. "I suspect a coup. You're a refugee now, Terran, and something is going on in the Embassy. Something bad. When I first read the cards, not too long algo, I caught sight of you in my vision. We ran into each other on the street, like when we had first met. You're supposed to fix this awful system, which is why I need you. I *beheld* the corruption and the hate and deceit firsthand."

"My head hurts. This is all crazy, you know that? Was that a vision or a dream or—"

"Pick one."

Terran pulled his hands away from his eyes and welcomed the headache that played on the forefront of his temple. The King pulled out a few cards from his deck. He set them adjacent to one another on his desk, face down, gesturing to them like a stage magician.

"Just one?" Terran inquired. All this magick, or whatever it was, gave him a blistering headache. A tingling sensation shot up his arm when his fingers brushed a card, and when he flipped it over, he looked upon an illustration of a guard on some kind of animal, brandishing a shield and riding into battle. The King's eyes flickered with surprise as he took the card and replaced it, sitting at his usual seat.

"When I first encountered these cards, I acquired them from a man I had never met. I stumbled upon him, lying in the street covered in blood. He had been shot by an Elite as he was attempting to steal food for the poor. I witnessed the entire thing: him crashing into the street, the blood, the guard spitting in his face as he died, the looks on the faces of the people he was trying to steal for. He had motioned for me to come closer as he passed on, and from his pocket he produced these cards.

"I took them and drew one, not knowing the meaning at the time, and a specific card shimmered before my eyes. 'Justice,' he muttered before he died. As soon as I touched the cards, the flashes hit me just as they hit you. I saw two people I had grown up with being murdered, and I watched the city degrade from glory into poverty and filth. Then, I was running, running to the aid of a boy I had never seen before. I felt dazed, in a dream, but I went home after that, packed up my things, and walked away from the Embassy forever."

"You were a part of the Embassy?"

He nodded and said, "I held the position of Councilman, not a district leader or anything of that sort. And the whole thing lasted very briefly. The whole system made me sick when I set foot in the first meeting."

"I've never seen you before."

"I dipped out before you were born and have been on the streets for as long as you've been alive."

"You knew my parents then. My mother became Sovereign before I was born."

The King replied, "I went to school with them."

"So, you lied to me. You said you only knew them from the political side."

"I *did*. Don't accuse me of lying when you don't understand anything at all," he huffed as he pointed deliberately at his red hair. "If you're *different* in the Embassy, no one talks to you. Your *parents* were just as subjected to the system of prejudice and hate as the rest of them."

"Okay, so what? The cards showed me that someone overthrew my family. You're bitter and old and pissed that somebody made fun of your hair. Boo, hoo."

"Don't you use that tone with me, young man. You know *nothing*. Your parents drowned you in privilege, and you benefited, too. I need to show you everything that's wrong so we can actually *do* something and fix it, help repair it while the people it's killing die in the streets. I was bullied for my hair, but people of dark skin, people simply choosing to love, are being strangled to death in alleyways. Remember that I'm in charge and that, despite what you want to think, we're in this together. I'm going to teach you how to use them, the cards, but in return I'm going to need you to stick with me."

"You're not afraid that I'll betray you? I'll use this magick, kill you, and run?"

"You wouldn't last two seconds against me."

Terran said nothing and swallowed his pride; The King spoke the truth, and if Terran was going to run, he should have done it long ago. Besides, new questions burned in his heart, and the shock that the cards had delivered sparked curiosity in his mind. How had no one discovered their powers when something as fantastic as magick existed? How did The King know how to use them? And... what could he possibly mean about the system? Nothing The King said made any sense to him. Terran wanted to unravel the mysteries of the cards, and Segeno, for himself.

With solemn submission, he asked, "How do I use them?"

Falling
Parisa

The Palace, June of the First Year

"Daddy, all I'm asking for is ten minutes of your time. You haven't had a long conversation with me in *weeks*, and I wanted to show you this assignment I've finished that I thought you would like."

"Can't you see I'm *busy*?" Lord Talbot barked as he gazed at a map of the city, the sprawling expanse of Segeno laid out on a single piece of parchment. The War Room held its spot as one of Parisa's least favorite places in the palace, due to its cold nature and the grim sensation she felt in the pit of her stomach whenever her presence was required. It was adjacent to the throne room, a small space where the Sovereign and his Councilmembers would meet to discuss matters of conflict. Her father had been holed up in the War Room for days, strategizing ways to exterminate the last Sovereign's only remaining heir and the rebellion that brewed throughout the city. This reclusive behavior, Parisa observed, cultivated insanity, and she had hoped that she may be able to bring him back from the brink.

"But you're *always* busy!" Parisa retorted. She had been impatient for a very long time, and she could no longer stand it.

"I don't understand, my dear," Lord Talbot said as he stood from the table and took an aggressive step toward his daughter, "why it is so difficult for you to catch me at a time when I am *not* trying to protect us from rebels who want to kill us?"

"And *I* don't understand what you want from me, Father. You tell me I need to show improvement and progress, but you don't want to discuss my work. You say you're interested in how I'm coming along, and when I come to visit you, you couldn't be more disinterested. What do you *want* from me?"

Lord Talbot opened his mouth to speak but held his tongue. After a few moments, he replied, "The Sovereigns before have been almost entirely removed from their children. The children are educated by tutors, are raised by servants, and then perform their royal duties without question. *I* am involved in other matters and *do* not have time to socialize."

"Oh, so you want me to go away? Is that it? You want nothing more than for me to be a pet bird? Did you stop caring about me *before* or *after* mother died?"

"Your Majesty," Master Esmond, who stood adjacent to the table in silence, interjected.

"No, Parisa, I want you to do what you're told. This has nothing to do with your mother, so leave her out of it."

"If you don't want to see me," Parisa snapped, "then tell me. Don't lead me on like this."

Master Esmond stepped forward timidly and coughed to

clear his throat, mumbling, "Sir, perhaps it would be best if you listened to—"

Lord Talbot inhaled like a bull and moved over to Esmond, huffing, "Are you suggesting, Master Esmond, that you know how to deal with my daughter better than I do?"

"No, sir. I—"

Lord Talbot grabbed Master Esmond's wrist hard and twisted his arm around with such force that Master Esmond yelped out in pain. Lord Talbot leaned in close to Master Esmond's face and hissed, "*Never* tell me what to do."

Parisa swallowed thickly and gripped what schoolwork she had in her hands as if it were a rope hanging over a ravine. Esmond's knuckles turned white as Lord Talbot held him there, like a python she had read about in one of her books.

Lord Talbot released Esmond and moved to Parisa, who instinctually stepped back against the wall. Her father flew into rages like this often, and when he did, she knew he was not to be meddled with.

"*You* are to go to your lessons. You are to entertain *yourself*," he spat. "You are to play *by yourself*. If you ask me again to play with you, you'll be locked in your room with nothing to do. Do you understand?"

Parisa's lip trembled. Her father's rage hardly ever resulted in violence, but it seemed that today had been the exception, and Master Esmond cradled his twisted wrist as he observed the scene, ready to jump to Parisa's aid. Parisa's nerves caused her chest to shake as she breathed, and she strode, with dignity, over to the table again and slammed her schoolwork in front of where her father had been sitting. Master Esmond took Parisa's hand and escorted her back to her room while her father seethed with hatred, rooted to where he stood.

The walk down the hallway acted as torture itself, with their footsteps echoing through the stone hallway as they moved toward her bedroom, which was on the bottom floor of the palace. Lord Talbot did not permit Parisa to live with him in the Sovereign's suite, despite their immediate relations. She instead had been given a small room in the back of nowhere, where he would never have to see her, hear her, or be near her. She understood why now and felt sad, not because of the way he treated her, but because she had not known sooner. Red marks gleamed on Esmond's wrist where he had been grabbed like wine on dyed wool.

"You fell, didn't you?" Parisa inquired, afraid that she already knew the answer. How could her father have been so violent and, furthermore, was he the cause of Esmond's other injuries?

Esmond said nothing and simply nodded, closing her bedroom door behind her.

Burn
Terran

Atsa, December of the First Year

"These ones?"

"Those."

Terran pointed at a silver deck of cards at the back of the jewelers. Thousands of small cogs and tickers whirred and clicked in a unanimous cacophony of mechanical sound. Mechanized eyes, animals, wings, and other automated contraptions ticked and moved as tiny wound motors brought them to life. Many of the pieces were protected behind glass cases; Terran assumed the jeweler made enough from his trade to afford such a luxury. In the back of the shop more wonders resided, and it was there where the jeweler sold mysterious decks of cards. The sets themselves were locked away in wood cases and kept out of the public eye. Superstitious, the jeweler said, and his hands shook as he revealed the chest's treasures.

The silver cards had glinted in the corner of the box as

Terran's eyes grazed over the chest, decks bound by ribbons and twine nestled inside. The King told him he could not learn the magick of the cards without first picking his own deck. The King was not yet ready to give up his deck, the deck that had once belonged to a dying man, so Terran got a new deck instead. Less than a half dozen decks rested in their velvet coffin, protected from light and dust for who knew how long.

"How have I not known about these? Why hadn't my family ever taught me that they exist? How does that jeweler have access to them?" Terran asked and ran his fingers over the top of the cards as The King gave the jeweler money. No imperfections marred the metal plating and Terran's fingers glided over them like ice.

"These cards represent an old magick," The King replied, handed over a pouch of silver, and turned to leave the store. "A long time ago, people would use these cards to tell the future. Then, someone somewhere discovered the magick within them, or maybe rediscovered. Those who didn't believe couldn't use them. That's why. Nowadays, people who haven't seen the power of the cards do not grasp that something of the sort is even possible, let alone exists. Most don't even make them anymore. The people hunting me think that I've made pacts with spirits or demons of the desert because of the things I do. Little do they know, I would be powerless without these cards."

The King led Terran back down the stairs into the tavern, and then into the back room where he now spent so much of his time. Nearly a year had passed since Terran had come into the care of The King and, for his sixteenth birthday, The King bought him whichever deck suited his eye – a generous gift. Apparently, The King held in his possession more money than he let on, and coins seemed to flow from his pockets like water. He purchased goods by money of his own devices, and it never ceased to amaze Terran how much there was. He never suspected that thievery could be such a lucrative business and wondered how much cash flowed through The King's hands on a day-to-day basis.

"That card you had me pick months ago," Terran began. "You haven't let me touch your cards since. What did it mean?"

"Oh, The Knight?" The King huffed and treated it like it was of no importance. "It represents who you are, as a person. I am called The King because when I drew from the cards like you did, I was given the King of Swords, someone who is very much like me. You drew the Knight of Wands and, now that I know you more, it seems to fit you perfectly."

"Have you ever let anyone learn about the cards before?"

"No."

The King took the cards from Terran's hands, pulling out the Knight of Wands as if he knew exactly where it was in the deck. "Right now," he said, "uncovering how deep the Embassy corruption goes is of the utmost importance. I understand I've been harsh and that this has all been new to you, but your destiny led you here."

Terran shook his head. "I still don't under—"

"Sh."

The King moved behind Terran and pushed him down into his chair. Terran flinched as The King's icy fingers moved his hair away from his neck. The King continued, "I'm going to give you a present, but it will hurt."

"What—"

Terran's skin exploded in sensation, a singeing pain he had managed to avoid all his life, until now. He had never burned himself, fire on skin, because his parents had never let that happen. Now he knew exactly what it felt like, and something burned into the skin at the back of his neck. As he tried to pull away, The King tightened his grip on Terran's shoulder so that the boy could not move. Eventually, the pain died down and The King replaced the card into the deck. Terran looked up at him angrily, hot, welling tears in his eyes. "What did you *do*?"

The King turned around and lifted the long waves of ginger hair from his own neck. On the flesh, a dark circle carved of the same, swirling symbols on the back of The King's cards were emblazoned there in the form of a dark scar. Inside an inky circle, a long dagger's tip broke the border of the mark, and behind it sat a large, sturdy-looking crown. The image reminded Terran of a coat of arms. "When I first received the cards, I read every book I could find on the subject, which wasn't very many. The books I *did* read told me about significators," he explained. "That mark will allow you to use the cards. Without it, they are only paper."

The King held up a hand mirror and walked Terran to a standing mirror so he could investigate the reflection. Metal twisted itself into a clear, simple illustration of a shield, upon which was a tree branch that tangled into a staff. Behind it a sun rose. The imagery bumped out of his skin, almost as if the metal had been welded into his flesh, and the spot felt sensitive to the touch. His heart leapt into his throat as he realized that there was no turning back now. "Will this ever go away?" Terran asked.

"Never," The King said. "It's with you for the rest of your life."

Betrayal
Parisa

The Palace, January of the Second Year

"Happy birthday!"

Master Esmond took his hands from Parisa's eyes, and what she saw made her giggle due to the oddness of the thing. On the white sheets of her bed lay a small, silver dagger, inlayed with aquamarine stones, and Parisa cocked her head to one side to get a better look at the gift. Birthdays held some strange wonderment for Parisa, as the presents she received tended to be from Master Esmond and were often just as quirky as he was. Esmond had chosen the presents that she had gotten from her father when she was young, and she had always known it. Her father never paid enough attention to ascertain what she would want for a gift, so he left the task to his closest advisor.

Parisa thought herself rather lucky to have someone like Esmond around for birthdays. Esmond spent a lot of time with Parisa's mother when they were young, and it was Esmond who had been chosen to be her godfather. Esmond knew Parisa from back to front like a book and, for most birthdays, his presents were eerily accurate, which showed nothing more than his astute observational skills. This year, however, the gift made almost no sense to Parisa, and she spent a moment attempting to solve the riddle, which she was sure it was.

She picked up the dagger cautiously, as to not cut herself on its sharp edge, and smiled. "So, what's this all about?" she prodded.

Master Esmond shrugged, "I know it's an odd present to receive on one's fourteenth birthday, but I wanted to get you something practical. This year is not the year for books, I'm afraid, and I feel you may need it one day."

"What do you mean?"

"It's a cruel world out there, Parisa, and I would want a young lady to be able to defend herself."

"Esmond, I've never taken a self-defense class in my life. Father won't allow it."

"He may if I prod."

Parisa looked the dagger over in her hands and mused, "It *is* an odd present, but it is pretty. Thank you."

"You are *very* welcome. May your birthday be as merry and bright as your spirit."

She laid the dagger down onto her dresser and gave her teacher a hug. Esmond's chest was warm, and she felt her head rise and fall with his breath. "At least," she said, "you *remembered* my birthday."

There was a quiet knock on the door and Master Esmond turned to open it. The swinging door revealed a page who trembled in his boots as though he was prepared to be shouted at.

"Good evening," Esmond addressed.

"Lady Parisa, Lord Talbot requests your presence," the page said.

"Thank you. We'll be right there."

The page clicked his heels together in a tight bow and scuttled off, bustling away to some other busy task.

"Maybe you spoke too soon." Master Esmond smiled and pushed Parisa toward the door. "Go on. I'll be waiting in my study when you're finished. I have another surprise for you."

Parisa followed the hallway down, her heeled boots clicking on the stone, and a knot formed in her gut. Her father had not celebrated her birthday with her for three years, so the fact that he had changed his mind now made her uneasy. A guard opened the heavy, glass door to the throne room where her father sat on his place of honor, gazing out the window. Solicitude clouded her father's expression, something that Parisa noticed often as of late, and he drummed his fingers on the rest of the chair. The guard presented a salute in front of him, bending into a deep bow, and reported, "My Lord, Lady Parisa."

Lord Talbot glanced in Parisa's general direction and straightened up. "Parisa," he breathed, as though a weight rested on his chest. "I need to have a talk with you."

Talbot waved a hand and dismissed the guard and Parisa curtsied to her father. "Yes, Papa?" she asked.

"Don't call me that."

"Well," Parisa felt her throat knot up as she replied, "would you prefer Father?"

"At this point I would prefer Lord Talbot. Do you

74

understand?"

"I suppose, My Lord, but—"

"Now that you're of age, you need to actually start being useful. I figured because your grades are so poor, I simply cannot have you seated in a dignitary position and your lack of qualifications would make a mockery of me. I assume what you lack in mental skill you may make up in athleticism, so I am placing you into the Elite Training Program."

"W-What?"

"I know a woman has never been in the Elite Guard before, but I feel you will do well there. Also, if someone else is training you, I won't need to babysit you like I have been. I want you to train hard, you hear? Treat it like your life. I want you to be the face of viciousness and discipline, so a change of lifestyle is in order. Your room is being cleaned as we speak, and your dolls thrown out."

"Daddy, don't throw away my—"

"Don't' address me that way," Lord Talbot threatened, stood, and began pacing. "You will train only. That is all. If I see you doing anything otherwise, you will be severely punished. Playing is for little girls, and you are no longer a little girl, are you not? Master Esmond will no longer be in charge of you. This is Commander Crevan."

Parisa spun around when the sound of clanking, metal boots filled her ears to meet the eyes of a tall, broad man whose hand gripped the hilt of his weapon and whose long, dark hair knotted taught behind his head. Wrinkles and canyons created by burnt skin marred his face and scars etched his chin and cheeks like roadways on a map. "My Lord," he barked.

"This is Parisa. I want you to treat her no differently from the other boys. Understood?"

"Yes, My Lord."

"When we are done here," Talbot continued and returned to his throne, "you are to go get your schoolbooks from your room and go out to the barracks. Commander Crevan will instruct you from there."

"Father, let me attest for my ability. I promise to work hard in school and never disappoint you again," Parisa pleaded. "Please don't put me into the guard."

Talbot waved his hand at her like she was nothing more than a trifle, a gnat in his face, a passing thought. "You are dismissed."

Parisa stood there for a moment in consternation, hot tears in her eyes. She curtsied curtly, turned to leave the room, and slammed the door behind her. How could he make a decision like that? Horror stories circulated throughout the Naa'a district of the conditions at which the boys were trained, and, more often than not, the boys died. For most, the training was so rigorous that their bodies would often fail, and the draft pulled normally from the Dza'ya district, where the boys were starving to begin with.

Perhaps, Parisa hoped, if she spoke with Esmond, he would get the whole thing sorted out. Or had he known the whole time? Had he gotten her a dagger to protect herself because he knew it was coming? The elevator moved too slowly and Parisa tapped her foot in exasperation as she waited. When she burst through the door to Esmond's floor, tears fresh on her cheeks, Esmond shot to his feet and wrapped his arms around her as she clung to him. "Good heavens, Parisa!" he exclaimed. "What on *earth* is the matter?"

"I will never see you again!" Parisa tried to articulate through her sobs.

"What?"

Parisa shook as she lowered herself into Esmond's chair, stuttering, "Father said I'm going to train instead of s-study. M-My new guardian is Commander Crevan and I-I've never seen him before in my life. Father told me I wasn't allowed to call him that anym-more – I'm to become an Elite Guard and... a-and..."

"Sh..." Esmond comforted. He placed his hand on the back of her head and held her as she shook. "We'll get through this. Did he say you weren't allowed to see me?"

"N-No," Parisa stammered and shook her head, but did not believe what she said. "He said if he caught me doing anything besides training and studying, I'd be p-punished."

"I'm sure he doesn't *mean* it, Parisa. You know how your father is, cold and—"

"Am I merely an a-animal to h-him? D-Did I not perform well enough?"

"Your grades were fine, Lady Parisa."

"Ap-parently not, because he sees fit, due to my lack of *intelligence*, to throw away my things and turn me out. H-He said he didn't want to b-babysit me anymore."

Esmond yanked a piece of wrinkled parchment from the desk, took his ink pen, and dipped it in the well near Parisa. He drew something on the paper with precision and continued, "I suppose your other present will have to wait, then. I wouldn't want it to get thrown away. Once you complete your training, you'll most likely be put on patrol. There's a well in Dza'ya where women wash their clothes and their bodies, pretty easy to spot. There's a loose stone on the edge of the well, on the eastern side, and those of us who are accustomed to it exchange letters there. Using this, we will be able to communicate without endangering your position with your father."

"Why not use the post?"

"Some things government eyes are not meant to see."

"I don't understand what's happening."

"As always, you're welcome and safe here, so if anything happens come straight to me, no matter what."

Esmond blew on the parchment to dry the ink and handed it to Parisa, who folded it in her hands, which were trembling. "Remember," he affirmed, "you aren't to let anyone catch wind of this. Do you understand?"

She nodded and left his study with a heavy heart. She could not bear to say goodbye, and she was too upset to stay. It would only be too painful. In her room, she quietly gathered up her books, hid the silver dagger in her boot, and headed for the courtyard in her royal attire. How shameful it would be, she guessed, to look upon the crown heir to the throne of Segeno marching across a cold field in fresh mud toward the barracks. At every step she took, she felt her identity stripped away, bit by bit, and soon even the clothes she wore would be gone. She figured that she would get new clothes and other accommodations when she arrived, and that people would soon forget that she was Lady

Parisa, daughter of the Sovereign of Segeno.

It was bitter and cold outside, like her father's eyes, and it was nightfall, the stars obscured by the fading light. She clenched the paper tightly in her hands as she went but before she got to the barracks, she slipped the paper into the front cover of her Philosophy book. When she arrived, she took a deep breath, trying to calm her shaky gasping, and knocked on the door to the commander's building.

She had only ever visited the barracks once when Esmond taught her briefly of military strategy. The military was Segeno's pride and joy, one of the most well-funded parts of the clockwork that ran it all. When the first Segenites emerged from the underground safe havens that protected them from the deadly meteor shower that struck the earth, Segeno had been the first place they went. The city had been relatively untouched, and its insides held technology beyond their wildest dreams. While they had to start over with agriculture, literature, and construction, at the very least the Embassy Palace stood tall, albeit missing some glass and in need of repair. Storage rooms underneath the city had contained what the ancients called guns, as well as supplies and computers, technology from long ago. These resources were salvaged and put to good use. They were the backbone of the Segeno military.

It pained Esmond to be in the barracks, Parisa had seen it on his face, and to watch the boys he looked over as the Dza'ya district leader put to such a monumental task. Commander Crevan had screamed at those boys then, who struggled to exercise in the monsoon-season rain. She never imagined that one of those boys would soon be her.

Commander Crevan threw open the door and glared down at the girl, eyes devoid of compassion, and the warm electric light from his quarters rimmed his shadowed figure. Parisa gazed up at him, fear apparent in her eyes, and her hands shook. He no longer wore his armor, and she became quickly aware of how strong he actually was. If she attempted anything, he could overtake her in an instant. His face wrinkled into a scowl. He sneered, "You the runt of the litter, or what? Are you his only child?"

"Yes, sir."

"Speak up." Crevan did not invite her inside. "Are those all your books?"

She nodded and shuddered a little, despite her trying to keep her sobs inside her chest.

"I *said* speak up. Do you not know how to speak to your superiors?" Crevan demanded as he closed the door behind him. The warm light from the cabin was quickly shadowed by the cold of the night, and Parisa shivered.

"And *stop* sniveling!"

Before Parisa could protest, she was hit hard across her face. Commander Crevan had struck her with the back of his hand, but Parisa held her composure and straightened up after she recoiled, raising her voice. "Sorry, sir," she replied with resolution.

Parisa had never been hit by anyone before. Her father had gotten close, but never brought himself to do it. Commander Crevan's hand hit her cheek like a rock, and the spot swelled and warmed. It stung for only a moment, but as the bruise formed and the skin broke under the surface, a dull pain pulled through the spot every time her heart beat.

"That's better," Crevan grumbled and clasped his hands behind his back. "Your bunk is this way."

Parisa followed him to her new room; a small, ramshackle building that looked like it could barely stand. The room contained a small bed, a dresser, and a bathroom, but nothing more. It was not the same as the other buildings, which were long and looked like they slept many. She probably was assigned the shack because it was inappropriate for her to sleep with the other men and boys. It seemed as though they had just been told that morning she would be assigned to the Elite Guard.

"You have your work clothes in the dresser. Put your books wherever you like as long as I don't trip on them. You're to be up at dawn."

Commander Crevan slammed the door as he left and Parisa crumpled into sobs. She let her books fall from her arms as she sank to the floor, shuddering into her misery. Being betrayed, especially by someone from her own family, burned worse than fire on skin.

Odd Jobs
Terran

The Tavern, January of the Second Year

"Terran, I need you to run some errands for me," The King absentmindedly spoke as he shifted through some papers. It was a lazy, chilly afternoon, the kind of afternoon where a bowl of hot stew and a cup of hot chocolate are the only company you need. Terran dunked a large hunk of bread into his piping hot soup and sat in the fake window, watching as The King worked.

"Errands?" Terran asked, muffled through a mouthful of hot food. The King had never let him leave the tavern without his supervision, and he gazed at his papers with no distinguishable emotion in his eyes.

"I didn't stutter," The King replied and handed Terran a piece of paper. "I need you to purchase these things from the blacksmith and bookkeep. Can you do that? Everything I need is on that list."

Teran took the list and looked it over in his hands. "Of course, I can."

"And take this to the tailor," The King added and handed him a sealed envelope. "Here's the money."

A sack of gold came flying through the air and Terran tied it to his belt. Terran paused for a moment, awaiting further instruction, but The King looked up at him expectantly after he had not left. "Go on," he urged. "You haven't got all day."

The door to The King's room clicked softly closed and the quiet hum from the tavern filled Terran's ears. People always talked in murmurs and whispers in that place, and the raucous harshness that Terran normally associated with taverns or general spaces of personal gathering was missing, replaced by eerie silence. A few patrons bowed to Terran as he passed, and he opened the inn door to freedom.

Outside he hustled down the streets, mingling with people and not daring to stray from crowded areas. Dza'ya, due to the thatched roofs of the buildings, remained impassable above. Alone, Terran was wary of walking the rooftops. In the crowd, he was just another ratty little boy with no one to love him. One of The King's spies had heard the Guard was avidly looking for him, so it was better to go unnoticed. Despite his anxiety, he was happy and excited to wander the city.

Dza'ya crawled with disease, Terran learned, and often he would use any spending money he received from The King to pay for medicine for the sick. He understood now why The King did what he did, and where most of his funds went. Terran also discovered the little things, too, the beautiful things. Food in Dza'ya was like nothing he had ever tasted, laced with intricate spice blends and hot flavors, whereas the food from Naa'a seemed lacking in comparison. It bothered Terran deeply that his parents, or the entirety of the Embassy, for that matter, had never let him or the other children experience the lower parts of the city.

This was where people worked hard, sweat on their brows and callouses on their hands. Terran respected their work ethic and loved to wander and watch the intricacy and skill of Dza'ya's artisans. Most manufacturers of the clothes that the Embassy wore, the armor that Naa'a used, and the utensils that graced the upper district's tables all came from Dza'ya. When Terran arrived at the blacksmith, he knocked on the wall of the shop to let the blacksmith know he had a customer. The forge stood in a stall next to the shop itself, and the blacksmith hammered away with determination at a flat blade on the anvil. Terran felt as though he was interrupting something, like he had no place there, and he knocked again, louder the second time.

"What do you want? Can't you see I'm..."

The blacksmith lumbered out from behind the forge and gazed at Terran, his eyebrows furrowed into thick confusion. He asked, "What the hell do you want?"

Masters of the trade, those whose parents learned from parents whose grandparents worked as engineers before the Great War, crafted the arms in Naa'a. They were specialists, the most learned and skilled men in Segeno. Terran did not speak often with the smiths in the lower districts but found that they were full of gall and struggled to make their arms, created with low grade materials and old, broken forges. These brazen types of folk used to make Terran uneasy, as the residents of Naa'a approached conversations with poise and courtesy, and the lower people started conversations with fists.

Or, at least. That was what he had thought. Terrible stereotypes pervaded deeply into Naa'a culture. Rumors spread about the denizens of Dza'ya and how they were loud, violent, and eager to commit crime. As Terran moved among them, he found the opposite to be true. They were some of the nicest people Terran had ever met, and though loud and forward, were no more violent than anyone else.

"I'm here for The King," Terran began, took out the list, and read it. "He's in need of a breastplate and greaves."

The blacksmith roughly took the sheet of paper from Terran's hands, his dark fingertips blackened with soot from the forge. "All right, all right," he barked. "He should know I'm overwhelmed as it is but come back in a day or so. I'll work on 'em when I can."

"Thank you. The King appreciates your time."

Terran moved out of the shop and back onto the street, but when he spotted a group of guards, he nervously lowered his head to the ground. Elites, they were, and they analyzed a map, discussing amongst themselves strategies and future plans. They combed for Terran, and he knew it, but they paid the ratty boy no attention. He looked only like a beggar to them.

The book keep's shop was nestled far into the Atsa district, near a pleasant outdoor market. It surprised Terran how different the two districts really were from each other, Dza'ya and Atsa, and when he arrived at the book shop, the owner rapidly read the list over with his tiny, beady eyes and scuffled into the back to get a couple of books. When he brought them back, he surprised Terran with the diversity of the stack. Amongst the books were a couple of fantasy and astrology novels, which did not seem useful to The King's cause, but Terran shrugged and took the books with him to the tailor.

The tailor's shop sat at the border between Naa'a and Atsa, which gave Terran butterflies as he slunk his way through the door. The place was cluttered and crowded with bolts of fabric and garments, which allowed Terran to keep his face hidden while the tailor himself opened the letter and read its contents quietly.

"Ah... ah... yes, I see," he muttered. He was a thin, tall man with awkward limbs and long, curvy fingers, and he touched fabric like one would touch a lover. "Drop the books. On the floor is fine."

Terran rested the books on the floor, concern on his face, and when the tailor pulled out a measuring tape and began to measure Terran's body, he was even more baffled. "What are you doing?" he demanded.

"You're to be fitted. That's what the letter said, at least."

"But—"

"Hush. These old Embassy clothes are much too small for you, anyway. You look like an overstuffed sausage. How did you expect anyone to respect you like that?"

Terran hadn't thought of it that way. In a year, he had gained nearly two inches in height, and his pants rode halfway up his shins. The material had turned almost black in some places from coming into contact with mud. Terran was sure he looked disgusting. After an hour of poking, prodding, and pinning the tailor scooted him out of the store, books in hand.

"Come back in a week."

"A week for the tailor, a day or two for the blacksmith..." Terran muttered to himself. When he returned to the tavern, and then to The King's office, The King didn't raise his head from his work. He seemed troubled, like he had heard bad news, but spoke anyway.

"How did it go?" he asked.

"Are all these things for me?"

The King stood and took the fantasy books from his hands. "Not these, but the astrology book, the armor, and the clothes, yes."

"Why?"

"For someone who was spoiled as a kid, you sure do question gifts. Because I *like* you, Terran. Is that a good enough answer? You're one of my closest associates. You need to present well. Right now, you look like a dirty dishrag."

Terran smiled. "Well, thank you."

"You need to learn the magick behind the cards in depth. I want you to read that new book, as well as *these*..." The King continued, and handed Terran a small stack of books, "by the end of this week. All right?"

"That's so much to read!"

"Well, then, you better hop to it."

Induction
Parisa

Barracks, January of the Second Year

"Rise and shine!"

Bang! Bang! Bang! Bang! The echoes of the rattling door shook Parisa's tiny shack, and she leapt out of bed, covering her head out of fear. Commander Crevan's gravel-throated voice grated beyond the door, and he yelled, "Outside in ten!"

Parisa took a moment to recover there, on the floor, shaking, and eventually stood to look around. The shack appeared much more dismal in the daylight, beams of sun floating through the spaces between broken shingles. The night had been cold and unwelcoming, winter air permeated through the cracks and holes. Her breath formed clouds as she stood, and dust motes floated through the light as though they were lost. Winters in Segeno were not cold for long, and the day would be warm before she knew it, but the night had been relentless and dry, and she wanted to be at home in bed with her books.

She almost forgot what had happened and expected to

wake and see her breakfast in her lap, just like yesterday and the day before. Here she stood, in the cold, and it took her moments before she mustered the courage to open her dresser, an old, wooden thing, and see what lay inside. She pulled on a pair of trousers that were too big for her and cranked a belt down around her waist to help them stay up. The shirt's sleeves were too long, and she rolled them up to keep them from slipping over her hands. On the floor rested boots that laced up with hard soles and scuffs in the toe, not new, and white leather gloves that barely fit her delicate hands. She had no mirror to examine herself, but she was sure that if she did, she would look like a clown in her oversized getup. She laid her Embassy dress and shoes, a memento of the old, into the bottom drawer of the dresser and dashed out the door.

On the lawn of the barracks stood the garrison, and, lined in a neat row, only a dozen or so men. Most of them were her age or a little older, from what she could see. All of them were young boys, and Parisa could not believe what she saw. When she had last visited with Esmond, the men that stood there had certainly been *men*. One of the soldiers before her now barely came up to her shoulders. What had her father been thinking, recruiting ones so young? Most of the guards that she had ever known had been old men, and she could not imagine why they were lowering the draft age requirements. The only threats to Segeno, as far as Parisa knew, were sandstorms and thieves. The number of Elite Guards grew and grew each year, and for what?

She shook at the end of the line, sticking out like a sore thumb next to the dark-skinned, fit boys that stood like statues adjacent to her. A gust of wind came, shook her curly hair, and she hurried to pull it from her face. With shaky and hasty fingers, she used some curls to pull back others until her blond ringlets were out of her face.

Commander Crevan paced in front of the boys, his stern eyes examining their every flaw with disgust. When he stepped in front of Parisa, he touched her hair with his large fingers and bent down to meet her face.

"What is that?" he demanded.

"My hair, sir."

He reached for her hair again and she reflexively flinched, not caring to have him touch her again, but he grabbed her shoulder hard. With a massive hand, he ran his fingers through the curls in her ponytail.

"How is it that your hair is so light?"

"I was born that way, sir."

Commander Crevan flicked an eyebrow in curiosity and released her. "We'll have to cut that mop off your head. I'll leave a pair of shears for you in your bunk."

"Y-Yes, sir," Parisa replied, her voice wavering. She met eyes with the other boys, whose hair had been cropped close to their scalps, and knew hers was next.

"Now, you all are here to be inducted into the Embassy's Elite Guard. This branch of our great military is one of rigorous training, blood, sweat, tears, mud, and pain. I know you all are young and most of you are here for the high pay. Despite your motives, you all have been selected because you are the best of the best. You've surpassed your other peers and deserve to learn more specific skills. Are you ready to partake in the biggest challenge of your worthless lives?"

Parisa glanced down the line again and realized that every boy she stood with must have come from Dza'ya, for they were all of dark hair and skin. The rings of Segeno had always been divided, but her lessons had taught that it was by choice. People liked to live with others that looked like them, and therefore the residents all maintained similar characteristics for generations.

Her skin separated her from her peers. It always had. Her mother had been from Dza'ya, with glimmering, auburn skin and dark ringlets that formed a cloud around her head. Parisa was nothing like the people from Naa'a. A stone dropped in her stomach as she began to wonder how much their skin and hair had affected their lives, and how hers would affect her own.

"We live to serve the Embassy!" the boys chanted.

"Good. Today we'll be running an obstacle course. Elite Guards are defined by their ability to move over any obstacle and chase targets, even on rooftops. That bastard thief, The King, utilizes sneaky tactics among his men, and we need to train to meet them. This exercise will be used for me to rank you, best to worst, in terms of athletic skill, and we train until everyone completes the course in five minutes. Go to it!"

It was then Parisa saw the structure. The boys moved in a line to another part of the barracks and the training course came into view. A makeshift obstacle course grew up out of the ground like an urban jungle and ran the length of the training green. Parisa followed after the boys, hands trembling and knees shaking, and got a better look at it all. The course consisted of high walls, low crawling spaces, ladders, slippery surfaces, and a large pool. They all lined up at the start. Commander Crevan started a timer, and the first boy ran for it. Parisa swallowed hard, bottling her fear and her pride. She had never done anything like that in her entire life, and she did not understand how her father expected her to now.

The other boys in line had been in the regular guard, street patrol that was assigned to businesses to prevent petty theft, investigate complaints, and keep the streets safe. Through an application process and physical tests, they had been welcomed into the Elite Guard with open arms because of their prowess and ability to follow orders. Parisa had done no such training or tests and had been placed here. Perhaps her father hoped she would fail so he could humiliate her more.

The boy in front of her in line shifted excitedly as he waited. He looked like he wanted to run forever, bouncing on his toes and shifting his heels in the sand. He stood tall and thin, and the sun bounced off his black hair, the blackest that Parisa had ever seen. He had long, dark eyelashes that protected him from the sun and eyes darker than pitch. His hair was straight, unlike the other boys, and even though he appeared thin with hunger, he bounced with energy. Parisa's eyes trailed down his arms to his wrists, which were barely wider than her own. She shuddered at the sight of his bones and wondered how long he had gone hungry.

A few of the boys returned to the line behind Parisa because they had been too slow. Commander Crevan shouted and the boy in front of her bolted off. He ran faster than anyone Parisa had ever seen. He attacked the course with such agility and speed that the other boys stopped to stare. Commander Crevan even looked impressed. When the boy finished, mud-stained and smiling with perfectly white teeth, Commander Crevan stopped his watch. "Two minutes, fifteen seconds."

The boys whispered with contempt as he sat off to the side with the other champions, those who finished the course in three or four minutes. The boy now held the record and beamed as he sat in the sand.

Before she could blink, it was Parisa's turn. Her heart pounded in her chest and her hands shook as she readied herself.

The commander held up his watch. "Go!"

Parisa tried to remember what the boy before her had done and she jumped to grab the wall in front of her. It was around six or seven feet high and as she scrambled up it, she slipped, hitting the ground hard squarely on her backside. The second time, she heaved herself up and over it, arms trembling and hands sweating. After making it over, she hopped across large rocks in a pool of water as if it were a game. She was happy that she had not yet injured herself, but she moved like a tortoise and she knew it. And it was only the beginning.

The rest of the course was straightforward and simple until she reached the rope. The rough hempen twine tore her hands underneath her gloves and as she climbed, she bled. At the top of the rope, however, the course only climbed higher. Mesh acted as a handhold and she continued upward, with no safety net. Her knees trembled and she dragged herself up onto solid ground. The worst was yet to come.

At the top of the platform, the only way down was to jump from the ten- or twelve-foot ledge into a pool below. She stood there for a moment, absorbed in the terror of it all, thought about what she had to do, and fear choked her up.

"Come on, girly!" a boy called. "Afraid to get your pretty hair wet?"

"I think she's afraid she'll soil her frock, boys!" another joked.

She glared at them and grimaced. As she met eyes with the fast boy, his face flooded with compassion. He nodded. His smile seemed to say, *Go on. You can do it. It really isn't that bad.*

She swallowed her fear and jumped, trying to land as gracefully into the water as she could, but with no luck. It was warmer outside, now that the sun had begun to rise, but the water in the pool was frigid and the shock of the cold choked her up as she floundered to the surface. Loud splashing mingled with boisterous laughter and she came up coughing. She had swallowed water; she paddled pathetically and wished that she had learned how to swim.

She swam as fast and as best as she was able toward the final challenge, crawling and vaulting. The fast boy had slid underneath all the sharp wire and metal that blockaded the path, but she knew she could not do that. She pulled herself from the water and began to crawl, trying as hard as she could to not cut her face. The sandy ground stuck to her clothes and face and when she finally came out, Commander Crevan shook his head.

"Back to the line," he barked.

She shivered and walked past all the boys who laughed, and she stuck her tongue out at them. He did not disclose her time, and the back of the line was a lonely place for a princess.

She would go to do the course twenty-five more times

after that. As the other boys went off to lunch, she miserably sat at the end of the course as Commander Crevan looked down at her, sighing, "You don't eat until you get it under six minutes."

Parisa shuddered as she sobbed. She jumped when a hand touched her shoulder, and she expected to get hit again. Her face still swelled with the mark that Commander Crevan had left, and her discomfort made her uneasy. When she looked up, she met the warm, black eyes of the fast boy.

"Can I give you some tips?" he asked.

"W-What?" She rubbed her eyes, smearing more sandy mud onto her face. She would not bear to have any of the other boys see she was crying.

"Tips – you know, to make you faster?" he added, and crouched next to her. She nodded childishly, felt like such a helpless little girl, and she hated it.

"When you go to jump across those blocks," he continued, "don't stop running. If you keep your momentum, you can clear two at a time sometimes. And... I understand you're scared to jump into the pool, but if you can think about making your body an arrow, you'll cut the water better. It'll also hurt less."

Parisa nodded and said, "T-Thanks."

"I'm Perseus," he smiled, and stuck his hand out for her. It was covered in a little bit of sand and he had such large hands compared to her petite ones.

"Parisa." She took it, expecting him to kiss her hand, but when he shook it, she did not understand. That custom was reserved for businessmen, not princesses.

"Back up out of the dirt! Come on! We don't have all day!"

Commander Crevan barked from across the field.

Parisa stood, brushed off her pants, and moved back to the front of the course. Her arms still had one more run in them, but she was sure if she continued, they would give out. Perseus gave her one last encouraging grin and called, "Remember what I said!"

Parisa took a deep breath and waited for her signal. Her entire body ached and cried out for a break, but now she could not stop. Commander Crevan would not let her stop, and she did not want to be hit again.

"Go!"

She dashed for the goal, remembering what Perseus had said. At the dive, she still trembled, but she managed to not hit the water as hard. At the end of the course, Commander Crevan stopped the timer and huffed, "Four minutes, forty-five seconds. Go eat, soldier."

Parisa smiled, wobbled her way to the door of the mess hall, and leaned on the doorframe, catching her breath. Her feet felt as though they were caught in an earthquake, even though the ground stood still. Perseus strolled up beside her and clasped his hands behind his back.

"Thanks," she huffed. "For the advice."

"You'll get better. I promise. I've been running like this for my entire life," he said.

"Have you eaten?" Parisa was shocked when Perseus followed her into the mess hall and grabbed a plate of food.

"No. I was waiting for you."

"That's sweet of you."

Parisa grabbed a plate of the most unappetizing food she

had ever seen and sat at a long table with a rudimentary fork and knife set made of wood. Perseus followed and sat across from her in the empty room. All the other boys had gone outside to continue their training, and the cook stopped making plates and turned off their stovetop.

Perseus took a few bites of his food without saying anything, eating hastily like one who knew what it was like to go without any kind of food, but then he looked up at her. "So, is it true?" he asked. "Are you really from the Embassy?"

Parisa nodded, but it almost embarrassed her that she *was*. She was not of royal blood, though, but a half-breed as her father often said, one born of poverty and privilege. He never let her forget it. When she put the fork in her mouth, the food tasted cold, but the flavor was not half as bad as it looked, and she swallowed a mouthful of it. "Yes," she said through her food, disregarding all the precious etiquette training Master Esmond had so heavily insisted upon. "I am."

"Really?"

"I'm the Soveriegn's daughter."

"You're kidding."

"No," she sighed. She poked her fork into the food, and it wriggled like it could have been alive. "My father told me yesterday I had to train to become an Elite or I would be severely punished. I'm bad at school and not good at anything else."

"And you're the only girl in the entire guard?"

She nodded, and replied, "Today's my first day. Is it yours?"

Perseus finished his meal nearly as fast as he ran. "It is. How are you adjusting? Don't your people live off chocolate and whipped cream?"

"It's awful. I would rather be studying and reading than fighting."

"At least you have that choice. Most of us are forced into the guard due to poverty. I'm just lucky that I was fast enough to be placed as an Elite."

"And you *are* fast. You're the fastest person I've ever seen," Parisa added and pushed her plate away from her. The plate was only half-empty, but the food lacked flavor and disinterested her.

Perseus pushed it back. "You need to eat," he insisted. "If you don't, your body will fail. Hunger will overtake you and then you'll be kicked out."

Parisa glowered at the plate.

"I know you're probably used to ritzy food, but at least try."

She continued to eat, despite the horrible food, but she appreciated his concern. She asked, "What district are you from?"

"The Dza'ya district."

"Really?" she smiled. "I hear that's a nice district."

Perseus nearly spit out the water he was drinking. "Nice for bugs, maybe," he choked.

"I don't follow." Parisa wondered if she had offended him.

"You really *are* from the Embassy," Perseus scoffed.

"What's *that* supposed to mean? I don't understand what I've said to upset you."

Perseus shook his head and sighed, "Let's get back out onto the field. We need to keep training and it sounds like Commander Crevan is giving out instructions."

He left without saying a word, storming out into the

blazing afternoon sun and onto the field. Parisa scoffed, threw away her uneaten food, and with low spirits, marched back outside.

Pure Power
Terran

Atsa, February of the Second Year

"I'm on him!"

Terran turned his head for a moment to look behind him in the direction of a shout to meet eyes with a street guard and felt his heart begin to flutter. The guard pointed in his direction and called for other members of his squad to begin pursuit. Terran sneered and shoved past two women bickering over peppers underneath the brick eaves of a crumbling roof. People were no barrier as he shoved past them in the crowded marketplace, and the guards followed with equal aggression, armor bashing against unarmored flesh.

Terran knew the pursuit would not be difficult for the guards, as he shone in his new and audacious wardrobe. He moved slowly enough that the guards could keep their eye on his colors. He wore a tribute to his district, fabrics of bright blue and shining silver draped on his body, and the garments were fashioned after The King's. Armor covered his skin; protection from rogue arrows and swords, and his blond hair had been tied up and out of his face so he could run. Terran had never had such long hair, and to keep it long enough to be pulled back, as short as it still was, would have been a disgrace to his royal upbringing. It was all part of a statement. He had changed a lot over the course of the year, and he felt proud to be the symbol that he now was.

Terran shoved past people in the crowd, trying to be as gentle as possible, and pardoned himself as his armor and momentum knocked civilians around. He heard the clank of the guard's boots behind him and caught a glimpse of The King's shadow as his master moved above him. Terran had not been caught that day. It was merely a lesson.

Sharply, the student turned into an alleyway and into the shadow of a falling building, preparing himself for his task. When he entered the hollow, out of sight of the average citizen, he turned and whipped the deck of cards from his pocket. His hands shook as he drew his first paper weapon. The card bore a picture of a five-pointed star on it, in which was a horned goat with blood-red eyes. Below that knelt a woman and a man who looked away from the terrifying figure.

Terran smiled and flipped the silver card over, placing it onto the back of his hand as he had seen The King do before. The silver of the card whipped out like snakes, wrapped Terran's hand as though they formed a gauntlet, and when it was finished, the pentacle and the goat were visible on the dorsum of the glove. In a burst of flame, the pentacle appeared underneath his feet in a crimson color and a pillar of light shot up from it. Terran held his breath in the flame and a crackling light brushed up his skin, changing his flesh into molten rock. When the light faded, in his hand he found a chain that was hotter than the whitest hot metal and lava dripped from his fingertips.

The guard peeled around the corner but stopped cold when he locked eyes with the beast he saw. "Oh, my gods... W-What... what are—"

"I am a message," Terran's voice grated like cold steel, "a message for the Sovereign of Segeno. Tell the Sovereign that the true heir lives and that he is coming for the throne. Change is inevitable, and the deceiver will fall."

The guard bolted out of the alleyway before Terran could say or do more, and the card wore off, the metal unwrapping itself from Terran's hand and the fire receding. The King hopped down from the roof and smiled, clasping Terran's hand. He joked, "You *would* draw The Devil on the first try, wouldn't you?"

Terran smiled and shrugged as they walked calmly back into the crowd and headed toward the tavern. He replied, "I'm a natural, eh?"

"The first one I ever got was the six of swords, so yeah... I'd say you're something special."

"Did I do well?"

"I'd say."

"What dictates how long they last? The cards?"

"The cards have eyes, my boy, and they just *know*."

"What if that gets me killed?"

"Then Justice made her decision. The cards giveth, the cards taketh away. You'll be fine, particularly in the dangerous situation I've devised."

Terran looked at him curiously. "And what dangerous situation is that?"

"We need to infiltrate the Embassy."

"So soon? I've hardly learned the cards. This is day two of card training, Your Majesty, I—"

"You'll be *fine*. The cards are pretty base in their mechanics, so I would not be afraid." The King reassured and nodded as they moved back into the tavern. "You'll need to practice on the go. Based on the sources I have, we're losing time... and fast. They're looking for you and the Sovereign is training new Elites to be more like us, running on rooftops and stealthy approaches..."

"Well, what do we need to do? Who's going to be the spy?"

"We need to plant *you* inside the Embassy, make you one of them. I've mulled it over, and unfortunately, I cannot take my men and women and create false identities for them. The Embassy is too exclusive for that, and newcomers are scrutinized... unless they fit perfectly. I may not be able to make a poor man rich, but I can make a rich man into another rich man. We're going to change everything about you, Terran. Your face, especially. You'll fit right in. Hell, you've lived it, so who better to place?"

"You don't think it's risky? If they find me out, I'll be killed."

"You have to survive. The cards said so."

"Well, *assuming* I live, and *assuming* I don't get killed in my sleep, changing my hair color will not be enough. Am I going to wear a mask? Won't that be obvious?"

"You're thinking too literally. Think abstractly."

Terran spluttered, "I-I don't—"

"The cards, Terran," The King affirmed and grabbed Terran

by the shoulders, deviance in his eyes. "The cards will protect you, just as they've protected me all these years. Do not lose faith."

The Well
Parisa

Naa'a, March of the Second Year

A hawk screeched out as it circled above, dipping into the blue sky, and Parisa gazed out over the desert, shielding her eyes from the blistering, blinding sun. Far in the distance, blue mountains peaked over an endless sea of tan, nothing but dirt and rocks, and soft, white clouds roved their way across the sky, like they had not a care in the whole world. Parisa wondered if the earth had always been that brown, or if the Great War caused the place to be devoid of all vegetation.

She sat in silence on the Naa'a rooftop, pondering the events of the last few months, and closed her eyes in speculation. The sunlight danced across her cheek and she smiled.

"You're pretty in the light," a boy said. Parisa looked to meet eyes with Perseus, who munched on a plum, and he continued, "Your skin is really lovely, I mean."

"Thank you."

"Now that we're not dirty all the time, we both look pretty

good, huh?"

"I think so."

"People don't take me seriously, though. They assume I'm a kid playing dress up. Has that happened to you?"

"It's even worse for me. People see my face and think I ran away from home, or sometimes they don't believe me when they say I'm the Sovereign's daughter. I look nothing like him, so... I get it."

Parisa was surprised at how different she looked now. At first, she had feared the drastic change of lifestyle, but Perseus proved to be a fast friend and good company. With help from him, after she made up and took back what she said, she had become the second fastest and hardest working soldier in the Elite Guard. Perseus had been promoted from soldier to Captain and he and Parisa worked closely together, taking care of investigations of robberies and patrolling the streets.

Elites, Parisa had learned quickly enough, only worked in the Naa'a district, to protect the rich and the royal. Parisa found this strange, seeing as the entire city could make use of increased help and protection. Perseus and Parisa spent most of their time chasing down thieves before they disappeared into the other districts and guarding large amounts of goods and money as they moved from one place to another. The Elite Guard were at the Sovereign's beck and call and did not serve the people.

"Man, this job is so *boring*," Perseus huffed.

"I think it's quite relaxing."

"Nothing bad happens in this district, other than tax fraud. I wish I was in Dza'ya busting bad guys and helping people."

106

"We *are* helping people."

"Not the people that matter. We protect property. We don't serve the citizens of Segeno. Not really."

Parisa pondered on it and looked out over the desert again.

"You know what's the worst?"

"What?"

"I never thought I would end up working for the guard, because we all hate them down there, you know? The guard ruins everything: they destroy businesses, tear apart families, wrongfully accuse. I was sure I'd never be one of them, and here I am."

"It can't be all that bad."

"You Embassy kids just don't understand," Perseus continued and bit into the plum as the two of them sat together. "You get taught that everything is perfect and pretty in the city to cover up all the ugly... and there's a *lot* of ugly."

"Like what?"

"Poverty, mostly. The Embassy sucks money out of people's wallets through tax, while they themselves don't pay a dime. You end up with hardly enough to pay for your house, let alone anything else. If a family member gets sick, you're done for."

"How is that possible? I've watched my father pass reforms that benefit everyone and make it easier for all people to live."

Perseus simply shrugged. "You're asking the wrong guy. All I know is what I've seen, and I've seen a lot of fat, rich, light-skinned Embassy goons get away with murder."

"What do you mean?"

"Down there, if you even look at a guard wrong, they take everything from you. You either walk away with no money, no stuff, and a bunch of black marks on your record, or you don't walk away at all."

Parisa turned to look at Perseus, her eyebrows scrunched together in the center of her forehead. She said nothing, and when he looked at her, he seemed confused.

"What?" he asked.

"What do you *mean*, you don't walk away at all?"

"They kill you."

Goosebumps shot up Parisa's arms. A hawk circled overhead and cried out, lonely and solitary in the sky.

"I don't understand why they hide the horror from us instead of making it better," Parisa whispered.

"Me neither! I knew that joining the guard was a bad option. I didn't want to associate with them at all. I *hate* them, but... the pay for an Elite is higher than I could have ever imagined. A day of work sets my family for months, and as someone from Dza'ya, the best jobs I had to look forward to were shoe shiner, page, or a stable boy, if I was lucky."

"But everyone has the freedom to get whatever job they want in Segeno."

Perseus laughed and coughed on a piece of plum. "If," he said, "You find a boss up in the other districts that doesn't hate dirty street rats, and unfortunately *your* people don't want us contaminating their stock."

"There are laws to prevent employers from—"

"It gives us equal opportunity, girl. Doesn't mean they have to hire us."

"But that's how it was in the ancient times. Before the

Great War. It doesn't happen—"

"Look around you," Perseus said as he gestured to Naa'a. "Nothing's changed."

Parisa's heart panged as she looked at Naa'a and realized that there was no one who walked the street that looked like her. She was unique, a mother from Dza'ya and a father from the Embassy, which left her in the in between... alone.

"When I become Sovereign," she said, "I'll change that."

"Your dad has to die first."

I hate him, Parisa almost said, but she stopped herself. Instead, she asked, "What's your family like?"

Perseus sighed, "It's just me, my mom, and my dad now. My sister died a year before I was eligible to work."

"Of what?"

Perseus shrugged. "We don't know... we didn't have the money to take her to a doctor. She just got sick, that's all."

Parisa said nothing for a while and adjusted her armor. "I understand how you feel. Losing family is the worst."

"Do you?"

"My mother left when I was five, and my father doesn't care about me. I really have no family."

Perseus smiled and gently socked her on the arm. "So," he laughed, "we're in the same boat then, eh, Princess?"

"Don't call me that!" Parisa giggled.

Perseus had called her that since the day they had met, and Parisa at first found it endearing but also a constant reminder of the things she hated. Only a year ago, she had been a regular girl... no. Not a regular girl. She had been a very wealthy girl living in a house all alone with a servant. Something to be ashamed of. And now she could not escape a title.

"When you call me that," she continued, "it makes me sad."

"Why?"

"It reminds me of what has been robbed from me. It reminds me of the time I spent with my mother, and how my father never wanted me around. I was a princess, sure, but... only by title. I didn't feel like a princess at all."

"Perhaps you just need someone who will treat you like one."

Parisa's cheeks turned bright pink and she stammered, "W-What did you do for fun as a kid?"

"Steal, mostly, for good reasons, I promise," he laughed, "but I used to climb trees a lot, actually. If I didn't have anything to do, friends to play with, I'd climb the trees in front of the Embassy gates."

"Seriously?"

"Yeah, they'd yell at me, too. The guards. They always thought I was trying to break in. I got rocks thrown at me more than once, but luckily never shot at. What about you?"

"I used to own this doll..." Parisa hadn't thought about her best friend in a long time. "Before I had any friends, Theophilia used to be my only playmate. My mother got her for me for a birthday, a long time ago, and when she died, I used to imagine that Theophilia was her emissary, that, as an angel, my mother could see me through Theophilia's eyes. We'd do amazing things together. Go to faraway lands, host tea parties..."

"That sounds nice, for a girl," Perseus laughed.

Parisa socked him on the arm, harder than he anticipated, and he recoiled. She laughed, and he laughed, and their laughter echoed across the flat rooftops of Naa'a. He knew how to push her buttons, but in the best kind of way. He did for her what Esmond did, listened unconditionally and with no judgement, even when he jested and made her smile.

"But," he amended, "it does sound nice. My parents didn't have enough money for toys, and we played with sticks and rocks. Who were your friends when you were young?"

"I only really had one."

"Yeah?"

Parisa closed her eyes and did her best to remember the smell of the sage of Esmond's study, the gentle touch of his caring hands, and the fond gaze of his eyes. She continued, "My tutor. His name is Esmond."

"And you were friends with your *teacher*?"

"Yes. He is like a father to me, better than my father could ever be, honestly. He actually listens to what I have to say and is always there for me. Can I... tell you a secret?"

"Of course. I won't tell anyone."

Parisa pulled a piece of paper from her breastplate, something she kept on her at all times. "Now that we're on patrol, we can go wherever we want, right?" she asked. "Do you figure they'd question if we went to Dza'ya?"

"I don't think so, if we say we're following a lead. Like, if we saw someone pickpocket a rich person and we chased them down." Perseus leaned over to look at the drawing and tossed the pit of his plumb aside. "Why?"

"Do you know where this well is?" Parisa inquired and showed Perseus the drawing.

Perseus nodded and replied, "Yeah, that dirty thing is by my house. It's tucked away in a back corner of Dza'ya. Women bathe there."

"Let's go then!" Parisa stood. "Lead the way!"

Perseus smiled and stretched his legs. "Think you can keep up?"

Before she could reply, Perseus was already off running and she had to push herself to match pace. Perseus' legs were lean and long, and his endurance proved relentless. Parisa loved running with him and felt free as they darted together, like fish in a river. After a long while of dashing across rooftops, roofs turned to thatch and Parisa saw for the first time the atrocities that the Dza'ya district had to offer.

She had never expected any district in Segeno to look the way that the Dza'ya district did. As she and Perseus dropped to the ground, she had to cover her mouth to keep herself from gasping. Tears came to her eyes as she witnessed the poverty that surrounded the people of the district. Perseus glanced at her and muttered, "See? I told you it's not all marble and flowers."

"I-I... I just can't believe..."

"So, you're telling me they *never* told you what Dza'ya was really like in the Embassy?"

"Never," Parisa stuttered and wiped her eyes. "I was always taught that all the districts in Segeno prospered."

"Who writes the history books?"

"I've read several by Naa'a scholars."

"There's the first problem. And who prints the books?"

"The... The Embassy."

"Now you understand."

After a few more minutes of walking, Perseus led her to the well that Master Esmond had drawn, which had been dug near small wooden shacks. A woman threw her chamber pot into the street and Parisa lifted her arm to protect her nose from the stink. "This place is horrible," she said.

"This is my home. Do you suppose we have a moment to visit my family?"

"Let's go."

Perseus strode, proud in his gleaming armor, to his house, where he called through the thatch and wood building, "Mom! It's me!"

He pushed the door open and a wave of aromatic scents escaped into the chilly outside air. Parisa took a deep breath in, experiencing the new smells, and met the eyes of a woman with skin the color of dark clay and bruised eyes. "Oh, Perseus!" she exclaimed. "What a surprise!"

"I was in the neighborhood and thought I'd stop by."

She rushed to him, wooden spoon in hand, and enveloped him in a hug. "Look at you," she smiled through tears, "so professional in that uniform."

"Thanks, Mom. This is First Lieutenant Sauveterre."

"Parisa, please," Parisa added.

"Parisa. Aren't you a lovely young lady? Such hair! Perseus, where did you find such a lovely thing? I wish my skin looked like yours, baby. It's so pretty! Would you like some stew?"

"No, thank you, ma'am. I don't know if we'll be able to stay and eat," Parisa replied, resisting the urge to pull up her hood.

"Oh, but you *must.*"

"I'll come back, Mom," Perseus assured and kissed her on the cheek. "For now, I have to go, but I'll visit soon, when Dad's home."

"Have a good day, honey. I love you."

Tears came to Perseus' mother's eyes as she kissed his forehead on tiptoe, and she opened the door for them as they left. Parisa took in the home one last time, and the meagerness of it all. The thatch roof harbored holes and their bed was merely a mat in the small, one-roomed hut. Perseus hugged his mother tightly, picking her small frame up off the ground and twirled her. She laughed like a songbird, loud and joyous, and when he was done, she opened her arms to Parisa. Parisa returned the hug, a warmth spreading to her fingertips, and before Perseus' mother closed the door, Parisa said, "For the record, you look a lot like my mother, who was one of the most beautiful women in the whole world. I would give anything for skin like hers. I look forward to meeting you again."

A smile as wide as the moon spread across Perseus' mother's face as she closed the door. Perseus pointed toward an old, crumbling wall, and led Parisa to a small square. The well sat in the middle of it, stalls and bustle around it as women poured jars of water over their naked, glistening bodies and dunked their children to get them clean. Parisa gazed among the group, not seeing what she had expected. Perseus had described a place filled with people like him, and there were, but that was not all. People of all skin shades and face frames, eye shapes and hair texture visited the pool... except... Parisa strained and only found one person that looked even remotely like her father.

All others had skin ranging from tawny to umber, a rainbow of accents and types of people she had never seen before, but no one that looked like they were from the Embassy. Parisa bit her lip as she looked upon the crowd, watching smiling children splashing in the dirtiest water she had ever seen, and knew something was wrong. Parisa pulled out a piece of paper and pencil from her pocket and began scratching a note.

"What are you doing? Are you going to throw it into the well?" Perseus asked.

"Sh," Parisa hushed.

After she finished writing, she searched the rim of the well on the eastern side, found a loose rock, and, when she lifted it, she found numerous pieces of paper underneath it already. The notes were from various people, names she did not recognize, some letters written in languages she did not read, and she discreetly added hers to the stack. Perseus crossed his arms, and his weight sank to one hip, suspicion in his eyes.

"I don't think your teacher is a teacher."

Parisa shrugged and replaced the stone. No one paid her any mind. "I don't know. Maybe he is, maybe he isn't. All I know is that he is one of the dearest friends I have, and I must stay in touch with him. Let's get back to the palace before they realize we're gone."

The pair rushed their way back to Naa'a as though they had never been gone, and when they arrived, they climbed back up to the spot they had been before. Nothing was out of the ordinary. It was nearly dinnertime and two other boys that Parisa had trained with soon replaced the two. Parisa and Perseus walked, inseparable, back to the barracks and, at the dinner table, the two of them exchanged no words. Someone talked to Perseus about moving troops to Dza'ya, which he refused, and Parisa kept to her dinner.

Parisa was unsure if Perseus felt Esmond was a spy, and that she herself was a traitor, or if they were both too exhausted to speak. The other officer left, and Perseus returned to silence once more. After she finished her meal, Parisa started to stand to put her tray away when Perseus' hand rested on hers on the table.

"Wait," he said.

"What?" Parisa looked back at him. "What is it?"

"You know you're my only friend, right?"

"Perseus, I—"

"I've never known anyone like you, and I feel like I have known you my whole life. You have to promise me you'll always be my friend, all right? You wouldn't betray me, would you?"

"Is this about Esmond?"

"This is about everything."

"I wouldn't."

"*Promise.*"

"I promise," Parisa affirmed and smiled at him as the sun began to go down. He took a moment to watch her eyes, his own darting back and forth, hoping to pull the truth from her face, until he stood without another word. He returned his tray to the bin and walked off by himself back to his sleeping quarters.

Rune Guildenhart
Terran

The Tavern, June of the Second Year

"Everything is prepared, yes?"

"I think so."

"Clothes?"

"I got a brand-new wardrobe from Naa'a last week."

"Alibi?"

"Due to Councilman Guildenhart's sudden death, the Sovereign called for a replacement. As his... 'son,' I am his replacement."

"Perfect," The King said, and pulled out his cards. They glided past his fingertips as he shuffled them. "We have prepared nearly two years for this, Terran. Are you sure you can handle it?"

"I'm sure."

"Remember what our goal is," the King muttered and leaned closer to Terran. "You're to find the Sovereign, and you're to find out whatever foul play he's got tucked in sleeves. You've got to become his best friend, Terran, and then we can take him down from the inside out."

Terran gazed at the candle behind the fake window, burden weighing on his shoulders. He had never done anything this important in his entire life, and guilt hung in his heart. He felt as though he were planning a coup against his parents, though they were already gone. "I know."

"Now, for your disguise..."

The King picked up Terran's deck and drew The Magician on the first try. "Remember," he said, "the card only lasts at maximum... twelve hours. Dawn till dusk, or dusk till dawn. As soon as it wears off, you're discovered."

Terran swallowed thickly and joked, "This is like a story I read in an ancient book, about a princess who became beautiful using the magick of a wise woman, but the spell wore off at dawn."

"Here's to hoping this card doesn't turn you into a beautiful princess."

It wouldn't. Terran knew it wouldn't. He had read every book he could on the cards, and now better understood their rules. They were intuitive, but he, as the card user, still had some control. Though the cards worked differently for everyone, certain cards, the Major Arcana, had set spells attached to them. The Magician was one of them. With The Magician, a card user could change their appearance at will, transforming into anything that they needed. With intent in mind, the card user could control the outcome... to some extent. The Magician would last as long as The King had detailed, dawn till dusk or dusk till dawn, and that was all. Terran could draw the card at will from the deck, just as The King did, with the proper practice and this card was about to become his weapon of choice.

"Let's do it," he said. "The cards will make it right."

The King handed Terran the card and Terran placed it on his hand. The metal uncoiled and wrapped itself around his hand like thin, metal fingers, and on the back of his skin a five-pointed star surrounded by odd symbols revealed itself. When the card finished, Terran looked at himself, expecting a great change, but saw nothing. He did not feel any different. The last card he had used had been something incredible, but now he felt as if nothing had happened at all.

Then, The King started to laugh. When Terran looked up at him, he held out the small hand mirror and Terran looked at himself. The face he saw there he did not recognize. It was far older, and his white-blond hair had been replaced with fire locks, much like The King's. The King chuckled, "If I didn't know any better, I would have guessed you were my own kid."

Terran smiled, "So, I just head to the front gates of the Embassy palace, then?"

"Yes. But remember... wander first. If guards are watching, we want it to look like you were just shopping."

"I need to get my story straight."

"You're from another settlement, somewhere far away."

"Sulphur."

"Right, Sulphur."

"But Sulphur is full of raiders and criminals, exiles from Segeno. Why would the son of a Councilmember be out—"

"You're a creative kid. I trust you. You'll come up with something. And Terran—"

"Not Terran. Rune Guildenhart, son of Adriann Guildenhart."

"*Terran,*" The King affirmed, stood, and grabbed him firmly by the shoulders, "be *careful.*"

"Are you actually saying you care about me?"

The King straightened up and frowned, a scowl plastered on his otherwise youthful lips. "I'm not saying any such thing. You're just a large part of my operation, is all, and if I lose you, I'm sunk. You're only a street rat, remember?"

"Of course." Terran bowed. "I won't fail you, Your Majesty."

RECOGNITION
Parisa

The Palace, June of the Second Year

"Parisa," Lord Talbot ruminated and leaned on his elbow, "I hear from Commander Crevan you are out of training."

"Yes, My Lord," Parisa reported and kneeled before her father respectfully. She was unsure if she even considered him a father anymore, and the only thing that connected he and she as related were the shapes of their faces and their eyes. "He tells me all that remains is experience."

Lord Talbot nodded and continued, "Then I have a new job for you. You and that other Elite boy who's Captain... Perseus, was it? You two will be the Embassy's personal guard. He will be required to keep up on his duties as Captain, but he should be able to order around a bunch of other boys from the inside, no? My spies have picked up word on an assassination attempt that is brewing amongst the common folk and I fear The King is up to something. I'm satisfied with your performance in the guard and appreciate that you're better at running than at school, so I trust

121

you with the responsibility of protecting me and my colleagues."

Inside, Parisa felt relieved that Perseus was the one picked to work with her. She replied, "Yes, My Lord. Thank you, My Lord."

"I had not expected you to come so far in so little time, and Commander Crevan reminded me that Perseus is an ignorant illiterate. I'm assigning Esmond to him. I will not have my best men unable to read books. That's an embarrassment to Segeno. You two will live here from now on, and when I need you or when I get a lead on the traitor, I will summon you, you will go to him, and you will stop him dead in his tracks. Otherwise, you must stay here and watch over the palace, keep an eye out for any intruders. Do you understand?"

Parisa felt her heart flutter with happiness and she could not believe that she had come across such good fortune. "Yes, My Lord," she said.

"Captain Perseus is on his way. You are dismissed."

Parisa stood and bowed too fast for it to be polite, but as she moved down the hallways that led to her old bedroom, feeling the walls she missed so much, her heart skipped a beat. When she entered the room she had once called her own, she found that nothing had changed, save the fact that the bed was larger and many of the frivolities of her old life had gone. When she checked the drawers, she found combat clothes in place of all the Embassy gowns she had once worn, and there were a few sets of formal attire, but not many. She flopped down onto the bed and stared at the ceiling, ever so glad to be home.

And then she remembered.

She leapt to her feet and dashed into the elevator to head toward her teacher's room. He sat at his desk, his silver spectacles lightly falling off his nose as he read, and when she knocked on the door frame, he glanced up and then returned to his book, seeming a little surprised that there was an Elite guard in his study. "Yes?" he asked absentmindedly. "What do you need?"

"Master Esmond! It's me! Parisa!"

Esmond raised his eyes from his literature and when they met Parisa's face he gasped for breath. He jumped to his feet, rushed to her, and hugged her tightly, lifting her from the ground. "I hardly recognized you!" he exclaimed. "You've grown so much! What happened to your hair? What are you doing here?"

"Father said I can stay here and that he'll call me if he needs me. O-Oh, and my hair?" Parisa rain her fingers through her short curls. "Commander Crevan made me cut it. It's silly, I know—"

"It's beautiful."

A smile pooled across Parisa's face and she took his hand. "Did you get my message from the well?"

Master Esmond moved to his desk and pulled out the piece of paper she had written on only a few months ago. "Of course! I still have it here. Did you get my response?"

Parisa shook her head and replied, "I haven't had the time to check."

"Well, no matter. You're here and that's what matters," he said and hugged her again. "Are you to study with me?"

"Not me, but Perseus, my Captain. Father thinks it's shameful that he is uneducated, but I can help him study. He helped me survive training."

"Any friend of yours is a friend of mine."

"I don't think he's arrived yet. I'm just happy I can let go of a few worries and take my time during the day, patrolling the palace grounds instead of running in the streets."

"You should go get some rest. I have a surprise for you when you have the time, and now we have all the time in the world. It's good to see your face, my dear."

Master Esmond returned to his desk and Parisa slipped off back to her room without saying goodbye. There was no need, now. She had never been happier, and as she changed into her nightgown, one of the kinds that she used to wear, a knock rattled on her door.

"Come in!" she called, and she went to sit at the vanity. *It's Master Esmond come to give me a surprise,* she thought, *or Perseus.* She did not need to turn to see who stood at the door. Whoever it was opened it and his words boomed around the room.

"Sheesh! This place is so covered in silver I'm afraid I'm going to wake up made of the stuff!"

"How do you like it, Perseus?" Parisa laughed as she spun around on her stool.

Perseus sat at the edge of her bed and stuttered, "It's... incredible, but almost scary. I can't believe you people live like this. I mean, I actually had a servant come up and ask me if I wanted anything to eat or if I wanted fresh towels in my bathroom. I told them to bring me the entire kitchen and as many clean towels as they had."

Parisa laughed and began to rub her favorite mixture of

yarrow and sweetgrass into her hair. Perseus gazed at her in a strange way, head rested on the palm of his hand and his eyes trained at her face. He blinked slowly, mesmerized by her, and a smile crept into the corner of his mouth.

"What?" Parisa asked.

Perseus sighed, "Do all of you Embassy people have white hair?"

"Most of us, yes," she replied. "I'm lucky I got my dad's hair. Some of us are born with wild, red hair, and kids make fun of those who are different relentlessly. I'm lucky *I* didn't get made fun of for the way I look... not heavily, anyway."

"You're beautiful, so if anyone ever says anything, I'll break their face," Perseus mused, "but you're right. You don't look anything at all like your dad."

"My mother was one of the only people that looked like you on the Council. Her father had been elected into the Embassy by not the last Sovereign but the Sovereign before, which was incredibly rare. He brought his wife, who was also from Dza'ya, and had my mom. She had legal claim to the position as Councilmember in the Embassy, despite her parent's origins. My father then married my mother and married into the Embassy, so here I am. My mother was of royal blood, and he is not."

"Oh!" Perseus' eyes drifted around the room. "I didn't know that."

Another quiet knock echoed throughout the room and a servant opened the door. "Captain Sherazi, your supper is ready."

"Captain Sherazi?" Perseus grinned like had been caught with his hand in a cookie jar. "I'm going to go eat. See you later,

Pri... P-Parisa."

"Bye!" Parisa chuckled, rolled her eyes, and was about to get into bed again where there was yet another knock at the door. The servant opened it again, drowsiness in his eyes.

He said, "A Master Guildenhart is here to see you."

Guildenhart. Parisa recalled the family name from her studies and knew that the Guildenhart family had owned a seat in the council for generations, but she had seen the funeral procession for Councilman Guildenhart through the Naa'a district, so it could only be a vague relative of his. Parisa sighed, a little annoyed, and sat up again. "Send him in," she huffed.

Before long, a man stepped into her room. His features were striking, and he carried himself like a stork, elegant and long. A silk tunic draped over his shoulders, audacious in color even for someone in Naa'a. A single gemstone pierced his eyebrow, and he smiled genuinely as he stood in the doorway.

"Good evening," he began. His voice fell over his lips as smooth as his clothes. "I hope I am not disturbing you."

"I've just been trying to get to sleep, but it's no problem, really. I suppose I'm not that tired, after all. Is there something you needed?"

"I wanted to come and introduce myself before it got too late. My name is Rune. I'm new to the Embassy and I felt I should get to know my colleagues."

"I am not a colleague," she retorted. "I'm not a part of the Council. Never was. I merely serve the Sovereign. You need not pay any attention to me or what I do."

"On the contrary," he retorted. "I think you're the most

fascinating part of this place. I should like to take a day to spend some time with you, if you'll let me."

"You cannot simply expect that I will be free of my duties for an entire day. I am no longer allowed the same leisurely pleasures you are, My Lord. My father would not have me be absentee for a day," Parisa sneered.

"I'll see if I may obtain the proper permissions, then."

"Good luck."

"You... disagree with him?" Rune wondered. "You seem unhappy."

"*What?*" Parisa argued. "What on *earth* gave you that impression?"

"Your tone."

Parisa shifted out of the bed and made herself less vulnerable. She knew that she could bring him to his knees if she needed to, and she snapped, "I don't think it's appropriate for us to be speaking in a lady's quarters."

"I meant no offense. I was just—"

"Goodnight, Lord Guildenhart," she huffed, closed the door in his face, and not another word was said.

LIES
TERRAN

The Palace, June of the Second Year

"Lord Guildenhart?"

Someone rapped on the doorway and Terran emerged from the throes of sleep, rubbing his eyes and stretching as warm sheets encapsulated him. He remembered where he was, and he pulled the puffy, down sheets up to his chin, a smile on his face. The sunlight streamed in through his window, the wavering glass casting fanciful patterns onto the floor, and he breathed in the scent of orange peel and cinnamon. When the knock sounded again, he startled himself from his half-dream and stood, alarmed. It only took one look in the mirror to tell him that his disguise had worn off, and he fumbled for the cards in his pocket as the rapping on the door continued.

"Lord Guildenhart, I have an urgent message for you from Lord Talbot."

"One moment!" Terran stumbled to his feet and, as quickly as he could, Terran drew a card from the pouch around his waist.

He had no time to check if it was The Magician, and he knew he had to trust his cards. The first card he drew was the one he used, and just as the card finished its magick, the servant opened the door. Terran stumbled into a pair of pants. "Sorry," he apologized. "I had a long night. I had not yet awoken."

"My apologies for waking you," the servant added and nodded in a rote fashion as he opened the door wider. "Lord Talbot wished for me to inform you that he is holding a feast in your honor and instructed that I return with your response. It will be later tonight, but he wanted to make sure that you would have time to attend. He understands you are busy adjusting to your new life."

"I'll be there," Terran sighed and flopped down onto the bed. "Send my regards."

That had been incredibly close, he thought to himself as the servant closed his door again. He was banking on dozens of lies to get him through however long it would take for him to complete his mission. He was not sure if he was comfortable with it or not, but he knew it must be done.

He had forgotten how much he missed the Embassy, and he enjoyed the moment to himself a little longer. Soft beds, warm sheets, and large open windows leading to warm summer nights called to him like a dream. The Embassy Palace, as far as he was concerned, was the most beautiful building ever made, and each floor of the crystalline building served a different purpose. The first floor contained the courtyard, the throne room, and a few guests' bedrooms. The second floor held the kitchens, the dining room, and the servants' quarters, and above that there were floors of suites, each belonging to a councilmember. Esmond, Councilman Wolff, and now himself occupied these floors as leaders of districts, but the rest of the suites remained empty.

Terran wondered, when wandering these empty floors, why Talbot had refused to elect new members of the Council. The process was straightforward. If the Councilmember had an heir by blood, they took the position. If not, then an election was held to determine who would replace them. Each district offered up the best candidates and a vote was held. Why Talbot refused to move forward with the election process was beyond Terran. Seven empty chairs tucked under the council table on the ninth floor, and Terran had wondered the day before who would fill the seats.

Days ago, when he had been assigned his mission, Rune's face masked his for the first time, and he wandered the city like a tourist. As Terran passed through the districts, he kept his eyes to the skies as he gazed upon the Embassy tower. Once in Naa'a, he passed through the gates of the palace into the outermost courtyard, which was flanked by Russian Olive Trees, those that appeared white in the right light, blue hydrangeas, delphinium, bluestars, and bellflowers. The entire courtyard itself was enclosed in glass so all manner of plants could grow, regardless of the weather.

The gates to the actual palace, beyond this small garden, stood tall and intimidating made of silver and woven into the emblem of the Embassy, an eagle. He looked into the throne room through the glass doors that led into it but did not enter. He feared the room, and memories of his parents haunted him, their ghosts playing in the light of the afternoon. It was the grandest room in the entire palace, except for the Sovereign's bedroom, but every corner and every nook and every particle of dust that flitted down from the ceiling reminded him of something that no longer was.

He loved the bedroom he was assigned as Councilman Guildenhart, though, with its huge down bed and beautiful metalwork. Because he now held the title of Councilmember as of yesterday, he occupied an entire floor. The suites comprised a small living room, an enormous bedroom with a large bathroom, as well as a study. What he loved most about the Embassy was the soft, warm bed he now called his own, a treasure compared to the small, hard bed provided to him by The King. He had been sound asleep the night before, so deeply that he could not plan what he was going to do with his day. He was nearly asleep again when he forced himself to get up.

Terran stood with hesitation and then dropped into twenty pushups before getting changed into a fresh set of Councilman's clothing, clothing that had been readily supplied by Lord Talbot. They were gorgeous and of finer quality than even The King's clothes. Even though he had grown fond of the vibrant colors, Terran had missed the soft blues and whites of home.

While he changed, Terran noticed a smudge of darkness on the back of his neck in the mirror, behind his ginger hair. The tattoo, one made by his significator on the back of his neck, was still present even after he had used The Magician, and he tried to cover it with the collar of his shirt. If he were sitting and someone were to pass behind him, they would be sure to see it, and he would need to come up with an excuse as to why it was there. To make things worse, the winding metal of The Magician hugged the back of his hand. In his drawers, he found a pair of plain white gloves and used them to cover his hands.

He had already come up with Rune's story. Because of his red hair, Councilman Guildenhart, Rune's "father," had wanted nothing to do with him. Rune took it upon himself to go and explore, see what the world had to offer. He settled in Sulphur, where Terran had never been, to research the wastes. Sulphur was nothing more than a rumor among the people of Naa'a. It certainly was a prison camp, where the worst of Segeno's criminals were stuffed, but it also was the only hope for exiles. Somewhere, miles beyond the city, Rune Guildenhart had found his refuge among the worst of Segeno. Simple enough.

After he had milled about a bit, wasting some of the morning, Terran made his way back to the quarters of Lady Parisa in hopes that she would be there and searched for a way to compose his thoughts. Parisa was an interesting case, certainly. *The daughter of a usurper turned princess, then stripped of her title and thrust into a place where her father could forget about her, but why?* Terran wondered. *And what kind of leverage does she have against him?* His primary goal remained to pull Talbot apart at the seams, bit by bit, until he disintegrated into nothing. His hand hesitated at the door, until he knocked.

He heard another voice from a boy, probably someone not much older than his usual self, and Parisa laughed. She laughed loud and long and hard, and it brought a smile to Terran's lips. He was glad that, even in such a horrible situation, she still found someone who made her happy. He knocked again. When the door opened, it was the boy who answered, his dark hair immediately betraying him as a palace guard. "Whoa... Parisa, who's the stiff?"

Parisa leaned over on the bed so she could look past Perseus at whoever stood in the doorway. When she saw him, she sneered, "Ah, Lord Guildenhart. What a pleasant surprise."

Ouch.

"I just wanted to apologize for my rude introduction last night," Terran started, "and I wanted to make sure we got off on the right foot, seeing as we'll be working closely toge—"

"We won't be, as I said, but that's a nice sentiment."

"Oh?"

"I'm not allowed now that my status is that of an Elite, so I will not be following in my father's footsteps replacing him after his time is done. That is at least what I have been relayed."

"Besides," Perseus interjected, "the guard is a much more respectable position, if I do say so myself."

Terran chuckled and smiled at the boy, a firecracker, he was certain. "My," he added, "you've got quite the mouth. Exactly what this place needs. Not enough people standing up for what they believe in."

Parisa's eyebrow flicked, a betrayal of her stone-faced countenance, and she eyed him as though she were looking for flaws. "Most don't like insubordination in the guard," she said.

"I didn't say he was insubordinate," Terran clarified. "He's bold and stated his opinion. It's about time Naa'a had a shake up, wouldn't you say, Lady Parisa?"

"Perseus, meet Rune Guildenhart. He is the newest

133

member of the Council," Parisa gestured. Caution coated her words and her suspicion betrayed her.

Perseus saluted Terran and said, "An honor to serve you, My Lord."

"You both are on guard here, I assume?" Terran asked.

"We're here to protect my father, yes," Parisa affirmed. "At the moment, we're on break."

"First woman in the Elite guard. That's quite the achievement and nothing to shake a fist at."

Perseus laughed, "That's what *I* said. Don't be fooled, though. She's the best soldier in the guard, under the Captain."

"Who is the Captain?"

"*I* am," Perseus beamed.

"You are a little *young*, aren't you?"

"I am, but that doesn't mean I'm not as good as any older man. All the older soldiers have retired and so they've needed to enlist younger and younger boys. I'm faster, stronger, and have better endurance than them, besides."

"A little overconfident, too," Terran nodded and smiled. "Well... sorry for interrupting. I'll be leaving. Perhaps we can enjoy a meal together one day, the three of us. My treat."

"If you would like a private meeting to speak with me, Lord Guildenhart, perhaps after the feast tonight would be a good time," Parisa suggested.

"That would be fine. Good day, Lady Parisa, Captain Perseus."

The door closed softly behind him and he moseyed along, hands in pockets, whistling, back to The King's home base. He figured it would be good to keep in touch with The King, let him know all he had learned in such a short time. He would perhaps suggest ideas for the direction they should go. The only obligation left on his plate was the feast in his honor, and there remained more time in the day than he needed. No one paid him any mind as he meandered through Naa'a, and then into Atsa, where he did not differ from any of the other rich men who did as they pleased when they pleased.

Those in the tavern did not question him, as Terran was sure they had all been alerted to The King's new schemes, and a few, after glimpsing his tattoo, nodded in recognition of him. After a few knocks on The King's office door, Terran wondered at the silence. He may have caught The King at a poor time, he imagined, or his master may have been out.

And then he ascertained a female voice inside but was unsure of whose it was. His brain scanned memories of every woman under The King's employ he had ever met, but the voice did not ring a bell. After knocking again, he could hear movement, but was hesitant to believe someone was moving toward the door. He began to feel a knot form in his stomach as he tried to open the door, only to find it locked.

"Your Majesty?" he exclaimed.

"What the *hell* do you—" The King opened the door just wide enough for only his body to be partially seen. "What are you doing here?" he hissed. He moved his body around to prevent Terran from seeing inside, and someone moved away from the crack in the door.

"Checking in," Terran reported, offended. He had never

seen The King like this and did not understand why he would keep secrets from his closest associate. "Like you said."

"After only a few days?" The King barked. "Now is *not* the time."

Terran pushed the door open, despite The King's resistance, to find a woman sitting in his usual chair. Her eyes were crying, her cheeks stained with tears, and her dark hair would have indicated to Terran lack of nobility, but her dress would not have... and the bruises. Her arms, hands, and face were covered with them, and her body trembled with sobs. Her hair knotted at the root and her Embassy gown tore at the edges as though it had caught on something. She was rather beautiful, though; tall and thin, the definition of elegance. Terran stood, stunned, and recalled a vague memory of her, but was unsure of exactly who she was. "Who is this?" he demanded.

"*I* told you. It is *not* the time," The King spat back.

"You're Rune Guildenhart, aren't you?" The woman shuddered as she spoke. "Councilman Guildenhart's son?"

Terran nodded. "Yes," he replied. "I arrived last week."

"He is *not* Rune Guildenhart," The King huffed as he attempted to close the door against Terran's arm. "Vena—"

"So, he's one of yours," Vena whispered and stood. "Are you the one he talks about so much?"

"I don't understand," Terran admitted. He could hardly find the words to explain his bewilderment.

The King frowned and replied, defeated, "Yes. This is Terran La'Hall."

Vena nodded and the shadow of a smile crossed her lips. "I

am glad that you are safe."

Terran knew he remembered her from somewhere. "Are you Alvena Wolff?" he asked. "Your husband is on the Council, isn't he?"

Vena frowned like she was going to be sick, and she sank back down into the chair again, sobbing.

The King shot him a dirty glance. "Nice going."

"What did I say?"

"You need rest," The King cooed as he lifted Vena gently by the elbows to stand and handed her one of the books that Terran remembered purchasing a few months before. "Read this. It's new... I know you'll love it."

The King led her into Terran's room and quietly closed the door. After the door was shut securely, The King whipped around and snapped, "When I say it is not the time, it is *not* the time."

He stormed past Terran, who followed, and sat at the bar at the back of the tavern. The tavern hushed for a moment, all its patrons assessing their leader's condition, and within moments things returned to normal. Terran shut the door to the back room softly behind him and sat next to The King, who gestured something to the bartender. Terran pried, "So those books were for her?"

The King said nothing and when his drink came, he sipped it, eyes glued to the wall.

"How did she get hurt? Is she all right?"

After another shot, the drink was finished, and The King ordered another.

"Why won't you answer me?"

"You may be disguised as a man, but you are a *boy*, Terran." The King glared at him with cold, grey eyes, much like the day they had first met. "The law says you are a man, but you do not *understand* the affairs of men."

With that, The King took his drink and went back to his office, closing the door behind him, locking it with a loud click, and Terran was left sitting at the bar in a sea of people alone.

Small Talk
Parisa

The Palace, June of the Second Year

A knock resonated off Parisa's door, and she took a moment to finish fastening her necklace and to look herself over in the mirror. While she was not in the most elegant dress in the whole world, she looked nice. Her toned arms would give her away in any crowd, and even though she was going to a fancy dinner, a party, nothing more, she still kept her knife slipped into a sheath on her thigh. If she had to, she could tear the dress and stab anyone foolish enough to put her or anyone else in danger. Her father had done his job, she supposed. He had made a weapon.

Even though she wore nothing too far out of the ordinary, it was still not her uniform, and that made her happy. She missed clothes like these. An errant curl tried to spiral its way off her head and Parisa grabbed for more hair butter to keep it in place when the knock rattled off again. Once she was certain she looked presentable, she opened the door.

Rune Guildenhart was there, dressed for dinner. He bowed

and smiled as he had before. "Good evening, Lady Parisa."

"Good evening," she replied, her own curiosity betraying her. What could he possibly want?

"I was wondering, if you'll let me, if I could escort you to dinner," he inquired.

"Sure, I suppose," Parisa replied. She was actually quite disappointed. She had hoped Perseus would come to escort her, but he was nowhere to be found and terribly late. "You're very kind."

"I wish to make as many friends as I can. With what happened to my father and all, I feel rather awkward, replacing him as though he never existed."

"How did he pass?"

"He drowned, strangled by thugs and tossed into a well."

"How horrible."

"Truly."

"It can't possibly be that hard, though," Parisa mused as they walked. "You must have everything I ever wanted."

"In a den of coyotes, perhaps," Rune replied. "Here, you play by others' rules or you get eaten. A good first impression is everything."

"So that's all this is? Another good impression?"

"You misunderstand," Rune fumbled and tripped over his words. "It is not just that."

"You should choose your words more carefully, Lord Guildenhart. If you continue conversations that way, you will have more enemies than friends. And you can stop calling me Lady Parisa."

"Is that not the correct title?"

"As I said, I am no longer the Sovereign's daughter. You may call me Lieutenant Sauveterre, as that is my title."

"You're critical, Lieutenant, and that is why I am nervous. I respect you the most out of anyone in this place, and I suppose my lack of poise comes from my desire to befriend you."

The glass elevator doors opened and the two of them stepped into the tight space. Parisa's hand brushed the top of her knife under the skirt of her dress and she sighed. The servant in the elevator pulled the lever and the two of them rode up a floor.

Parisa laughed, "You're full of bull. No one here respects me. I'm the trash my father threw out."

"That is *why* I respect you, because no one here understands in the slightest what it means to be tested. You must be tough."

"What do you mean?"

"I have been thinking... about your being in the Elite. I know I would not be able to do it. You must be strong-willed."

"Well, thank you," Parisa edged out. He confused her, with his eloquence and understanding. Since she had been born, her father had not seen her as anything more than a doormat and the only people she knew that seemed to give a damn were Perseus and Esmond. Now, here came this newcomer who seemed to know everything about being stomped on. *How could he?* she wondered. *He has been raised off milk and honey, just like the rest of them.*

The doors of the dining hall opened and Parisa smiled as she remembered having countless birthday parties in that very room. Rune led her to a seat that was set for her by her father and he, after pushing her chair in, sat next to Lord Talbot himself.

Perseus sat in the seat to Parisa's right, an expression plastered on his face that she could not quite decipher, and once everyone was present, Lord Talbot stood and smiled.

"Welcome, everyone!" he greeted. "It is good to see you all. Tonight, we leave the past behind us. Though we mourn the death of our dear former Councilman, Adriann Guildenhart, we join here not only to celebrate the new admittance of Rune Guildenhart to the Council, but to welcome my daughter back from rigorous training."

The Naa'a residents at the table clapped. Parisa recognized Councilman Wolff and his wife, Vena. She gazed into the tablecloth as if she wished to disappear. Esmond was present, and a few of the Embassy's wealthiest philanthropists also held seats at the table. Rune Guildenhard looked like quite the outcast with his red hair, but Perseus and Parisa were the darkest people in the room. Parisa was thankful for people like Esmond and Alvena who were divergent from the Naa'a crowd, outsiders.

"Would you both stand and say a word?" Lord Talbot asked. "I'm sure everyone here is dying to hear what you have to say."

Rune and Parisa exchanged glances and Perseus gripped her hand under the table as her heart backflipped. Was her father actually welcoming her home?

Rune stood and smiled, warm but too sweet, and he said, "I am so pleased and honored to be here. Though I am still mourning my father, who was a great man and a friend to me, I agree with Lord Talbot. It is time to move on. The future is ahead of us and I hope to make it brighter for all Segeno. Thank you."

Rune sat again and Parisa caught Lord Talbot smile, a smug, awful thing, and her stomach churned. She had sworn to herself that she would never see that horrible sneer ever again, but here she was. After the guests at the table had delicately clapped and a moment of awkward silence followed, Lord Talbot coughed and gazed at Parisa eagerly. Perseus squeezed her hand again, and she then stood to follow up on her father's request. "Though the training has been difficult," she began, "I feel as though I have grown much as a person. By the will of my father, I have sworn to protect all at Embassy Palace and within Naa'a, and I will stick firmly to that duty, even if it means my life. I am proud to be the first woman to ever hold the position of Elite Guard. Long live the Sovereign."

People clapped once more, and the appetizers were brought out by servants. Most of the guests broke out into conversation, but Parisa swallowed her tongue when she sat, nausea bubbling in her throat. She was not grateful. She was not proud. She hated him, but could say nothing, and she remained trapped in Segeno regardless. No one ventured outside of Segeno into the wastes, out of fear of dying. No one except the residents of Sulphur.

Sulphur was a mystery to most of Segeno. Parisa had learned about it in her studies. It lay far in the desert, past the safety of Segeno's walls. When sentenced for a crime, the worst sentence of all was banishment to the wastes. Supposedly, those who survived had created a settlement: Sulphur. It was a barbaric place, from what was written of it. No clean water, hardly any food, and rampant violence were things that often were mentioned. No one survived out there, and Parisa realized that in the dining hall,

143

though feral and hostile in its own way, was still ultimately safer. She had been out of that crowd for months, and she feared what she was up against. Rune began chatting with her father, and she strained her ear to listen.

"So, a brighter Segeno, hm?" Lord Talbot asked and began to eat.

"Well, yes. If that means pushing and shoving a little. I'm not afraid to do what I have to do," Rune replied as he cut into his food.

Parisa raked her brain for memory of him and found none. Perseus had briefed her before his arrival, and claimed he was from Sulphur itself, which seemed impossible. The trip would have been brutal, and why would Councilmen Guildenhart abandon his son somewhere else?

"So, Sulphur?" Parisa asked as she sipped her wine. Perseus pricked up next to her as she entered the conversation. She wanted answers. "It must have been quite the trip."

"I've lived among the Badlanders for some time, now. Once you get used to things, you simply pack enough water and rations for the trip, cover your face in the sun, and you can make the trip in two days' time," Lord Guildenhart replied.

"What on earth were you doing out there?" Lord Talbot asked, pushing his empty appetizer plate aside.

"Because of my red hair, my father thought it more appropriate that I find something to do other than linger around Naa'a and soil our reputation," Rune joked. "I decided I wanted to understand the wastes better, learn about the flora and fauna beyond the walls. Sulfur was the perfect place for me to do so, so

I moved out."

Certainly, all his habits fit a royal, Parisa thought; the way he ate, the way he spoke. Even the way he looked, though his red hair proved suspicious, and his facial piercing looked foreign. He was fair enough, however, and had the blue eyes of one born of royal blood.

"Have you heard of what we're planning for taxes this year, Rune?" Lord Talbot asked.

"No, My Lord, I have not."

Lord Talbot leaned in. "Well... the people complained about food quality around the city. Lots of bad sandstorms earlier in the year, and the greenhouses just can't take another beating. I want to bring a tax to the table that increases the quality of the food, puts more into agriculture. What the people don't know is fifteen percent of all food sales will go to the Embassy. We're fueling expeditions and tunneling out below the wall around Segeno, recovering weapons of old that the ancients left behind in the tunnels. They're powerful, Rune, more powerful than you could imagine, and we will be the only city in the west with them."

Rune smiled and pushed his plate away. "Clever, My Lord."

"I like you, boy. You'll be a great addition to the Council."

Parisa gritted her teeth and turned her attention to Perseus, who shook where he sat. He watched how everyone ate and copied them, trying to match exact movements. Parisa leaned in close and whispered, "Be yourself."

"I've never been around this high caliber of people before. Not only that, but I do *not* do well in crowds." Perseus' trembling hand caused the fork to rattle against the silver plate and he

145

quickly put it down.

"Take it easy. I'll give you hints..." Parisa watched as servants replaced the appetizer with a small salad. "For the salad, you use *this* fork..."

The rest of the dinner went on like that, with Parisa teaching Perseus the customs of the upper class and eavesdropping on Lord Guildenhart, who she disliked more and more every minute. He was a slimy snake, just like her father, who was only interested in funding his research. To think, she entertained the idea for a moment he would differ from the rest of them.

After dinner was through, she stood to return to her room, hoping to avoid her previous engagement, but was stopped by a hand. Rune Guildenhart took her arm and smiled at her as he escorted her through the door. "You promised a meeting, Lieutenant."

Parisa frowned and started to walk toward the elevator. "To the library, then?"

"That sounds lovely. I've missed the library."

"You have been to the palace, Lord Guildenhart? I have never seen you here before." Checkmate. Parisa gleaned his face for lies as she had been trained to do. She wondered if he realized who he was up against.

Rune seemed to choke on his words. "I mean," he spluttered, "I missed it when I toured the palace earlier."

"Ah." Parisa watched his eyes, and they glanced around the room as though they searched for something. His arm tightened ever so slightly as he shoved open the library door with his free arm. The enormous library swallowed them up and Parisa had to admit that it put her slightly at ease. It was one of her favorite places in the whole world. The Embassy library even contained books from long, long ago, like H.G. Wells' *War of the Worlds* and other tales of ancient battles. Parisa enjoyed these ancient manuscripts, and the library was full of them, treasures salvaged and protected by royal decree. After the Great War, most knowledge had been lost, and even names of common animals, such as the Mammoth, had slipped into the realm of forgotten memory.

Most of what was contained in the old world, such as ways, customs, and technology had been lost in the great blasts that shattered the earth. But Parisa thirsted for this knowledge, and she reveled in anything she could read. She would have loved to enter the library and be by herself, but she had to get rid of Lord Guildenhart first.

"Now, is there anything of dire importance you need from me? I have things to do," she snapped as the doors closed behind them.

"Snippy," Rune remarked. "What happened? You were so friendly before dinner."

"Things changed."

"Did they? I'm sorry if I've offended you."

"Is there anything you wanted to discuss?"

"I wanted to exchange a little small talk, to get to know you. You seemed awfully quiet at dinner."

"I don't find delight in conversing with those kinds of people."

"Do you not? You grew up with them."

"No, I didn't," Parisa barked. "I was sheltered. My father

kept me away in our house in Naa'a as much as he could. He told me it was to protect me, but it seems my life in Naa'a may as well have been an invisible one. *You*, however, seem to fit right in here."

Rune raised his eyebrows and asked, "How do you mean?"

Parisa held her tongue. "The people seem to adore you... especially my father."

He moved closer to her to get to books. She felt the hair on the back of her neck stand up as though something full of static energy had passed over her skin, and he grinned at the title of a book. The more she looked at him, the more she lost the ability to read him. Before, he had been decent, but any friend of her father's was no friend of hers.

"Thank you," he bowed. "I'd say I've made a good start for myself here."

"I didn't say his adoration was something to strive for," she spat, all the hatred she held for her father spilling over her lips. "Lord Guildenhart, my father is as despicable as a rattlesnake, as dangerous as a scorpion. If you want to rule this place, getting on my father's friendly side is a sure way to claw your way to the top."

"He's that ruthless, eh?" Rune mused and sunk down into an armchair. "You have a bite, it seems. You and Perseus make quite the pair."

"Don't talk about him."

"I don't understand why you stay. It seems you all have built a pretty prison for yourself, where you are both those who run it and those who fill it, and what you don't realize is you can walk out any time you like."

"I am *no one's* prisoner."

"Are you not?"

Parisa said nothing, and she did not have to endure his company any longer. As she tried to leave, he grabbed her elbow, not hard enough to hurt her, but hard enough to make her stop. She spun around, and before thinking, drew her knife. Rune, startled for a moment at the presence of a weapon, froze long enough for her to strike with her free hand across his face.

Two Faces
Terran

The Palace, June of the Second Year

"Get your hands *off me!*"

Parisa had smacked him as hard as he had expected. He put his hand to his face as his lip swelled. He grinned and pulled his fingers away, blood forming in his mouth. "Great strike!" Terran praised.

"What the *hell* is wrong with you?" Parisa demanded, putting her knife away.

"I'm sorry, I didn't mean to startle you so. I merely wanted to apologize and wish you goodnight. It seems I struck a nerve."

The door swung open. A man with silver spectacles that wobbled precariously off his nose looked about the room for any threat. "What is going *on* in here?"

"M-Master Esmond," Parisa stuttered, out of fright or anger, Terran did not know.

"I heard yelling and came at the sound. I was on my way to do some late-night reading," Master Esmond muttered as he ripped Terran's hand away from Parisa's elbow. "Conduct like this will not be accepted in this palace. This kind of behavior may be acceptable in Sulphur, but not here."

Parisa glared at Terran with such spite he thought for a moment she would hit him again, but instead she stormed off. Master Esmond turned his enraged eyes to Terran and demanded, "You stay away from her."

"Rune Guildenhart," Terran said as he stuck a hand out for his colleague. "I know you. You're Esmond Middlestriker, aren't you? Councilman Middlestriker? You oversee the Dza'ya district."

"Yes," Esmond affirmed and brought his finger close to Terran's face. "I possess a good deal of power in this place and if you touch her, I *will* have you executed."

"I mean no harm," Terran sighed and sat back in the reading chair. "All I wished was to get to know her, and I had no idea she would be so touchy."

Esmond huffed, "She is none of your business."

Esmond left, slamming the library door behind him, and Terran let out a heavy sigh of relief. He knew what he had to do to understand people's positions in all situations and pushing people's buttons was one of the easiest ways to get into their heads. He wanted to know Parisa, but he would not bother her anymore. He now had learned more about Lord Talbot and the threat he posed. If Talbot really had killed his parents, he understood why. He was oppressive, greedy, spiteful, and full of contempt for all those who dared to stand in his way. Terran had to become just like him. If he wanted to become close to Lord Talbot, he would have to become like a son.

Shadows
Parisa

The Palace, June of the Second Year

Parisa tapped her toe in anticipation as she rode the elevator down, anger chiseled into her face. The servant manning the elevator tensed as she stood there, her dress ruined, and a large slit torn up the side of it. She had ruined the dress to get at her knife. *How could I have ever agreed to talk to such a pompous, perverted, irritating-*

Parisa was lost deep in her thoughts when she came through the elevator doors, and she bumped right into Perseus, who was coming into the elevator at the same time. Perseus reached out his arm to catch her, and when they locked eyes, Parisa saw sadness there.

"Oh," he sighed, a heavy sigh that was laden with nervousness and covered-up disappointment. "Hey Parisa. Where have you been?"

"Talking with Lord Guildenhart," Parisa spat.

"Yeah, he seems like a great guy."

"Great?" Parisa hollered as she paced in front of a painting in the hall, which depicted a geyser that erupted from the ground not too far from the city. Perseus paid her no heed as she stomped, huffing, "I could find hundreds of words to describe him, but not great."

"You mean wonderful, or charming, or tall, or royal, or—"

Parisa laughed, "No. More like gross, rude, and shallow."

Perseus perked an eyebrow up and asked, "So, you don't like him?"

"Of course not!"

Perseus sighed as though a huge weight had been lifted from his shoulders. "Well, that's... um... great. I-I mean, interesting, not great. I was wondering if tomorrow you would maybe help me a little bit."

"Help you? With what?"

"I... I want to fit in. Be like one of you. I hate feeling so low class. People look at me funny."

"Sure," Parisa agreed. "I'll help you with manners and things like that, but there's no changing you deep down. Don't expect that. And I wouldn't dare change you. Not for the whole world."

Teammates
Terran

The Tavern, September of the Second Year

"Terran... you haven't checked in for months," The King huffed and gazed into his false window. He would not look Terran in the eyes, and he drummed his fingers on his desk with impatience.

"I didn't want to come back without good information," Terran snapped back. His heart still stung from how he had been treated the last time he reported in. Since the day Terran interrupted The King and Alvena Wolff, The King had been curt, aggressive, and unfriendly. Terran showed nothing but the utmost respect and did not appreciate how he was treated.

The King stood and motioned to the door. "Walk with me," he offered.

Once the two left the tavern and were a good distance down the road, The King turned to him and said, "I'm sorry."

"That's all well and good, but I don't think it's fair that I haven't even been *home* and you're still treating me this way."

Home. Terran rolled the word around in his mind and supposed that, yes, the tavern was his new home. Now he was back, with his own face, not Rune's, and still felt unwelcome. Perhaps that was why The King's blatant cold shoulder had been unbearable.

"I shouldn't have to explain myself. There's a lot happening you don't know about and it's best it stays that way for the safety of the mission."

"You're playing that card, huh?"

"What did you learn?"

"Don't just write me off."

"What did you *learn*?"

Terran stopped walking for a moment and put his arm out to prevent The King from moving any further. When The King shot Terran a look, one filled with ice and steel, Terran lowered his arm and continued to walk. "Well..." he begrudgingly continued, "Lord Talbot's awful. I recently helped pass another tax law to hike up the price of water to the city. He proposes profit disguised as law. All the money seems to go to projects, whether that be public works, tunnelling under the wall, or otherwise, and all of it disappears. I suspect, directly into Talbot's pockets. He has a daughter, Parisa. I'd say she's about my age."

"Not Rune's?"

"No, mine." Terran had to check himself to make sure he did, in fact, look like Terran. He dared not to go see The King with Rune's face again. It was simply too risky, and he wondered if that mistake was what had made The King so incensed, or if it was something else. "He's basically disowned her, sent her off to be a guard. She's friends with the Elite Captain, who's just a touch older than me. Her guardian is Esmond, the Dza'ya district leader."

The King's eyebrows peaked with interest, but he said nothing about the matter. "How does she feel about her father?"

"She hates him."

"Interesting... and what have you been doing?"

"Acting exactly like Talbot. So far, he likes me. I've received gifts this month from him, books and clothes and the like."

"Perfect." The King made a turn and Terran realized they were heading toward the Dza'ya district. "You're getting closer. Does he speak of plans for the future?"

"Sometimes, but not often," Terran replied and looked around, watching passersby and merchants. "So... what's the deal with you and Alvena Wolff?"

"I'm not finished with you yet."

"And I'm not going to answer any more questions until you tell me what's wrong with you. You can't expect me to just ignore it."

"How dare you speak—"

"Oh, don't be like that. After two years, you can't tell me what's wrong?" Terran asked, earnestly.

The King sighed and looked down at his feet as they walked. "She and I go way back."

"How far back?"

"Childhood. She and I were good friends. We grew up, and I realized she meant everything to me. We wanted to be engaged when I was just a little older than you, but her parents had other plans. They told her they had arranged a marriage between Alvena and Jacob Wolff. I was heartbroken, but I knew there wasn't much I could do about it. They were married, and I realized I had nothing holding me to the Embassy anymore. I no longer had any attachments, and I hung around for a while afterward, to be closer to your parents, but then Talbot chased me out. This was maybe a few years before your parents died. As it turned out, Wolff is an awful husband. You saw an example of that the last time you were here."

"Her husband did that?"

"I believe that every one of the Councilmembers represent a sin. This is the fifth time she's come to me, now."

"She keeps going back to the palace?"

"She insisted... next time, I won't let her. I won't let him touch her anymore."

The King stopped and leaned on an old well that barely held itself together with its beaten, weathered rocks and mortar. Women huddled around it and pulled up water, washing their curly hair and eyed Terran and The King as they approached. Men kept their distance from the well and the women moved to the other side of it to avoid being looked at. "Why are we here?" Terran asked.

"I have been waiting to show you this... mostly because I wanted you to be ready."

Terran raised his eyebrows and replied, "For a well?"

"For what's in the well. This well holds dozens of people's wishes, from the past and the present." The King removed a stone, revealed two letters, and continued, "This is the Castle stone. Here

I send letters to the rest of our organization. All outgoing mail goes under this rock." The King placed a letter that was addressed simply to "E," and Terran glanced at the label on the other letter. It was partially smudged by dirt, but Terran saw the letters, "Par."

"Whoa, whoa. Wait. Who's that one to?"

The King stopped Terran's hand before it reached the letter. "The one rule of this well," he advised, "is that we do *not* go poking around in others' business."

He replaced the stone and moved to another. "This is the Flight stone, for anyone in my organization to send us letters."

A question occurred to Terran that he had never thought of asking. "How... how many of us are there, exactly?"

"Hundreds. All of those in the tavern are a part of the highest ranks in my organization. They are all fighters, at least I've trained them to be. It is their job and duty to train others. When the time comes, they will be at our side."

"Why didn't you teach any of them the power of the cards?"

"Because," The King stopped, looked at Terran with a quiet truth in his eyes, and replied, "it was not in the cards."

Terran looked across the faces of the letters under the Flight stone and saw that there were many addressed to The King. He grabbed those and after he removed them, the remaining read "E" and "TL."

The King handed Terran the latter, leaving the other letter alone, and said, "This one's been here for years. You can read it where you want."

Together, the two walked in silence back to the tavern and Terran folded the letter over in his hands. He recognized the handwriting on the front, and it terrified him. When they got back to the tavern, Terran noticed Alvena waiting in The King's office, so he instead went to sit at the bar. He tore the wax seal on the envelope as The King closed his office door.

Inside the envelope were several pieces of paper, and the first document was small and had been torn out of another notebook or journal. On it were only a few words:

Poverty is only a state of mind. True richness comes from the heart and home.

Terran set the paper aside only to find another, similar one.

Truth lies with loyal friends. Loyalty comes from being true.

And finally, a third paper in the envelope.

Betrayal of loved ones is the sharpest sword.

The final document in the envelope was a letter.

Dearest Terran,

We can only imagine what you've been through. We never wanted it to come to this, but if you're reading this, then the worst has occurred. When your mother began her rule as Sovereign, tragedy befell us. You were only six. Talbot, leader of the Naa'a district, became too close. He had been such a good advisor for so long, and it surprised us at first. He tried to push his way into the Embassy and into the Sovereign's seat, to the point where he attempted to arrange a marriage between you and his daughter. The discomfort was unbearable, but we could do nothing, and we did not know if he was truly conspiring against us or if he was simply invested in Segeno. Then, your father caught a whiff of conspiracy, information provided by your father's top spy,

Lexus. Someone aimed to remove us from power and eliminate any remaining heirs: you.

We could not stop the wheel that had been set into motion. Of course, if you're reading this, the deed has been done, but you're in safe hands. We hope that Lexus is treating you well.

From Mother:
*You will be such a **wonderful** leader, Terran. You showed signs of that when you were very small. Remember to follow your heart. That is the **most** important thing I ever wanted to tell you. I love you so much, darling.*

From Father:
Son, you'll have to carry on without us, but I'm sure you'll be just fine. I know you'll turn into a fine young man one day. Remember, everything that Lexus does is for the best. Put your faith in him as I have.

We love you more than all the stars in the sky.

Mother and Father

It took a few moments for Terran to process what he was reading. After reading it over again, he quietly folded the letter back up and replaced it in the envelope. After gathering up the other pieces of paper, he took a deep breath, stood, and made his way to The King's door, his heart as heavy as steel in his chest.

He found it was unlocked, and when he opened it, Vena

and The King sat at the window seat. Vena sat on his lap, her head resting on his, and he read a book aloud to her.

"Lexus?" The name felt odd on Terran's tongue when he said it.

"Yes?" The King responded as though he had been caught in a dream, like he had not heard his name in a very long time.

Terran nodded, feeling sick and uneasy, and asked, "They knew he was going to kill them?"

The King sighed, closed the book, and watched Vena leave the room. She closed the door behind herself, and he replied, "Yeah, it was more of a when, not if."

"Why didn't they leave?"

"They couldn't leave you. And who would rule this place? They did not want to give into Talbot so easily."

"Who else is wrapped up in all of this?"

"Esmond Middlestriker, myself, and Vena. We were the only ones who were told."

"Wait," Terran muttered. "Told what?"

"Talbot told us to kill your parents."

"*What?*"

"You – just wait a minute—"

"*You* killed my parents?" Terran hollered and grabbed The King by the collar. "*Why?* They *trusted* you! They did *nothing* to you!"

"Terran! I didn't kill your parents!" he choked. "I'm a spy!"

Terran shoved The King back down into his seat. He was not sure if he was really that strong or if The King was being passive. "So, who tried?" Terran demanded. "Esmond? Vena?"

161

"*None* of us. Cool your head. We received the order, but none of us acted. We loved your parents too much. Eventually, Talbot got frustrated that none of us made a move, so he did it himself."

Terran sighed and sank into his chair. "I can't believe this..."

"Well, now you have more reason to kill him."

"You knew the whole time? You acted like you had no clue what Talbot was doing."

"I knew what he had done, not what he was going to do. And... you had already been through enough. I didn't want to burden you with this yet."

"What do these mean?" Terran asked, revealed the envelope from inside his vest pocket, and pulled out the three slips of paper.

The King took them and looked them over. "Clues. They're clues. Your parents knew Talbot was going to destroy everything that had to do with them once he took over. They were worried he would burn, melt, and discard precious family heirlooms, so they're hidden around the city. Once you claim these things, you can better understand your family's origins... or something. That's what your mother told me once, anyway."

"I better start one at a time."

"No," The King replied and took the papers and letter from Terran. "First you must win him. Talbot. Then you can look."

Terran sighed and stood, replying, "I better go. I'm sure they're wondering where I am by now."

"Go. You're performing beautifully." The King opened his mouth as though he were about to say something, paused, and then finally said, "I'm sorry for—"

"Don't be. You love her. You were worried about her. It's fine."

"Thanks, Terran."

"Don't mention it. Besides, I know you couldn't live with yourself if I didn't forgive you."

Duty
Parisa

The Palace, November of the Second Year

"Here... I have this for you."

There she was: porcelain face and decadent dress, just as Parisa remembered her. Parisa pulled the doll from Esmond's hands and into an embrace and exclaimed, "Theophilia!"

Esmond smiled as she cuddled her doll, and said, "I've been meaning to give her to you sooner, but I wanted to make sure you were settled."

"I thought she'd been thrown away!"

"She almost was, but I rescued her."

Parisa smiled and hugged her teacher as though he might disappear. "Thank you! *Thank* you..."

"Now, don't get too excited just yet. I don't know if you remember, but on your birthday, I told you I had another surprise for you. I never got to give it to you."

"Another surprise?"

Master Esmond pulled a gilded box out from underneath

his desk and set it on the table. "Happy belated, belated birthday."

Parisa tugged on the soft, silken ribbon and pulled the lid off after the fabric fell away. She found inside the box another doll. His skin glimmered in the same porcelain fashion as Theophilia's, and gold thread shimmered in the suit he wore. He was a perfect match for her little friend.

"He's so handsome!"

"I wish I could have given him to you sooner, but I figured you'd need the knife more. Has that been of any use to you or was it a mistake on my part?"

Parisa remembered all the times she needed to cut bandages, slice through an obstacle, or defend herself. "It's been more than helpful. Honestly, you could have gotten me a rock and I would cherish it. I appreciate all you do more than words can say."

"It's no trouble, really. Hopefully that new beau will be motivation to finish your last few books."

Despite her father's wishes, Parisa studied. Master Esmond had not given up on her yet. He had set out a secret course for her, as if he was preparing her for something. She now knew more than she needed about royal practices and functions, though she felt she would never need them, and she could write an essay so sharp it almost rivaled her combat skills. Perseus, too, had been studying hard. Talbot, after all, could not respect ignorant commanding officers. When Perseus had explained to Parisa that he had received no education, she was appalled. He barely knew how to read or write.

His education progressed painfully, but Parisa spent extra

time tutoring him, which she enjoyed. Every bit of his progress made her proud, and she reveled in the fact that she not only finished her studies but had also become an adept Elite. Her mother would be overjoyed.

"I should probably go," Parisa sighed as she contemplated the events that brought her to this point. "I need to finish my governmental studies homework."

"You make me proud, Parisa," Master Esmond added. "Don't you ever forget that."

Parisa took her books and dolls to her room, her heart overflowing with happiness. As she walked to the elevator, she felt a pang in her heart, just a small, momentary one, that she was not allowed in the Sovereign's quarters. From the day they had made their move from their house in Naa'a to the Embassy tower, she had maintained her own quarters on the ground floor. She knew it was because her father did not want her to be the last thing he saw before he went to bed. Her father was so distant from her she would not have liked to live with him anyway. She dreamed of something that did not exist and reinforced that idea in her heart as she opened her bedroom door. Her books dropped heavily onto her bed and she propped Theophilia and her new love onto a pillow so they could see the entire room.

She did not want to study at the moment and knew she could get her work done another time. Something else itched at the back of her mind and she decided to humor it. She moved into the central palace courtyard, the same place Esmond had promised to read her favorite book but had never gotten the chance, and she fell onto the crisp, partially-dead grass. The world was dull at that time of year, even in the greenhouse, but she still loved the outdoors and the tree still comforted her, even though it bore no leaves in its open branches. She wore a large coat so the cold did not faze her, and, in fact, she was quite comfortable and could have napped there if not for the *crunch, crunch, crunch* of dead grass.

When she looked up, Perseus' dark eyes were there smiling down at her. He leaned over her, hands on his knees, grinned, and asked, "What are you doing out here? It's freezing!"

"It's not that cold," Parisa laughed and sat up. "You would be warmer if you had your jacket on."

"I *hate* this weather."

Parisa grabbed his hands with her gloved ones and pulled him down onto the grass. "What have you been up to?"

"Reading," he spat. His mouth twisted into a sour frown. "I needed a break."

"You came looking for me?"

His face turned bright red and he spluttered, "What have you been doing?"

"I got Theophilia back."

"Your doll?"

"My best friend."

"That's great."

"Yeah, she has a boyfriend now."

"Another doll?"

"Yup."

"Neat."

The two lay in silence for a little while, watching their breath form steam in the air, until Perseus sat up on his elbow.

"Hey," he suggested. "We should do something fun."

"Like what?"

"A game."

"A game? Aren't we a little old for games?"

Perseus rolled his eyes and then winked. "Aren't we a little too old for dolls? No one's ever too old for games."

"How about... chess? Backgammon? Spades?"

"Truth or dare."

"I've never played that."

Perseus' eyes gleamed with mischief. "It's real easy," he started. "Pick one. Truth or dare. And then you have to do what I ask, whether it's answering a question or doing something crazy."

"Truth?"

As Perseus speculated on a question, Parisa enjoyed their momentary silence. After a breath, he asked, "Have you ever kissed a boy?"

"No."

Before Parisa could react, Perseus leaned in and pecked her on the lips. It was a short kiss, no more than a breath, and Parisa's heart back-flipped in her chest. The dead grass prickled the back of her head, but she didn't mind, and his lips were warm in the winter air.

Perseus laughed, flushed red, and rolled over again to look up at the cloudy, grey sky through the greenhouse glass.

"You have now."

Celebration
Terran

The Palace, December of the Second Year

Well, Terran, he thought to himself as he sat up on the morning of his birthday, *you've been doing this for two years. You're seventeen. How does it feel?*

He chuckled to himself and stood, using the card to change his appearance. It had been over two years since his parents' deaths, and he was not sure if he should be sad or excited. After he spent time combing his hair and getting ready for the day, a heavy knock resounded across his door. "Come in!" Terran called.

A servant scuffled in bearing a large box covered in white paper and an enormous white bow. "This has arrived for you, My Lord."

"Huh," Terran mumbled and took the box from the man. "Thank you."

After the servant left, Terran opened the box and sorted through the contents. On top of mysterious lumps covered in glittering paper sat a small card.

169

Terran,

*Another year older. Hardly, but finally seventeen. You still have a lot of
growing up to do, physically and mentally, so don't get your hopes up.
This isn't my way of giving you free rein or jurisdiction over anything.
Yet. Inside are things for you. I know you like blue and white, so...
there you are. I'm having armor fashioned for you. Stop by when you
have the chance to pick it up. Oh, and there's something in there from
Vena, too.*

Happy Birthday,
Lexus

Terran could not believe The King had actually
remembered his birthday. He grinned as he lifted a new set of
clothes from the box. They were in The King's fashion but were
in Embassy colors. Far too audacious for everyday Embassy wear.
He knew he would not be able to put them on until the card wore
off. Rune certainly—

"What odd clothes."

Terran jumped. Parisa stood at the door and Terran
dropped what he was holding.

"I saw a servant bring it up, and I wondered who it was for,"
she continued. "Don't tell me you wear things that ostentatious
every day, Lord Guildenhart."

"Oh! N-No... of course not," Terran recovered, folding the
clothes and putting them in his dresser. "They're for a costume
party."

"Costume party?" Parisa asked and raised her eyebrows

170

in curiosity. Terran regretted the words as soon as they came out of his mouth, and he did not understand what it was about her that made him say outright stupid things. Parisa prodded, "Why haven't I heard of it?"

"Because I haven't announced it yet. I'm planning on holding it this month."

"Well! I hope I'm invited. What's it for?"

"To tell you the truth, it's my birthday."

"How old are you?"

"Nineteen," he lied.

"And who are these from?"

Parisa sat down next to him, her arm brushing his. He didn't like her, no. Not like that. The fear of saying something wrong and blowing his cover was what made him fumble.

"A friend of my father's." Terran told her the truth. The King had always told him that the best lies stemmed from a little truth. "And his wife."

Parisa watched him pull out a leather journal with gilded pages. "Do you write?"

"No," he muttered and read a small note on the front. "But I might now."

He lifted a book out of the bottom of the box titled *Black Thorn*. Terran recalled reading a book by the same author in The King's study when he had gotten bored. Parisa's eyes lit up, and she exclaimed, "You enjoy McGullen's works, too?"

Terran opened the front cover of the book and a note fell out. *From Vena.* "Yes, I do." He could not believe she was having civil conversation with him. "What's changed in you, Lieutenant?"

"What? What do you mean?"

"You hit me in the face," he laughed.

"Oh. That."

"And here you are, sitting in my bedroom, uninvited and sharing my birthday with me."

"I wanted to give you a second chance. Esmond talked to me about it, and... I felt bad. After I explained the situation I clearly was in the wrong and shouldn't have jumped to judge you."

"I see."

She smiled as Terran revealed the last gift, a pad of stationary paper and envelopes, along with a new set of quill pens. A note had been tied to the quills: *For the well.* Parisa glanced over Terran's shoulder to read the paper, but he crumpled the note before she could get a good look at it. He stood and placed the book, the journal, the paper, and pens onto the writing desk that was tucked in the corner of his study.

Parisa stood and turned to leave, but stopped and said, "I hope you enjoy your book. I... I should apologize for my actions. I admit, I've been avoiding you. I feel awful, and I didn't mean anything I said. I didn't know you then and I don't know you now, so I have no right to judge you."

"Thank you. I appreciate—"

A knock, reserved, interrupted Terran and whoever it was opened the door without permission. Vena stood in the doorway, and the shock on Terran's face was equally apparent on Parisa's. "Vena! You're back!"

Vena hugged Parisa like an old friend. "That I am. I am sorry I was gone for so long. I needed a break from the Council and... other things."

"I've missed you! I've improved my knitting! You should see the scarf I'm working on."

"You'll have to show me," Vena said and curtsied to Terran. "You must be Councilman Guildenhart, yes?" she asked, as if they had never met.

"Yes, My Lady," he replied.

Her eyes looked around for the book she had bought him and found it on his desk. "You have a great taste in literature. That book by McGullen is one of my favorites."

"Thank you, Lady Wolff."

"Vena, please." Vena looked as though she would rather die than be associated with her husband. "I have duties to attend to, but I heard from a little finch that the new Councilman was stirring everything up and I had to observe the chaos myself. I'll see you later, Parisa. You'll have to show me what you've knit."

"I'd love to!" Parisa headed to the door to follow her out. She turned, and said, "Again, Lord Guildenhart, I'm sorry."

And then Terran was alone again. What a gracious turn of events. Terran had gotten on Parisa's good side once again. Now, there was only the matter of the made-up party, and he could not believe he had suggested such a notion. As he made his way to Lord Talbot's throne room, he cursed his lack of poise. The King made it look so easy.

The servant at the door in the hall asked him to wait for a moment as he told Lord Talbot that Lord Guildenhart had arrived to speak with him. After only a few moments of waiting, the servant beckoned him in through glass doors and Talbot greeted him with a warm smile. "Ah! Rune! What a pleasant surprise."

Terran felt himself become sick as he gazed at Talbot. It was the first time he had been in the throne room since his return to the Embassy. Talbot sat in his mother's throne and next to him was an empty chair, a chair that had once belonged to his father. He tried as best as he could to put on a smile. "Good morning, Your Majesty."

He had only ever called The King that.

"Come. Sit," Talbot welcomed, stood, and gestured to a chess table. "Do you play?"

"A little, My Lord." He sat across from Lord Talbot and Talbot made the first move. "Do you play often?"

"I play every day," Talbot replied as Terran matched his move. "Life is chess, Rune. There are pawns... and then there are kings."

"Of course, sir."

"As the king on the chessboard, I must keep my pawns in check... we are the only surviving human city, now, Rune, with any kind of sophistication. We have been for centuries. You know this, you've been out there."

"It's actually rather disgusting in Sulphur," Terran lied.

"Exactly. I want to make sure that Segeno flourishes and grows... but most importantly, that the best prosper."

"The best?"

"The Embassy. The doctrines that founded Segeno state that we are placed or born into the Embassy for a purpose, especially those who are fair of hair and skin, pure of blood. It's basic science. If we were not better than the carrion, then we would be rolling in the same putrescence they are. And we're not. Therefore, it is simple to assume that we were placed on this earth to rise to a higher purpose. Why not make our lives the best we can?"

Terran moved another piece.

"I want to move you, Rune."

"My Lord?"

Talbot tapped the knight piece on the board. "You'd be a great son, Rune. That's how comfortable I am with you. Every day you reinforce that with strong action and a level head. But you're lucky... you were born into this life. Do you know what I had to do to get here?"

"No, My Lord."

"Talbot, please."

"Of course, Talbot."

"Kill. I killed to get here. I don't care who I step on... and I think that is a quality of a great leader, don't you?"

Terran swallowed and recalled reading a book about just that, using powerful tactics to maintain dynasties by stepping on others and lying to the people. "It shows you have ambition."

"I see ambition in you, too, Rune. I was wondering if I could share my opinion with you on something."

"Of course."

"The Atsa district is shrinking. Half of them are former Naa'a citizens who fell from grace and the other rubbish from Dza'ya that have risen just too far in station. They use too much water, sucking it up like sponges. They use gallons of it every day. As I'm sure you're well aware, we live in a desert and water is precious. We could kill two birds with one stone if we put a small fee on the water and limit how much they use. Fine them for using too much."

"I see what you're getting at." Terran felt his heart break. He could only imagine the families when they heard the news. How were they going to pay for food when they could not even pay for water? Why was Talbot not investing money into pumping more water into the city? To Terran, that was the clear and easy solution. Divert some of the money away from the military and back into infrastructure.

"You agree?"

"I do agree. What would we use the money for, My Lord?"

"Why, it goes to me. For having such a difficult job, of course. And, if you'll let me... you."

Ah. Terran should have guessed.

"A little extra funds to pay for leisure would certainly not be a bad thing."

Terran moved a piece and found that he had rapidly locked Talbot into a checkmate.

"Well played, Rune. Now... what can I do for you?" Talbot asked, picked up a bowl of cherries, and popped one into his mouth.

"My Lord, I propose a celebration," Terran cooed and put on a convincing, bright smile. "The Embassy is doing better than ever, and we should enjoy it! Your news about this new tax has only lengthened our list of successes."

Talbot thought for a moment and then nodded. "That sounds marvelous. I could use a party for a little publicity. Something whimsical... a masquerade."

"Exactly what I was thinking, Your Majesty."

"We'll schedule it within the month. Here in the throne room. It works well as a ballroom, don't you think? I was never really one for parties, but here will do. I better prepare and announce this to the rest of the Embassy. Invite whomever you like, Rune."

"Thank you."

"Of course. Anything you need, just ask. We're in this together, now, my boy."

Façade
Parisa

The Palace, December of the Second Year

"Hey!" Perseus hollered and poked his head into the doorway of Parisa's bedroom. "The Sovereign is having a party!"

"That's lovely," Parisa mumbled and turned to the last chapter of the last schoolbook she would ever have to read. "When?"

"Next week. We're both invited!"

"Well, I'm glad he hasn't forgotten about me."

"I guess... invited is the wrong word. Lord Talbot wants us at the party in the crowd, so we need costumes."

"So... *not* invited."

Perseus entered and harumphed down onto the bed. "Well, hey... I was wondering if you'd help me get a costume."

"What's the occasion?"

"Guildenhart's birthday and a celebration of how amazing the Embassy is."

"How pompous."

178

"It's showy, for sure... but at least if someone attacks, we'll be the first available to defend everyone."

"Sure. I'd love to help you shop."

"Let's go! It's a beautiful day... it's snowing outside."

Parisa marked her page with a bookmark and smiled at him, mere words away from the end. She could never manage to be angry around him and his words always helped her forget the day to day hurt. She teased, "It's cold outside."

"Yeah, but it's *snowing*! It *never* snows!" Perseus laughed and handed her a jacket, gloves, and a hat. Even their everyday clothes had the Elite emblem stitched into the shoulders. Everything blue in Parisa's room and wardrobe had been stripped away, and the Elite guards were not allowed the blue of the Embassy Councilmember wardrobe. Perseus wore a set to match, telling everyone who saw them exactly who they were. He beamed as they left the palace and caught snowflakes with his tongue as he danced down the street.

Snow was so rare in Segeno that they sometimes went months without seeing a flake in the sky. The clouds would roll in, but it was just too warm and too dry to bring anything down. The snow would not last long, but it was enough to dust the ground in white powder. Perseus kicked up flurries, his warm cheeks melting snowflakes as they touched his skin, and Parisa smiled. His joy brought her more happiness than he could ever know.

"You're sure we're okay to be on leave?" she asked.

"Yeah, Bryant and Chalcedon have us covered while we shop, Talbot's orders."

Parisa could not wipe the smile from her face as they

meandered through the Naa'a district. "So... do you have anything in mind?"

"In mind for what?" Perseus asked and flushed when she looked at him. She noticed that he had been staring at her, and the snowflakes caught on his eyelashes, turning them white.

"Your costume."

"I honesty have no idea. I've never been invited to a party in my life, and I've definitely never had the money to go costume shopping."

Parisa turned toward a costume shop she knew. "My mother took me to a costume party when I was very little. The old Sovereign hosted it, and I got my costume from a place not too far from here."

"What were you?"

"A fairy, I think. You know... we should match."

"What?"

"We're not really Embassy, but we're not really guards, either. Don't you think our costumes should match?"

"I don't know *anything* about these kinds of events."

"I don't either. This whole thing is just... awkward for me. I wish I didn't have to go at all."

"We'll be together, though."

"At least we have that."

It took a moment for Perseus to speak past the sheepish smile on his face. "Does that mean you'll accompany me to the dance?"

"You haven't asked me."

"Well, I'm asking."

The door to the costume shop chimed as it hit a little silver bell when it opened. As costume parties were a common occurrence in Naa'a, costume stores like this prospered by renting out costumes for a single night, and most getups on the shelves matched the colors of the Embassy. Parisa began to browse around, not giving Perseus a straight answer. She hid a smile from him and covered her laughter, enjoying the momentary chaos her response had caused in him. She mused, "Most people go as animals, but a mask can say a lot about character."

Parisa thumbed through garments while Perseus sighed, "Birds? How about birds?"

"Maybe? Like owls... or swans? I feel like a lot of people will be doing that."

"Why does it matter?"

"Well, we want to stand out, don't we?"

"Is being high class all about standing out?"

"Basically..." Parisa huffed and put her hands on her hips. "How about fish?"

"That... is an awful idea." Perseus' face scrunched, but after a moment of thinking he snapped his fingers. "I got it! What if we were a cat and a mouse?"

"What?"

Perseus shrugged, embarrassed. "It was just an idea."

"I'd be the cat?"

"No," Perseus grinned. "You'd be the mouse."

Parisa nodded in agreement and said, "It's actually not a bad idea... better than fish. We need to find actual costumes, though."

After an hour more of searching, Parisa and Perseus managed to find pure white cat and mouse costumes and masks to match, thanks to the help of a kind store clerk. As they walked back to the palace, Perseus contemplated the mask in his hand. "I've never spent so much money in my life."

"It wasn't *that* expensive..."

"The cost of the mask alone could feed my family for a week."

Parisa said nothing, a guilty pang striking her heart. The snow made everything so quiet, and few people were on the street in the chilly weather. Their footsteps echoed off the adobe buildings in Naa'a and finally, as they neared the Embassy palace, she whispered, "To answer your question... I'd be very happy if you took me to the party."

Perseus flushed and smiled at her, triumph in his eyes. "Then let's call it a date."

Masquerade
Terran

The Palace, December of the Second Year

Terran recognized no one, and the sea of masked patrons all with silver-blond hair moved to the music like a wave that swept the hall. Only when a man with hair the color of desert clay, red like a stain, entered did Terran know who had arrived. Talbot had said to invite anyone, so Terran invited The King. Tonight, Lexus posed as Rune Guildenhart's cousin, Ruben, though he did not blend in at all. He was dressed in the brightest colors of all the dancers, splashes of red and green mixed in among the blue and white of the Embassy. He stuck out like a sore thumb. Terran realized he did not fare much better. His own robes had a much bolder blue on them than the normal Embassy colors. Luckily, no one had said anything. People seemed to think it... eccentric.

Terran's eyes followed The King's hair for a while, taking in every detail of The King's jester costume and mask, until a voice caught his attention.

"It's beautiful, isn't it?" Talbot asked.

"Yes, it is. This sea of white and blue is entrancing. The masks make it very difficult to identify faces in the crowd."

"That's half the fun."

Then Terran remembered where he sat, and his fingers glided across the silky marble on the seat he occupied. He had been invited by Lord Talbot himself to sit in the seat of honor, at the head of the party on a throne. He could only envision his father sitting there and was not sure if his nose played tricks on him or not, but he swore he smelled the cactus blossom of the cologne his father used to wear.

Every moment Terran spent around Talbot made his stomach ache, and his hands shook in high-pressure situations like this. He clenched the arms of the throne to steady himself and he smiled at Talbot in false delight, squinting only his eyes. His fear remained hidden behind the mask that concealed nearly his entire face.

Kingly robes draped over Talbot's body, and a thin, simple, silver mask lined half of his face. His white hair and lavish robe made him instantaneously recognizable, which Terran believed was the point. Terran adjusted the silver Bauta mask that covered his own face, a strong, masculine mask that turned his face into a stone edifice, and huffed a sigh. Now that another redhead swept the floor, he suspected a lot of the Naa'a guests were bound to mistake "Ruben" for Rune. "It's amazing how much of a person's face you need to see to recognize them," Terran mused. "Are you sure we are all safe? What if The King and his men get into the party?"

"Don't worry yourself, Rune," Talbot replied. "The only

way in is through the front, and that is heavily guarded, unless, of course, The King managed to get himself an invitation, but that is... very unlikely. Besides, we have Perseus and Parisa scattered in with the crowd, and every entrance and exit is covered by an Elite Guard. You must have confidence in me, my lad. We are impenetrable."

Terran chuckled to himself, invisible under his mask, and glanced around again.

"See there?" Talbot continued and pointed at a head in the crowd. "There is Councilman Wolff."

Terran followed Talbot's finger to a man in the crowd in a coyote mask, furry and gray, and the pelt trailed down his back. Dancing with him was a woman in a pelt as well, thought it was an albino fox upon her face instead. He held her wrist and hissed something into her ear. Terran's heart sank as he watched Vena dance miserably with her husband, and her body language said nothing of love.

"Stop," a guard near the throne said, pulling Terran from his daze. "You don't have permission to be up he—"

"I just need a moment of the Sovereign's time! Please, let me speak with him."

Terran turned his head to see where the ruckus came from and met eyes with someone he had only seen on street corners in passing. Her silver hair trailed down her back, and though the ivory told her age, her face was nearly devoid of wrinkles. Red dye, redder than any clay Terran had ever seen, was smeared across her face, staining her skin. A dagger swung at her hip and her red robes fell from her body in a puddle. Among all the white, she looked like a blood stain.

The guard attempted to keep her from approaching the Sovereign, but to no avail. Despite her hands being tied at the wrists by rope, she was surprisingly agile, and she threw herself to Lord Talbot's feet. "My Lord," she pleaded. "Please. A moment of your time."

"Ah... Widow Corine, can't you see we're having a party?" Lord Talbot replied. "You were invited because of your noble blood and your claim to your property in Naa'a, but I warned you if you made a scene in public again, there would be trouble."

Widow Corine. Terran had seen her only a few times before. He remembered now. She stood on street corners and screamed scripture at passersby. She had formed some kind of religion over the last couple of years. Terran had heard of the church in his studies while he was still with the Embassy, but it was nothing more than a cult then. After his parents had been killed, Widow Corine had risen to infamy as she preached from her pedestal with her hands tied and a smear of paint as bright as the Castilleja flower across her face. Terran knew nothing of the religion and The King had instructed him to stay away from her. Her fanaticism had already proven dangerous, and people had already died for the religion, despite it being new.

"I just need a moment of your time, and if not now, later. My god has shown me things," Lady Corine muttered, her hair blown wildly about her face from lack of brushing. "About your reign. About the world. I have had a terrible vision."

"We can set a date to discuss it if that means you'll leave me alone," Lord Talbot grated, his lack of care clear on his face.

"You are free to stay and enjoy the festivities. Otherwise, if you plan on peddling that nonsense that you claim as a religion, I'm going to have to throw you out."

"Yes, My Lord. A date would suffice."

"You'll receive an invitation at your... church. Mind you, if you miss the date, I'm not giving you another chance."

"Thank you, My Lord."

Widow Corine bent so low her forehead touched the ground, and she continued to bow as she backed into the crowd. Lord Talbot rolled his eyes and his chest rose and fell in a deep sigh.

"Who on earth was that?" Terran asked.

"A thorn in my side. Nothing more," Lord Talbot dismissed. "I would rather think about anything else in the world than some religious lunatic."

A diversion. Terran needed a diversion.

"Is that Esmond?" Terran asked and pointed to a man with a dark braid bobbing in and out of the white. He wore a simple, white mask that tied behind his head and a historical military uniform. Among all the rich costumes, he looked more like a sword for hire than a Councilmember.

"I believe so... there are Perseus and Parisa."

Terran spotted them as soon as the words left Talbot's mouth. As a cat and mouse, they danced, lacking the sky blue of all the other costumes. Widow Corine pushed past them as she left the throne room, and Perseus stumbled as he dodged around her in the crowd.

"Who's that?" Talbot asked and gestured to The King, who

conversed with some other Embassy guests. Terran choked on his words, preparing his lie.

"My cousin, Ruben, from Sulphur."

"He was out there, too?"

"Yes, my research assistant."

"How delightful. On your mother's or father's side?"

"Mother's."

"Redheads about in the Guildenhart family," Talbot chuckled. "You should go and enjoy yourself while I figure out what to do with this... Corine mess."

"Are you sure? I don't want to abandon you here."

"You're a dutiful boy, Rune, and I appreciate that. Go on."

Terran stood, bowed rigidly, and was ready to walk away when Talbot stopped him by placing a gentle hand on Rune's arm. "Actually, I wanted to ask something of you."

"Yes?" Terran turned and kneeled in front of Talbot respectfully.

"The truth is, I've been looking for someone to ask this question to for a very long time, and I feel you are a suitable candidate, Rune. Frankly, I do not want Parisa to ascend to the throne. I feel her time with that lowborn Elite has poisoned her mind. She is too reckless and has far too many brash ideas. The only way to avoid total ruin under her rule would be to marry her off... to someone like you."

"But My Lord, even though she is a woman, she would still have more claim to the throne than her husband."

"Not if she is married to someone who puts her in her place."

"Like me?"

"You are a lot like me, Rune, and I feel you are all I could have ever asked for out of a suitable candidate. Your defense of me in the Council halls and in meetings is inspiring. You understand how important it is to keep the Embassy pure, unlike the last maniacs who took the throne. How disgraceful it was that they allowed lowborns like Esmond and Alvena Wolff into the Council, not to mention the others."

Terran's mother had constructed a colorful Council, certainly. She was a female Sovereign after all. Alvena Wolff came from Atsa and had presided over the district until she married Jacob Wolff and completely gave up her title to him, her reasons for doing so unknown. Esmond was from Dza'ya, a specific ancestry native to the region before the Great War. Another individual on the Council, Alvena's assistant, had claimed no gender and refused to use he or she, setting a precedent in all districts. They were outsiders, all of them. Nothing like Talbot. Terran's mother had been hailed by some as progressive, like Terran's grandfathers, and by others the harbinger of the apocalypse.

"I have been thinking on a marriage between you and Parisa for some time now, and it surprises me that a bachelor like yourself has remained unmarried for so long. What are your thoughts?" Talbot continued.

"I would love to be your successor. Anything to uphold the proper standards for Segeno."

"Good. I will tell you everything, Rune. All of the Embassy's secrets. There are many tenants that the last Sovereign ignored, and I will not let anyone tarnish the sanctity of this great city. Then, you must do everything I say... understood? We need to work together if we want to keep this sinkhole from falling into the earth."

Terran at that moment understood Parisa entirely. First, Talbot showered those close to him in affection, but right after the hook was in, he owned whoever was on it. "Absolutely. We'll save Segeno together."

"Wonderful, but we shall speak of this matter another time. Go enjoy yourself! Flirt with her a little, would you?"

Terran bowed again and made his way over to a pillar adjacent to the dance floor where he tried to spot a few familiar faces. The crowd unnerved him and even as he stood, he feared a nightmare that had haunted him the last few nights would become reality. Dreams the past week had kept him from sleeping, dreams in which he forgot to use his magick or the card wore off at inopportune times. He checked his hands and ran his fingers through his hair, reminders that he could proceed without fear. When he spotted Parisa he moved toward her to not lose sight of her.

Though he had not gained approval from The King, he was moving forward with a plan. His goal was to bring Parisa into the fold. She was just a move away from being an ally, from being the perfect inside spy. He knew that she would switch sides as soon as she found out the atrocities her father had committed. He only just had to give her a little nudge.

Perseus stopped dancing as he approached, and Terran asserted over the crowd and the music, "May I cut in?"

Perseus nodded out of sheer politeness, but as soon as

he backed away from the dance floor, Terran watched the Elite captain's lips tighten into a thin line. Terran chuckled as the next dance started, and joked, "Your friend is getting attached to you, isn't he?"

"Ah, Lord Guildenhart. I'd recognize that hair anywhere. For a moment I wasn't sure if it was you, or that doppelganger. There's another redhead running around here, if you didn't notice," Parisa babbled, relaxed, her mind somewhere else.

"He's my cousin, actually. We're like two peas in a pod, he and I. Are you enjoying yourself?"

"Very much so. I'm glad this was your idea. I can't remember the last time I had any fun."

The music swept them across the floor in leaps and twirls, and Terran could not help but smile under his mask. There had been very few children around the Embassy his age when he was growing up, so to do something with someone his relative age was nice.

After a few moments of silence, Terran commented, "You know, dances like these always remind me of a scene from *Treachery* by Garnier. Have you read it?"

"I *love* that book!" Parisa smiled with her teeth, a full, happy smile. Terran had to tread carefully. He did not want to ruin it.

"This moment reminds me of Phoebus and Daniella, when they're at the ball."

"Aren't they lovers?"

"I mean, yes."

"What are you getting at?"

"We complement each other, I think. You're unpredictable,

an out-of-the-box thinker. I'm sensible and level-headed. I have government experience. You're from this city, I'm from outside of it. It's really a shame we don't work together."

"My father made sure that I wouldn't be involved in any way."

"If he dies, that's another matter entirely though, isn't it?"

The song ended and Parisa searched Terran's eyes. He took her by the arm to the edge of the crowd to move out of the way of other dancers and her chest rose in anticipation. "Your point?" she asked.

"You feel this city needs to change, don't you?"

"Well, yes... Segeno is going through a hard time."

"What if it wasn't just a hard time?" Terran whispered as loudly as he could over the music. "What if this was the way it was intended, built into the system from the beginning?"

"You're talking about conspiracy."

"I'm trying to uncover information. Your father has dropped some... interesting tidbits that are making me question the inner workings of this place, and I plan on raising graves if it means answers."

Parisa pursed her lips. "What are you asking of me, Lord Guildenhart?"

"We have a real opportunity to make something great of this place."

Parisa nodded, but said nothing, her lip trembling.

"We could do it together."

"That's flattering, Rune, but—"

"Listen," Terran whispered in her ear. He put a hand on

her arm, but she perceived it as a threat. Parisa attempted to lean away from him, but his hand tightened around her arm. "Don't move. Please don't make a scene."

"What is *wrong* with you?"

"Listen to me," Terran pleaded. "Your father wants us to be wed. He wants me to control you, to quell your desire for justice. You know things are wrong. I know you do. You've seen Dza'ya. I have a suspicion that this whole thing, the Embassy, Naa'a, how people come into power, all of it has been rigged from the start. Why do you think there were laws for so long preventing people from differing skin to marry?"

"If you don't let go of me, I'll stab you."

"It's your father's will and I can say nothing against it for now. I think we should work together and do what we can for the city. It would be much easier for both you and me if we just did as he said until he's out of the picture."

The music came to a lull again and Parisa ripped her arm from his hand. "You are absolutely horrible, you know that? Do you know how crazy you sound? Conspiracy? Built into the system? You've got sand lodged in your brain."

Terran raised his hands and took a step back from her. "Think on it. If we're to be wed—"

"I hope you rot, Guildenhart. *Never* touch me like that again."

Parisa stormed toward the door and Terran made his way to a nearby pillar and leaned against it. Just a nudge. And it wasn't conspiracy. His mother had been considered a radical and had been shot for it. He was not sure what kind of agenda

Talbot subscribed to, but it was a deadly one. He was one step closer to understanding that agenda, and once he did, all the walls would come crumbling down. He eyed the crowd for The King's flaming red hair. He figured Parisa's response was to be expected. He did not want to marry her, either, but once Talbot was out of the picture Terran could call the whole thing off and be done with it. Safety was of his utmost priority, and the last thing he wanted was to hurt anyone. At least he had tried.

Eventually, Terran spotted his master in a not too distant cluster of people conversing with Vena as if they had never met. Another dance finished and everyone clapped. Terran's master downed a glass of wine, his face flushed and barely visible under his mask. He smiled and laughed loud enough for Terran to hear it across the dance floor, and Vena mirrored his merriment.

The King took that momentary opportunity to make a move. He beckoned Vena to the dance floor and Terran saw Jacob Wolff clench his fists when Vena accepted the invitation. Terran smiled as he watched them dance. The King whispered into her ear and she giggled at everything he said. Her eyes told Terran everything. She leaned her head on his shoulder and Terran wondered what it was like. He had never seen two people so in love.

Giving Up
Parisa

The Palace, December of the Second Year

It snowed lightly outside, a soft kind of snow that did not bite at the skin, a gentle snow, a silent snow. Parisa had gone and sat at the fountain that was not too far from her favorite tree, tears hot in her eyes. *How could Father ruin my life like this?* She had to do everything he said because he was the Sovereign; she had no choice, and now she had to throw away her life to be with a jerk and a basket case she hardly liked.

What could he possibly be talking about? She knew things were bad. She had seen it herself; he was right. But what did he know? A foreigner from a den of thieves was all he was. She had seen Perseus' struggle, learned about the inner machinations of poverty and plight. The thought that something was systemically wrong had tickled her in the middle of the night, but she never took it seriously. She had studied the laws of Segeno back to front in her classes with Esmond, so unless there was some secret doctrine that only the Sovereign was allowed to see, everything was fine.

She ran through her options in her head. *I could run away,* she thought. *To where? Sulphur, maybe. It's the closest settlement and if Rune lived there and was fine—he's horrible. And Father would find me there. It's not like no one communicates with Sulphur. What would he do if he **did** find me? Execute me?*

She wiped her eyes when she heard the glass doors of the ballroom open. Someone came to sit next to her, leaving prints in the snow as they came. "I'm sorry you had to dance with him," Perseus huffed. "Are you okay? What did he do to you?"

"N-Nothing. He's... ugh. It's everything else."

"I'll go sock him if he said anything to you that—"

"It's not that, Perseus... we—we have to stop."

"Stop?"

"We can't feel like this anymore. Not for each other."

Perseus looked as though someone had burned his skin. "I-I don't understand."

"Father said I am to marry Lord Guildenhart."

"I... oh." Perseus pursed his lips and shook his head. "That can't be right."

"I'm trying to formulate what to do, and the best course of action seems to be 'just go with it.' Rune's crazy, but not as crazy as my father. My father probably wants me to give up my right and power as the heir to Rune, but even if I'm in a secondary seat of power, I might just save this place."

"But is it worth it?"

"It is if we can play the game. You'll have to stay away from me, at least romantically. My father will eventually die, and I

196

can kill Guildenhart in his sleep. You—you just have to keep your distance and let me work."

Perseus spat with resistance, "Never."

"You're just going to make it harder."

"Who told you? Who told you the news?"

"Lord Guildenhart himself."

"He might be lying."

"Doesn't seem so, Perseus. He told me some things that I... I need to think over. I don't understand him like I thought I did. I'm angry with him, but... there's something else going on."

Perseus leaned in, kissed her on the lips, and took her hand. The snow caught in his dark hair and when he pulled away, he sighed like the ocean rolling from the shore. "I am *never* going to let you go. We'll work it out. Won't we? We could run away."

Parisa laughed. "Where would we go that he wouldn't find us?"

"I don't know... we'll find somewhere, won't we?"

Parisa muttered and looked into the nearly frozen water of the fountain, "I don't think so, Perseus."

Soul Dance
Terran

The Palace, December of the Second Year

Terran watched The King move closer and closer to Alvena and tensed. If The King did anything reckless there, he would be dead, and Councilman Wolff looked more and more agitated by the moment. He stumbled just a little on his feet, and Terran suspected he was drunk enough to be stupid but not drunk enough to be out of his mind. When The King lifted his mask to kiss Vena's exposed lips, Terran reacted. He dashed through the dancing crowd, but it proved difficult. People kept twirling in front of him, and when Terran caught a glimpse of The King again, their lips touched.

Councilman Wolff had seen and charged his way through the crowd, a juggernaut. When he reached The King, his fist flew at full speed at The King's face, and the brittle, paper mache mask shattered with the first hit.

Councilman Wolff was a large man, so it was not a surprise when The King hit the floor hard, taken completely by surprise.

The partygoers scattered and stepped back from the scene, an organic ring of bodies around Vena, The King, and Wolff. Wolff huffed and puffed, his shoulders rising and falling under his pelt. He, too, looked not entirely sober, and Terran pushed his way to the edge of the circle to get a better look.

"Get up, Jester!" Councilman Wolff barked and shoved Vena out of the way, a little too roughly, as The King stood. The blow had cut his lip, and blood dripped onto his clothing and the alabaster. Rather than recoiling, The King began to laugh, a side-splitting laugh. Wolff rushed to him and yanked him from the floor with brute strength and roared, smoke practically coming out of his ears, "Who the *hell* do you think you are?"

The King merely chuckled. Terran was about to stop The King from doing anything stupid but held still. The King locked eyes with him in the crowd, and he nodded. Something else was afoot. This perhaps was a part of his plan.

"You know me," The King replied, "a rich man, royal, privileged, but I am also a poor man, the oppressed, the beat, the starving. I am a beggar, but I am also a king." The King took his mask and threw it to the ground, causing it to shatter. Those around him saw his face, and the ones who recognized him let out gasps of surprise or fear.

Ah, so this was all for show. It was a declaration. Terran stepped back only just a little to let his master work.

"Do you recognize me?" The King continued. "I am your brother. You threw me out, cast me into the shadows, a place where you *forget* things. Have you forgotten me? You all have heard the horror stories about who the guards suspect I am, how I was born of the filth of Dza'ya, how I am a ruthless killer. Would you have believed that I am one of your own?"

"Lexus? Lexus Haywood?" Wolff muttered as The King ripped the Councilman's hulking hand from the collar of his costume. Wolff studied his face, recognizing him from some time long since gone.

What was he *doing*? Declaring war? Terran ran his teeth over his lip. After all the times that Lexus had told him to lay low, this was going to result in a brawl.

"The shadows are more powerful than you would like to admit. I *know* the misery that your beloved *Sovereign*," The King spit the word out with such spite that a few people flinched, "has caused the people. Do you even *look* beyond the district walls? The Council is supposed to keep all people *safe* but are drowning out the voices of those that suffer most. Lies leak from his mouth like rats from a hole. I was on the Council! I saw all of the destruction he caused, and it's not just him..."

Talbot stood and a few guards moved to apprehend The King. The commander of the Elite Guard entered the room, the heaviness of his boots an indicator of his presence. Terran heard the doors to the throne room open and felt Perseus and Parisa rush up behind him. Lord Talbot held his fist up, signaling his men to hold. He smiled underneath his mask. It seemed this display amused him.

"It's the whole damn thing," The King continued. "It's rigged. There are documents that only the Sovereign's eyes are allowed to see, books and codes from the beginning of Segeno, and I'm sure they hold all sorts of secrets. I was onto it all, and what did Talbot do? Threw me out! He claimed that I had seduced his wife and driven her to madness. We all *know* who did that."

When The King locked eyes with Talbot, Terran saw Parisa second guess herself, her eyes darting from the stranger's face to her father's. Terran wanted to reach out and take her hand, comfort her, but now was not the time.

"I come to deliver a message. This wasn't my intent for the night, but, heh," The King chuckled to himself, "plans change. Opportunities present themselves. My heart's not done me wrong before. Change is coming, the truth will be exposed, and Justice will rain down upon those who are guilty. Brace yourselves. I suggest you all practice some penance for your sins and take some time to educate yourselves. Otherwise, you might just end up regretting everything you've ever done."

This was a declaration of war.

The King drew a card. Everyone flinched and gasped, afraid of the power. "I'm sure you all have heard of these," he continued. "You think I am a demon, cast out from hell and given glorious dark powers by Satan himself."

"Enough of this," Talbot spat. He had become bored. "Get him out of my sight."

Guards swarmed, pushing through the partygoers and royalty, and The King placed the card on his hand, igniting the paper and his flesh. The guards paused for a moment as a sword materialized in The King's hand. Some chuckled as The King turned the sword.

"Ready men?" Commander Crevan barked, drawing his blade. "Dice him to bits."

The King struck with such ferocity that the guard jumped back. Eight swords erupted from his back and The King used his weapons as extensions of his body to slash at all his targets at once, like some sort of metal tarantula. It was beautiful, really. Sweat dripped from Parisa's brow as she danced with The King, dodging blows to get close with her dagger. Perseus knelt in the crowd and drew his rifle, cocking the gun and waiting for an opportunity to fire. Terran watched all of Commander Crevan's men fall like flies. With one swift motion, The King grabbed Parisa's arm and spun her in front of himself, blocking Perseus's shot.

"You shoot, and she dies," he said. He turned and pointed to Councilman Wolff. "Now you... you remember me, don't you, you bastard? You took everything I loved away from me. If you touch her again, I'll end your life."

"I'll kill you," Wolff spat. "I'll kill you, you insolent—"

Parisa threw her head backward into The King's and knocked him back. The King's nose began to bleed and Parisa swiped at him with her dagger. He barely dodged the blow and pulled another card from his pocket. In an instant, golden, shining wings burst forth from his shoulder blades, tearing his costume. He flew through the doors at the front of the throne room, shattering the glass, and Parisa and Perseus followed, whistling for backup. Terran knew they would not catch him. No one would be able to catch The King.

Of Age
Parisa

The Palace, January of the Third Year

"You *are* of age to be married, and that is final. Lord Guildenhart is a suitable man to be married to, and I do *not* see why you are being so obstinate!"

"But on my *birthday*?" Parisa spat in a tone that should not have been used with her father, let alone the Sovereign. For months she fought with all her being to control her temper and keep her resentment buried deep inside her, but this obscenity was the final straw.

"You are *dismissed*," Talbot finished, and when his eyes met hers, they showed no sympathy. If anyone asked how Parisa felt at that moment, she would not be able to give a straight answer. Disgust, perhaps, or betrayal. Her father must not have cared for her at all, and all the love he had ever shown her had been a lie.

Lord Guildenhart stood next to Talbot's chair, slim hand on marble. She hated them both, and if she had to marry him, she knew she would loath him for the rest of her life. And yet, the things he said... had they been lies, too?

As she left the hall, she took a deep breath to try and calm her temper, but it did not work. When she arrived at her room, she took a pillow from her bed and screamed into it. She tried to let all her anger out in the form of air, shouts that turned to sobs.

Ever since the night of the party, her father had been out to get her. She and Perseus had failed to catch The King, and Talbot punished them for it. He had given Perseus a black eye, and Parisa was thankful that she did not have to see him get hit. Perseus wandered into her room after his meeting, eye swollen and purple, and they sat in silence together while she dabbed his face with ice.

She had been so naïve. How could she think her father was so good? And did The King mean what he had said? Had Talbot really had something to do with her mother's disappearance? She was led to believe that her mother left her father for another man and died in the desert. Was it true? The only person she could turn to was Esmond, but she did not have the strength to talk to him. As far as she was concerned, her fifteenth birthday was ruined.

Old Enemies
Terran

The Palace, January of the Third Year

"She took that rather well."

Terran sighed and sat in his father's seat, agreeing, "I think she did... at the ball she would hardly listen to me."

"Damn him," Talbot cursed, stood, and made his way over to a window.

"Who?"

"Lexus, that traitor, waltzing into *my* palace like he owns the place. How did he even get in? There's only one entrance, and he would've needed an invitation."

Terran chuckled in his own head, and he asked aloud, "What do you have against him, anyway? He's just a street thief."

"We've sparred before, in the Council Room. When La'Hall was Sovereign, I wanted to begin my work reshaping this city and proposed a good deal of laws to do so. I had found a book, something buried in a secret compartment behind La'Hall's bed. She must have had it built while she was ruling. This book, titled

The Old Way, outlined the way Segeno was constructed. The book was written by the original Sovereign, Lord Raith the First, and had what he called 'The Segeno Code' in it."

"You went through their room while she was still alive?"

"I had to. I knew they were hiding something. This code is God-given, Rune. It outlines everything we should hold dear as the Sovereign. There are rules we must abide by."

"Like what?"

"Firstly, we must maintain purity of the blood line. Lord Raith the First tells us that those of any skin other than white are lowborn, and must be separated from the stock. We must keep it pure. The science before the great war, according to Lord Raith, proved this as fact. Secondly, everything must be done to put money back into Naa'a. The lowborns are nothing more than cogs in a machine, my boy. Cogs in a machine."

Terran felt a stone drop in his stomach. He had to see this book for himself. "May I read the book?"

"In time. For now, I've hidden it in away so that no one unworthy of its wisdom may find it. I fear someone would destroy it. Why La'Hall hid it, I have no clue. Once I had that knowledge, I knew what I needed to do and what laws needed to be reinstituted. A lot of it La'Hall or her father had destroyed. Every time, she and Lexus would garner *just* enough support to shoot down everything I brought up. She said it wasn't good for the people. I asked, 'What about *our* people?' They didn't understand."

"How could they?"

"Exactly. Traitors, the lot of them. Lexus would attack me with his words, try to catch me doing something I wasn't supposed to. Eventually, I realized that La'Hall made the city sick, her and all her kind. She was destroying the Embassy from the ground up. May I share with you a secret?"

"Of course."

There was a knock on the glass door. Terran let out a breath as the conversation turned away from The King. He figured it was only a matter of time before Talbot put two and two together. The King had been disguised as Ruben, Rune's cousin, and things were about to get messy.

A servant opened the door and bowed to Lord Talbot. "My Lord, Widow Corine is here to see you."

Lord Talbot rubbed the bridge of his nose and sighed. "I had completely forgotten in all of this mess. Rune, would you like to stay and watch me deal with this nonsense?"

"Certainly, Lord Talbot."

"Send her in."

Widow Corine entered, her hands tied as before, and she knelt before Lord Talbot. Her red dress pooled around her as she fell to her knees, and Lord Talbot exhaled a sigh so long it became almost insufferable. "What do you want?"

"I have had a vision from my god, My Lord."

"And?"

"I saw something... concerning."

"Spit it out. I don't have all day."

"I saw great metal birds in the sky, and things that rolled upon the ground at great speeds. People wore strange clothes in a city made of metal and glass, and food flowed from all corners of the earth. I think it is a vision of the future."

Terran furrowed his eyebrows in interest. He wondered how she could have seen such things, or if she had merely had an elaborate dream.

"Why should I be concerned? It seems I launch Segeno into an age of prosperity, if that is the future of our city."

"I saw nothing familiar in it. Not Segeno, not you... my god was there. She took my face in her hands and screamed, 'Lies! All lies!'"

Widow Corine threw herself to the ground, taken by the emotion of it all, and Terran squinted at her, trying to figure her out. He had never seen anything like this. She raised her eyes to Lord Talbot and then looked at Terran.

"Zasdona sees all," she spat. "She can see through even through the cleverest of disguises."

Goosebumps shot up Terran's arms.

"And she can see through even the best hidden deceits. Tread lightly, My Lord."

"Is that a threat?" Lord Talbot demanded.

"Not a threat... just... a warning."

"Guards, get this crazy woman out of my sight."

Guards stepped forward and dragged Widow Corine from the room.

"It will all come crumbling down! Like melting ice, the truth will be revealed by The Deathless, She Who Sees!"

The glass doors closed, and Talbot rolled his eyes. "I hate fanatics."

"Is there any credence to her claims?" Terran asked. "Or to her ability to see the future?"

"Absolutely not. She's a lunatic. We all know there's only one God. The Segeno constitution says so."

Terran nodded and looked to the floor. "I'm so sorry we were rudely interrupted."

"I have a question for you, Rune..."

"Yes?"

"The King, it seemed, was not wearing a disguise at all. How is it that he got in with your cousin's invitation?"

"I haven't been able to find Ruben at all. I've already reported it to Commander Crevan. I walked with Ruben into the party, so I can only assume that Ruben went outside for some fresh air and The King must have..."

Terran put his hand over his mouth as if choking up. He needed to sell this lie and fast.

"We will search for your cousin. I won't let that murderer get away with killing any more of our own kin."

"Thank you, My Lord. That means more to me than you know."

Talbot crossed his legs and blinked slowly, as if lost in thought. "I want to tell you something important, Rune, but you must promise to keep it to yourself. Keep it so secure that not even a truth-seeking god could see it."

"Yes, My Lord."

"I murdered La'Hall and her husband."

Blackness danced into the corners of Terran's vision. He had known, but somehow hearing it in person and not being able to do anything about it was sickening. His stomach backflipped and the entire room spun as he sat still in the chair. "I see," was all he said.

"It had to be done. You know that as well as I do. Seeing as you weren't raised here in the palace, you didn't get to see firsthand what La'Hall did. Besides, before now, you were probably too young to understand... but I had to. The Embassy deteriorated in the hands of that cretin. I hired Lexus to do the job for me. He never finished his task, and I always suspected he was a spy. I got tired of my wife and she succumbed to certain... delusions from something she consumed that caused her to wander out into the desert. Because Lexus did not perform, I blamed it on him, and he retreated into the cavities of the city."

"I see."

"When he didn't get the job done, I confided in the people I knew I could break. Wolff and his wife, and Esmond. Wolff always backed my ideas and Esmond has always been too weak to disobey orders. None of them pulled through, so I shot them myself."

"Your rise to power has been... one of great planning, Talbot," Terran muttered, his hands trembling. He stood. "You have done much to get here."

"I have done more than most," Talbot added. Terran was not surprised to find no regret in his face. "Go along now... I need to think about how to trap The King, considering he made two of my best soldiers look like the children they are."

Terran bowed and said, "If you need my advice, sir, I am here. I know carrying the weight of a city can be sometimes more than one person can handle."

Talbot turned to look at Rune with eyes that for a

210

moment seemed to carry some semblance of emotion. The feeling disappeared as quickly as it came, and he said, "Thank you, Rune. Your presence is always greatly appreciated, and you mean more to me than you know. At least I have *someone* I can trust."

Old Friends
Parisa

The Palace, January of the Third Year

A knock tapped across the door and Parisa shouted, "Go away!"

She lay in her bedroom for hours, wrapped up in sheets and her own discontent, and had cried all the tears she thought possible to cry. Her eyes were dry now, her cheeks prickled with residue and salt, and she did not have the energy to move. She had tired herself out in her antics, and the bed was warm and shielded her from the world.

"It's me." Perseus' voice came through the door, and it opened. Parisa still had her face in her pillow and she did not look up. Perseus sat at the edge of the bed and placed a gentle hand on her back. "Hey, I brought something for you."

When Parisa lifted her head, she saw Perseus there with an enormous bouquet, beautiful beardtongue, bearpoppies, and blazing stars. Parisa took it and breathed in their sweet fragrance, her hands shaking. "Oh, Perseus... they're lovely."

She pulled him into a hug, extending her arm to be sure the flowers were not crushed, and pressed her cheek into his. He smelled like forget-me-nots and of cinnamon, and his shortly cropped hair and beard prickled her skin. Her fingers slid across his shirt and she felt home.

"I hoped that they would cheer you up," he said. "They were all I could afford. I know they're not jewels or dresses or other stuff that princesses—"

Parisa kissed him freely, and her face glowed brighter than the setting sun. "If it's from you, it's perfect."

Perseus smiled and wiped tears from her eyes. "Please don't be sad today... we need to go out and do something fun. What do you want to do?"

"I..." Even though the flowers had certainly made her feel better, her broken heart had not mended. "Perseus, I'm not up for anything."

"Are you sure? We could climb the palace, go and get some fried dough from the—"

"No, thanks... I'd rather just be by myself today."

Perseus nodded and moved to the door, taking the flowers with him. "All right," he conceded. "I'll... get a vase for these."

Parisa flopped onto her bed as he closed the door and released a heavy sigh. She simply lay there and did not want to move. She did not have the energy to move, and she was unsure how long she had actually been there when there was another knock on the door. It opened immediately, without permission, and Esmond stepped in. In his hands were Perseus' flowers in a new vase, and something wrapped in blue paper. "Hey," he said.

213

"Feeling any better?"

"No. I feel sick."

"It's because you're making yourself sick. You're giving up." Esmond set down the flowers on her armoire but remained standing. "You know, when I was married to Elsa, it was arranged. I had no idea that I would fall in love, and she turned out to be my favorite person in the whole world. It may be the same with you and Rune."

"But I *hate* him," Parisa spat and sat up abruptly. "He makes me feel dirty inside every time he touches me. *Dirty*. At this point, I never want to see him again."

Esmond paused and set her gift down on her bed. "That boy's stolen your heart, hasn't he?"

"Which boy?"

"Perseus."

"Is it that obvious?"

"Clear as day." Esmond chuckled and gazed at a painting on the wall. "You won't marry Guildenhart."

Parisa was unsure of his meaning. He had said it in a manner that did not suggest that he realized she did not want to. It seemed he thought that it was impossible and would never happen, almost as though he would prevent it from happening.

"What do you mean, Esmond? It's Father's will."

"A revolution is on its way, Parisa. A grand one," he said as he handed her a box of chocolates. "These are from Rune. The wrapped one is from me. Just hang on and keep your chin up. Soon... a revolution. I promise. Soon."

Wrath

Terran

The Palace, February of the Third Year

"Dammit! Why can't you do anything I ask? You worthless, ungrateful slut!"

The shouting was so loud it could be heard all throughout the palace. It was the middle of the night and the noise had awoken Terran from his sleep. He used The Magician and dashed out into the hallway and down a few floors in the elevator, where he followed the shouts to the door of Councilman Wolff's quarters. Terran trembled as he stood there, his hand hovering over his pocket where the cards sat. He knew he was about to witness what The King feared the most, and he knew he was going to have to stop it. His fingers tingled as they held there in the air, the magickal energy from the cards radiating out in an electrifying aura. It would be whatever they decided, and something told him it wouldn't be good.

"All I asked for was a glass of water, not for any of your excuses!"

215

Something crashed, a rumble that sent shakes through the floor. Councilman Wolff sounded undeniably drunk.

"Councilman Wolff?" Terran shouted at the door, but the yelling and crashing continued and he was ignored.

Terran took a deep breath, indecision in his muscles and his bones. The King would want him to act, and before he thought anymore, the deed was done. He threw his shoulder into the door a few times until it broke off its hinges, wood chips scattering onto the floor, and Terran entered to find Wolff had Vena by the wrist. Her face was red from where he had hit her. Furniture lay on its sides and glass scattered in fragments like ice on hardwood. The curtains had been torn from the wall and crumpled on the floor in a heap. It looked like a hurricane had passed through, and Wolff turned his eyes to Terran so viciously that it reminded Terran of a wild animal. "This is none of your *business*, Guildenhart."

Terran did not cower under his gaze, and just looking at him made him indescribably angry. With a hard scowl on his lips, he pulled a card from his pocket and laid it on his hand. There had to be justice. Before Wolff understood what had happened, Terran watched the flesh peel away from his limbs, leaving only bone, and one card traded itself out for another as his body transformed. Only a black cloak covered his now bare bones, and his corpse creaked and moaned as he moved. "You have hurt her for too long, Wolff. Do you even feel guilty?"

"W-What?" Wolff stuttered as he stumbled backward, away from Terran's horrifying visage. "What the h-hell?"

"You won't be able to hurt anyone anymore." Before Wolff could run, Terran grabbed his shoulder with a skeletal hand and whispered into Wolff's ear, "Do you know what card I drew? Death. I drew Death."

As Terran touched Wolff, all life from the Councilman began to fade. Color pulled from his face, his eyes, and his clothing until he was no more than a greyscale rendition of his former self. Then, he began to crumble into soot, gray dust that drifted to the ground and through the air like snow. Out of the pile of soot a caterpillar climbed, pulling its way from the dirt, and it inched its way along the ground until it hid under the couch, out of sight.

"Ashes to ashes, dust to dust," Terran commented.

"You *killed* him?"

The voice came from the door to the suite, and Terran turned to see who stood there. Esmond cowered in the doorway, pale as a sheet. The card faded and Terran first checked if he still looked like Rune, which he did not, and then glanced at Esmond warily, hands up defensively. Down the hallway, Terran heard the clanking of metal guard boots as they scrambled up the stairs. Esmond, Terran suspected, alerted the guards at the sound of the ruckus, but did not expect what he looked upon now.

"Esmond. Esmond, I'm a friend," Terran pleaded.

"Guards!" Esmond shouted as he hastily and weakly grabbed Terran by the shirt to prevent his escape. "Guards! Parisa! Perseus!"

Vena tried in vain to pull him off. "Wait! Esmond, wait! He's one of us!"

"I work for The King!" Terran interjected.

"Prove it!" Esmond's hands trembled and Terran knew he posed no threat.

"Check my tattoo! I'm a user of the cards! I'm undercover for The King!" Terran hissed this in a whisper. He could risk no one hearing.

Esmond spun Terran around and moved his collar. Once he saw the tattoo, he slowly released him, and Terran whipped out The Magician again, covering his true identity once more. At that moment, Parisa and Perseus, backed by a few guards, entered the room.

Parisa looked around for potential threats, dagger drawn. "What happened?" she demanded, authority in her eyes.

"The King killed Wolff." Esmond spoke before Terran had the chance to and motioned toward the pile of ashes. "Rune and I heard the ruckus and when we got here, The King had turned him to ash."

"And you did *nothing*?" Parisa spat at Terran.

"After him!" Perseus shouted and pointed to the open window. "We may still be able to catch him!"

In a flash, all the guards were gone, save for a few who moved into the hallway again, and Terran turned to Esmond. "So quick to defend a man who beats a woman?" he asked. "If Rune *had* killed Wolff, you would've turned him in?"

"I am eager to rid this place of evil," Esmond replied. "If Rune was a ruthless killer and had ascended to the throne, able to wield Death as a weapon and Talbot knew, the kingdom would be doomed. Who are *you* to speak of such things?"

"I am Terran La'Hall. You tutored me when I lived here."

"T-The Sovereign's son?" Esmond stammered and dropped onto one knee. "You're alive... I can't believe it."

"If Lexus hadn't found me, I wouldn't be."

"Come," Esmond beckoned. "We have much to talk about if we are to fix this nasty mess we are in."

Disgrace
Parisa

The Palace, February of the Third Year

"You let him get away... *again*...?"

Talbot had not opened his eyes once when Parisa told him the news. The King had gotten away again. Her father's jaw locked, and his hand gripped the chair as if he would crush the marble with his mortal strength. Parisa, even though she did not want to admit it, was chilled to the bone. Every word her father spat was a mental attack, and his face scrunched as though he were trying to imagine what had caused the failure. She and Perseus had searched the entire city, but it was as if The King had vanished, or had never even been in the room in the first place.

"You realize," Talbot began and made his way down the velvet carpet to where Parisa knelt, "that I oversee the smallest council in Embassy history, correct?"

"Yes, My Lord," Parisa replied and did not dare to meet his eyes.

"That council was helmed by me, Wolff, Esmond, and

Guildenhart. All of them I placed into power myself, and all of them I felt were allies at my side. Guildenhart died, and now he has been replaced by his son, who honestly serves me better. Vena I forced out because her husband was more powerful, and Esmond is mortified of what I'll do to him if he doesn't do as I say. Now Wolff is *dead*. I have the city in the *palm* of my hand, and I have clawed tooth and nail to get to this point."

Parisa flinched at every syllable. She had trained so hard, but he terrified her.

"Once it becomes necessary to replace people I trust, things begin to get *complicated*. I must scare more people or pray Vena isn't as much of a nitwit as Esmond. How did he even get *in* without you seeing? Hm?"

"Even—even the palace has blind spots, Your Majesty," Perseus muttered and kept his eyes glued to the carpet.

Talbot knelt and lifted Perseus' head by his chin, so they met eyes. "You're right. There are blind spots. I'm sorry. I should be more understanding. I understand that you need sleep as well, and the other guards aren't as suited for the job. I also understand that you should be *hung* for failing me as you have. The only reason I haven't *killed* you yet is because I can't get anyone as *fast* as you. Obviously, you aren't good enough."

"We're *trying*."

Perseus regretted the words the moment they left his mouth. Talbot's hand flew like a bolt of lightning and hit so hard that it forced Perseus to recoil a little. Talbot stood and gazed down at him with unrelenting eyes. "Try harder."

Parisa gave Perseus a glance to check if he was all right

and Talbot caught it. He grabbed Parisa's cheek so hard she almost bit it on accident. "Awe. And you feel bad, don't you?" he sneered. "You know, it's never good to fall in love. Perhaps I should lock you in a room, considering everything I tell you to do you fail at? I wanted to make you the front of feminine liberation, allow you to do what no woman has ever done before, and how do you repay me?"

"You threw me out," she retorted.

"You're right. I threw you out." Talbot teased her with a smile. It wasn't a good tease, the kind that belonged between father and daughter. It was the kind that occurred between predator and prey. "You're incompetent, impractical, and downright ungracious. You are refuse in my life. Frankly, I wish you had never entered into this world, but... mistakes were made. More importantly, you're expendable. I omitted you from the equation... or at least I thought I did. I was hoping you'd die, that the training would be too hard. But you pulled through, regrettably.

"And now here we are, back at the same place, except... something's different. You've grown up. Now you think you're better than me, don't you?"

"You're awful."

Talbot hit her the same way he had hit Perseus. It made her skin bruise, and he returned to his throne. "This is your last chance. If you two fail me again, you will be replaced. Permanently."

Alliance
Terran

The Palace, February of the Third Year

"So, you were masquerading as Guildenhart's son the whole time," Esmond stated and poured tea, his hands trembling and the china rattling. "That's impressive, and a damn good disguise, too."

Terran watched the swirling steam rise from the cup, and when he grabbed the warm porcelain, he looked absentmindedly at The Magician's symbol on the back of his hand. He had removed his gloves to prove to Esmond further still his identity. "It's all in the cards. I'm merely a vessel."

"You grew up."

"I hardly remember you."

"After your parents got suspicious, they locked you up. They didn't want you harmed. They didn't trust anyone – hell, they hardly trusted me, and it's understandable. I don't do well against force."

"You did pretty well against me."

"I'm getting better about it. To tell you the truth, I've just been praying for peace. When this whole mess started, I knew which side I would be on... and it was the side that offered the most protection."

"So, you just let my parents die?"

Esmond shook his head and sipped his tea. "Talbot hoped I would kill them. He figured he could scare me into doing it, some easy method like poison, my weapon of choice, but I upheld my beliefs and remained loyal. I didn't touch your parents. I loved your mother, she was the greatest woman I ever knew, and in times like these, times where the people are crying out for some sort of reform, she was just what we needed. Talbot tortured me for months to try to get me to kill them so his hands would be clean, and if anything went wrong, I could take the fall for him."

"He makes me sick."

"I know, but now that you're here, things will be better. I know they will. You'll start a revolution."

Terran sipped his tea, but the liquid was too hot for him to consume just yet. Esmond had taken him to his study, and the place seemed to yell every single one of Esmond's secrets.

"I understand what you're going through."

"You do?" Terran raised a skeptical eyebrow.

"He killed my wife, Elsa. Told me if I didn't kill your parents, he'd slit her throat in front of me, and he did. It was like part of my soul died, so I understand. You and Lexus and I, we're all very much alike. We've all lost someone."

Terran blew on his tea, and asked, "Who did Lexus lose?"

Esmond's eyes shifted to the floor, and he gripped his teacup. "You need to be careful."

"Careful?"

"Now Talbot's on his guard. He's like a snake, and he'll strike if he's even a little bit suspicious."

Terran put down his tea without drinking a drop. He was too nervous. "Thank you, but I need to get some sleep," he said. "I have to figure out what exactly I'm going to do to get everyone out of this mess."

"Good luck. You're going to need it, and it was good meeting you. It's nice to know that there's a card user within these walls."

Terran was about to leave, but then he stopped and asked, "Can you use?"

"No. I think only a select few can, and I've never tried, but I never had the courage. Lexus told me that hundreds upon hundreds of years ago, the people of this place would use the cards to tell fortunes and had no idea the power locked within them. Use it wisely. It's a force of the universe I don't believe we fully understand. Take... take care of her, will you? Parisa? I can't keep my eyes on her always."

"Thank you, and don't worry. I'll keep Parisa safe."

"I appreciate it. We just need to... remove Talbot from the equation. That's all there is to it."

Liar
Parisa

The Palace, March of the Third Year

Parisa ducked behind a wall as Rune glanced back in her direction, and she held her breath as he stood there, hoping that he would not come her way as she stalked him. She needed to keep an eye on him. She *knew* something was not right. What did he do behind closed doors?

The King would not have been able to get into the palace by himself, Parisa thought to herself earlier that week. *The only way he could have gained entrance to the ball was by invitation. The guards were on watch, and even **I** know **I** can't sneak past the guards through a set of glass doors. They're too well trained, and the entrance too obvious. The only way he could have gotten an invitation would be if he had an inside man. It's the same with Wolff. It was as if The King had vanished into thin air. The only way to kill an Embassy Councilmember is if you **are** an Embassy Councilmember. Rune and Esmond both saw Councilman Wolff die. Esmond I trust, Rune I don't.*

Rune kept walking. He had not noticed her and Parisa

heaved a sigh of relief. It was after dark and it seemed that Rune was heading to his chambers to sleep. Parisa planned on following him and waiting to see if he did anything suspicious. If he did not, then she would need to wait until he fell asleep. Then she would—

"Parisa? What are you doing?"

Parisa jumped as she turned, only to find Perseus standing there. She hushed him and pulled him behind the corner of the wall. "Spying on Guildenhart! Now he knows I'm here," she huffed. "Now I'll have to wait weeks before I can spy on him again."

"Jeeze... I'm sorry. Why... are you spying on him again?"

"I think he killed Councilman Wolff, and I think he's working for The King."

Perseus laughed boisterously. "Parisa, is this just because you don't want to—"

"*No*," Parisa spat. "Now, are you going to help me out or not?"

"Well, sure," Perseus conceded. "But you're going to have to do a *lot* better than following him to his room."

Sleepless
Terran

The Tavern, March of the Third Year

"You *killed* him?"

Terran had led Vena to The King's tavern from the palace and told The King what had befallen her husband. The King's face rippled with expressions of shock and anger, but after a few moments of silence, he stepped forward and hugged Terran, a strong, heart-felt hug.

Terran hugged Lexus in return, and asked, "Are you all right?"

"Thank you," The King replied and stepped back awkwardly. "Which card?"

"Death, actually. He must have *seriously* had it coming."

"Let's walk," The King said, and then addressed Vena. "There are a few new books on my desk for you."

The King said nothing to Terran as they walked, and when they got to one of the Atsa watchtowers, The King climbed to the top, Terran following. When he reached its apex, he took a deep breath and smiled, and he seemed as though his soul had been released, like nothing was holding him down. "Can you sense the change, Terran? Freedom. Rapturous, glorious freedom. Justice sure is sweet, isn't it?"

"Is that what this is?" Terran asked, scooted to the edge of the abandoned tower, and looked out over the city. "Sometimes I wonder if we're being selfish, carrying out bloody revenge. Sometimes I hate Talbot so much that I... I begin to wonder."

"It's only revenge if you're only helping yourself." The King took out his cards. "These cards don't discriminate."

The King drew a card from the top of the deck, The Lovers, and put it at the bottom. He waited for a few moments, and when he pulled the bottom card out again, it had changed to the Knight of Cups. "When I see evil, Terran, and these cards are in my pocket, I feel the need to use them. When I don't, my heart tells me I've done something horrible, like I should have helped. We've seen the evils that Talbot has committed. When I was in the Council, he pushed against every act that would level the playing field for people. If there were no benefits for the Embassy, then he would fight it, and most of the time he would win, too. His pack of dogs, members like Wolff, would gladly follow. When your grandfather died, your mother was ready to shoulder the burden. It was... inspiring."

"One of my grandfathers was from Dza'ya. The other was from Naa'a." Terran watched a Mammoth lumber down the street and remembered where he had been years ago.

"Legendary. The first two men to be married and rule Segeno. Wasn't that same grandpa from Dza'ya the inventor of

229

the washing machine?"

"And the hand mixer. Not to mention, he was the one who figured out how to repair those fancy ancient guns. Revolutionized the gunsmithing industry."

"Your mother inherited his morality, the perspective that most in the Embassy did not have. Suddenly, she was pushing new, great, life-changing ideas. Talbot fought it. He fought it hard, and he was the main reason your mother was consistently stuck in stalemates. Meanwhile, the people wandered along, sleepless, lost. Poverty has been getting worse. Soon, there will be no Atsa. Talbot is literally sucking the life out of people, like some vampire."

"I hear that."

"You're not killing him for yourself, Terran. You're killing him for the people. Who knows? Maybe the cards don't even have death in store for him. As long as you don't make it selfish, it's Justice."

Terran nodded, "I understand."

"So. You haven't checked in in a while."

"I'm at the peak of my relationship with Talbot."

"What makes you say that?"

"He told me to marry his daughter."

"Yeah, I'd say that counts as the peak."

"Oh, and Esmond blamed Wolff's death on you."

"Lovely," The King scoffed and pulled out the envelope that contained the letters to Terran. "We need to figure out what your parents left behind for you. They didn't tell me anything out of fear, I suspect, so I've no idea what they've hidden."

Terran took out the first scrap of paper and read it over

again. *Poverty is only a state of mind. True richness comes from the heart and home.* "I don't understand this. I never lived in poverty."

"And your mom and dad were both born into the Embassy."

Terran looked out upon the city and heaved a great sigh as his eyes met the Embassy Palace. "Maybe it's hidden in their room."

"If it is, Talbot's already found it."

"You're right. Apparently, he found some secret, terrible code book in there that's the how-to of oppression."

"We should try your grandfather's house."

"Wouldn't that be owned by somebody?"

"If we ask nicely maybe they'll let us in."

"I have until sunset."

The King and Terran made their way briskly across the rooftops until they reached the Dza'ya district where they could no longer tread up above. Once on solid ground, The King approached the stall of an old woman who sold ceramic pots. He smiled down at her and bowed. "Hello, ma'am. We were wondering if you might answer a question for us."

When the old woman tilted her head upward, she gasped in surprise. "Oh! Your Majesty!" Her head whipped to his counterpart, and her eyes welled up with tears. "Your *Majesty!*" She bowed her head in respect. "You look just like your grandfather."

Terran smiled as memories of his grandfather flooded his brain, recollections of freshly baked cookies and warm, handmade blankets. He remembered gazing out over Segeno from the palace windows with his grandfather beside him. To say he looked like his grandfather was one of the highest complements he had ever received.

"Actually, that's what we came to ask," Terran began. "We're trying to find out where he lived."

"We've actually turned his home into a landmark. It's not officially recognized by the city, but I would know it anywhere." The old woman pointed down a side street. "Head all the way to the end of that lane, and on the right. There's not much left there but wood and some old furniture. We made a plaque to honor him."

"Thank you, my dear," The King said as he waved.

"I hope you find what you're looking for!" she called.

As Terran approached the house, he was overwhelmed with a feeling of humility. He could not believe his family had started there, and the shack was not even as large as Rune's bedroom, not to mention the whole suite. When he opened the door, it creaked, and dust blew through the two small rooms like a ghost. There was an old table and a chair, a few shelves, and an old jug in the first room, and in the other, only a rickety bedframe and an empty fireplace remained. Terran could not imagine living there, and the condition of the building currently was a disgrace. If Terran had known, he would have made a decree to keep the place in tip-top condition. The King meandered around the space, and Terran asked, coughing on dust, "Now what?"

"Ask the universe," The King muttered and kicked an old spring that had fallen from the bedframe, sending dust flying.

Terran pulled a card from his pocket and placed it on his skin, letting the cards take him where he needed to go. The metal uncoiled and wrapped itself around his hand, the star that had been on the card pressing itself into his hand like a cookie cutter. A hollow, five-pointed star, lines etched in metal, replaced Terran's skin, leaving five holes to look through. When he peeked through the center hole, through his muscle and bone, the room registered to his eyes in black and white.

Terran swept his hand around the room, finding nothing out of the ordinary until he reached the fireplace. A small blue light, something reflective, gave off a faint glow inside the fireplace, no bigger than a small, twinkling star. When Terran looked outside of his hand, all colors returned to normal. He stuck his head into the dusty fireplace, running his fingers over every brick. His finger snagged on something, and he noticed a small engraving of a human heart etched into the brick. As he brushed his fingers over it, something began to thunk behind the wall in metronome time.

"What did you break?" The King demanded, rushing in from the other room.

"Nothing, I—"

Terran stepped back as the floor sank to reveal a set of stairs that led below the back of the house. The King smiled and remarked, "Your grandfather was a genius. Did you know he had a secret basement?"

"Nope, did you?"

"Nope."

The card wore off as Terran groped his way blindly down the dark stairs. The two fumbled through the darkness but, after the sound of a match being struck, Terran felt the warmth of a flame behind him. When he looked back, he found The King had used a card and held a small orb of light in his hand, which illuminated the way. The dark stairs led down into a large room with nothing in it but an old coin purse, no bigger than Terran's fist, resting on the ground.

When The King got to the bottom of the stairs, he swore. "Damn it! Someone already got here before us. Looks like they raided the place."

"I'm not so sure." Terran bent down and picked up the purse to see if there was anything in it. When he lifted it, another loud thunk echoed throughout the chamber. The King ducked when a small spear shot out of the wall, flew past his head, and shattered as it hit hard rock.

"Terran!" he shouted. "Stop breaking things!"

Terran dropped the purse and dodged out of the way of another projectile. Suddenly, spears were flying, and he and The King danced around each other trying to avoid getting skewered. Terran's heart raced as he felt death pass before his very eyes, and The King shoved him out of the way of a rogue spear. After what seemed like minutes, the last spear hit the wall and Terran tried to catch his breath, doubled over the broken spear shafts that littered the ground. "My grandfather was a genius," he huffed.

"In the next room, don't touch *anything*," The King spat.

"Next room?"

Just as Terran spoke, a nearby rectangle of stone pushed back into the wall, revealing another corridor. Terran cautiously made his way through the doorway and what lay beyond it made his heart backflip. A huge cavern had been carved underneath the streets of Dza'ya and was held up by only rickety supports. The path to the other side had crumbled and left many gaps that resulted in a drop of at least a hundred feet. Terran looked around in awe and shouted, "Hello?", listening to his echo as it bounced back.

"This must've been an old mine in the days when you could still find minerals anywhere near the city," The King mused. "I wonder how deep it goes."

"Either way, we have to get over there," Terran said and pointed to the doorway that stared at them from the other side.

"This place is unstable. Follow me exactly. I don't need you dying on me."

The King began to make his way across the cavern, high above the abyss below, making careful steps onto even the smallest rocks. He moved like lightning as to not apply to much weight onto the fragile earth. Eventually, Terran followed The King across. The King and Terran reached the center of the room, finding momentary respite on a solid rock, and The King caught his breath.

"There better be something damn cool on the other side of this," he panted. "Otherwise I'm going to be *really* disappointed. Are you keeping up okay?"

Terran swallowed, his throat tight from the run, and looked around. "Yeah," he said. "I'm fine. It's no different from running in Naa'a. It's darker in here, but I can handle it."

"Then keep up."

The King ran along a wall and Terran followed close behind. The surrounding rocks began to shake and fall, crumbling around them as they dashed for the other side. The boulders fell into the endless ravine, both from the platforms around them and from the ceiling of the cave. Terran shook as he thought of falling that far, but never stopped running. When they reached solid ground, The King braced himself against a wall as the final few rocks fell from the roof of the cavern, destroying their path to the other side. "Well, we're not getting back that way," he muttered.

Terran was not listening. He stepped into the next room, his eyes wide. An object in the center of the room reflected so much light Terran shielded his eyes, the warmth blasting his skin. As he edged forward and the flash grew less bright, he squinted through his fingers to gaze into the space. A suit of armor, gleaming in a beam of sunlight that shot down on it from some hole in the ground that seemed miles up, silver and white in the harsh rays, rested on a stand. The armor was surrounded by trinkets and other valuable items, as well as bags tied tightly shut. When Terran ran his fingers over the metal surface of the plate, a shock passed through his body. "Wow..." he muttered.

"It's beautiful," The King said and put his arms akimbo as he looked at it. "Nice score. Almost dying was worth it. This looks like your entire family's fortune."

"It was really clever of my mother to hide all of this here."

"It was. What's above us?"

Terran craned his head upward to see and found that a shaft extended upward. He could hear some kind of city noise but was unsure where the shaft led. "A dry well, I think?"

"We'll have to climb out from here."

The sounds of people hustling and bustling through Dza'ya above echoed down into the chasm, and Terran lifted a cloth next to the armor. He figured the rumbling of the rocks from the chamber before had knocked the cloth away, revealing the metal beneath. He whispered a silent thank you to the universe for keeping the treasure concealed for so long.

"Will you take it?" Terran asked and motioned to the armor. "I can't exactly take it back with me to the Embassy."

"Sure."

Terran ran his fingers over the embellishments in the metal, and each little engraving looked to him like a little card. "Did my parents know how to use them? The cards?"

The King laughed. "No. I was the first to show them their powers. We adopted it as our symbol, but I'm pretty sure this armor was fabricated after I left the Council. I suppose I'll have a team haul it out. At least there are handholds to get us out of here, but we'll need ropes to pull these things up. I'll take it, but you need to promise to keep Talbot under your thumb. Don't get distracted by this."

"Of course. I'll stay on task, Your Majesty."

Eyes Wide Open
Parisa

Segeno, July of the Third Year

There was a woman at the street corner who caught Parisa's eye. She was bone thin and could hardly walk, even though she was rather young. With her were four children, one a few months old, all clinging to her as if she were the last thing left on the earth. They were walking skeletons as well, eyes hollow and wrists small due to malnutrition. They hobbled down the street until they stopped and held out their hands at a street corner. No one gave them anything. No one had anything to give. And this was in Atsa.

"Is this how it always is?" Parisa asked.

"Pretty much!" Perseus bit into a plum that oozed juice onto his hand. "You get what you can, and you don't let go of what you have."

Parisa held her hand out. "Give them your plum."

"What?" Perseus exclaimed and hugged the plum into his chest. "No way!"

Parisa saw the same primal need to survive in Perseus' eyes. "Fine. Come with me, then."

The two of them made their way to the nearest market and Parisa bought as much food as she could fit into her arms. When she returned to the street corner, the family was still there, and she offered them the baskets of food she had. The woman seemed confused. "What's this for?" she asked.

"It's for you and your family," Parisa replied and gave a basket to one child. "You all really looked like you needed it."

Tears came to the woman's eyes. "Oh... oh thank you, Miss."

"It's no problem, really. I'm just more than happy to help."

Parisa and Perseus walked down the Atsa streets on their day off and Perseus sucked every bit of meat he could off the pit of the plum. Cloudy thoughts had fogged Parisa's mind the last few months. She had done everything she could to work through what Rune Guildenhart had said to her the night of the masquerade. No matter how hard she dug, she could not find anything misleading or manipulative in Segeno's laws. Unless there was some secret book somewhere that held other laws and rules, nothing looked wrong. She was not naïve; she understood that laws were only as good as their leader.

Currently, their leader was terrible. All of Rune's talk about rigged systems made no sense. And Perseus would talk on none of it. He was of the belief that she could not possibly understand, having never lived in Dza'ya, and it seemed the subject troubled him deeply. He would tell her that he *knew* they were being oppressed, some subtle laws were in place somewhere, and did not

239

believe her when she told him she could find no explanation to the divided districts. He would get teary-eyed and shake whenever she would bring it up, so she chose to drop the subject... for now.

After a few moments of silence as they walked, Perseus smiled and mumbled, "I hope your dad kicks the bucket soon."

"Why?"

Perseus looked at her with sincerity, his eyes bright. "If we'd had a Sovereign like you all along, we wouldn't be where we are now. Everyone would be fed and happy..."

"Well, I hope I can make it that way. With the way things are going, though, I don't think there's any hope for Segeno... especially if I have to marry Rune Guildenhart. He'll make sure things stay exactly the way they are."

"Things will get better. I'm sure of it."

Past Feuds
Terran

The Palace, July of the Third Year

"Damn it all!"

Talbot paced the throne room furiously and Terran stood at a distance, unsure what to say to quell the Sovereign's anger. "My Lord—"

"I've lost my *best man*, Rune! You and Wolff were top on my list! Now, without him, things will get *passed* and everything I've worked for will be *ruined*. It's all because of that *damn* traitor!"

"The King?"

"Yes, Rune," Talbot spat. He stopped and tried to take a calming breath. "Lexus used to be one of *us*. He was born into the Embassy. God knows how sometimes the seed can be bad. He was a good friend to the La'Halls. I had the hardest time with him for as long as I can remember, ever since I married into the Embassy. Every time I see him, I just want to *strangle* him." Talbot's anger escalated again, but he stopped to look at Terran with eyes that said he would strangle Terran too, if it proved useful. "You can keep that secret, can't you, Rune?"

"Of course."

Talbot drummed his fingers on the arm of his throne and then abruptly stood. "Rune, would you come with me up to my chambers?"

"As you wish, My Lord."

At that command, Terran followed Lord Talbot into the glass elevator, where the two said nothing to each other for some time. Talbot tapped his foot impatiently, as if the world could stop turning at any moment, and Terran had to exert a massive amount of effort to remain calm. He could not tremble before Talbot. He had to continue to convince Talbot that Rune was supportive of his efforts no matter the cost.

After the long elevator ride to the top of the Embassy, the two stepped into the Sovereign's chambers. Terran had not been there since he was young, and all the times he had ever spent with his parents in that room flooded his mind. Everything looked wrong now, all the furniture was out of place, and the whole suite was devoid of any happiness. Talbot approached his bed and moved beside the heavy frame. "Help me move this, would you?"

Terran did as he was told and stepped beside the bed. Together, the two of them shoved it aside. With a tap on an indent in the wall, Talbot pushed a switch that caused a compartment to eject. Once open, Talbot carefully removed a book, an old tome worn at the edges. He cradled it like a holy text. "This is it, Rune... *The Old Way.* This text holds all the first Sovereign's thoughts, ideals, dreams. It's more important than my life."

"I will never disclose its hiding place to anyone, My Lord."

Terran inched closer. If he could only get his hands on that book...

In a fit, Lord Talbot quickly stuffed the book away. He said nothing for a very long time and the silence was nearly unbearable. Terran would have loved to kill Talbot right then and there, but the guards would be quick to run to his screams. There were two standing at the entrance to his suite. And he had to wait for The King.

"I need rest..." Talbot sighed, as though he had long not slept. "You should rest, too. We have a lot to do if we want to fix the mess Lexus has made."

A sharp knock echoed throughout the empty chamber. Terran nearly jumped out of his skin.

"Yes?" Lord Talbot called.

"It's Commander Crevan, My Lord."

"Enter."

Commander Crevan entered, his heavy boots rattling along the floor as he went. He bowed stiffly and said, "We found Ruben Guildenhart's body, My Lord."

Terran's chest hitched and he turned toward the window as if mortified by this information. In truth, he had known this was coming. The King always tied up loose ends. Talbot stood and put his hand on Terran's arm. His fingers were ice old. "Rune, I'm so sorry."

Was he? Terran did not feel any real meaning behind the words. "I'm just... glad they found his body. Where?"

"A well in the Dza'ya district. He had been killed elsewhere and tossed into the water."

The King certainly was sending a message.

"We'll find him, Rune," Talbot assured. "We'll find Lexus and I'll strangle every last ounce of air out of him myself."

Lovestruck
Parisa

The Palace, July of the Third Year

"I have to do it."

"But it's... weird. And gross."

"It's necessary."

"But—"

"Don't."

Parisa put her hands on her hips and gripped the bottle of wine and glasses in her hands. "You know it's the only way for me to see if he does anything suspicious when night falls. Besides, you're just being jealous."

Perseus crossed his arms and frowned, the corners of his mouth pulling down to the bottom of his face. "If you weren't so damn pretty, maybe I wouldn't be."

Parisa kissed him on the cheek and pushed him around the corner. "You're too sweet. Now go!"

After knocking on the door, Parisa waited a moment. She heard some hurried shuffling and the opening and closing of drawers, which took too long in her opinion. She was already suspicious. Rune answered with a pleasant smile of surprise on his face. "Ah! Parisa. What brings you here so late at night?"

Parisa leaned onto the doorframe and replied, "I just came from my father... and I felt I should apologize for the way that I acted about us being married. I was being selfish. You're a great man and I'm lucky to even have the opportunity."

Rune's eyebrow twitched and he scanned the hallway with nervous eyes. "Well. I'm glad you changed your mind."

Parisa adjusted her collar and batted her eyelashes. She wore one of the formal gowns she had been given by her father, and while it was still modest, she hoped it was cute enough. He had to take the bait. "I brought some wine to apologize."

"Aren't you too young to drink?" he cooed.

"Do you *really* care?"

Rune nodded in the direction of his bedroom and went inside, not giving an answer one way or another. Parisa closed the door with a click after she entered, her heart pounding. The game now was to enact her plan without letting him go too far. Rune moved the book he had gotten for his last birthday from the bed. The lights on each of the bedside tables were on and Parisa started to uncork the wine as he sat on the edge of his bed. "My father sends his blessings with the wine."

Rune watched her struggle with the cork, and he stood and put his hand on hers, aiding her in getting the bottle open. She nearly flinched at his touch. The last few times he touched her, she had reacted so violently. She could not retreat now and did not want to blow her cover.

The wine bottle opened with a resounding, hollow thunk. Parisa smiled and turned her body away from his as he settled back onto the bed, pouring the glass in her lap. Quickly, with hands as fast as lightning, she pulled something from her sleeve, a small pill hardly detectable. With deft fingers, she opened the capsule and dumped its powdered contents into Rune's wine.

"Doing all right over there, Lieutenant?"

"Oh, just fine!" Parisa lied. "There was a smudge on your glass, but it's gone now."

And with that, she poured the wine. The powder in Rune's glass dissolved instantly, and the two glasses looked almost indistinguishable. She handed his glass carefully as she turned on the bed. "Thank you for helping."

"It's no trouble. Wine bottles can be tricky adversaries," he teased and took a sip from his wine.

Perfect.

"I've never uncorked wine before."

"So... what made you change your mind?"

"What?"

"You're like a flickering, old light bulb. Some days you like me, and others you don't. I must be doing something wrong."

"I suppose..." Parisa said, sipping her own drink. "I suppose there are some things I *do* like about you. Like—"

"You *don't* like me."

"I do *so!*"

Rune laughed so vigorously it shook the bed and nearly made Parisa tip her wine glass. Parisa's eyebrows furrowed as she watched him. His mannerisms did not match. Rune Guildenhart was gone and he was someone else. "You're denying it. You loathe me. I know it... I know it very well. I scare you a little, I think. Living with me scares you. I'm too much like your father, and besides, you like that other boy. I can see it in your eyes. I'll never get you from him. You're too wild. It's not a bad quality, not at all, but I know we don't belong together romantically."

Parisa was astounded. She did not know quite what to say.

"It is as I said at the ball. I know something's wrong, and I disagree with your father and the way he rules. I fortunately can speak my mind in the comfort of my own room. However, I do not wish to get exiled to the wastes. I never planned on becoming Sovereign. I... I feel like we could get used to it, though. Couldn't we?"

Parisa put down her glass of wine. She was not sure she wanted it anymore. After a moment of thinking, she turned in the bed and kissed him on the cheek. It was not the same as with Perseus, where the kisses were something wonderful and glorious, but it was not... bad. It was different, and she had to play along. He, unexpectedly, did not kiss her back. He smiled at her sweetly and moved away to take another sip of wine. Once he had finished his glass, it was only a matter of moments until he fell into a deep, deep sleep.

After she was sure that the valerian had taken its full effect, Parisa slipped silently from the bed and reached underneath it to reveal one of her uniforms and her dagger that she had concealed there. It had been easy enough to slip into Rune's room while he ran errands. After she had changed, she drew her dagger and waited.

Caught
Terran

The Palace, July of the Third Year

Terran awoke with the taste of wine on his tongue, the feeling of something missing beside him, and the worst headache he had ever had. He could also sense a presence above his forehead, and when he opened his eyes, he found himself looking directly into the tip of a dagger. His eyes darted about the room. Six other guards, including Perseus, all pointed patrolman's rifles at his head. A lump formed in his throat. He had planned on waking before her and using The Magician before she woke. Now he had overslept, he was just Terran, and he was in huge trouble.

"Move and I'll pluck your eye right out of your head," Parisa spat, her eyes trained on him.

"Look, I think we're all caught up in a bit of a misunderstanding."

"Who are you?"

Terran inched his hand toward his pocket.

"Rune Guildenhart."

"No, really."

"We should all lower our weapons and talk about this."

Terran felt the silvered edge of a card touch the side of his hand. He prayed it was face up.

"And I should have them shoot you."

Terran swallowed and flipped his hand over onto the card, waiting for a reaction. "Now, now... breathe."

In a flash, Terran felt something appear in his hand, a long staff, and as Parisa lunged with her dagger, Terran rolled to his side and the knife hit the pillow, sending feathers flying. He pulled the staff from underneath the sheets and twirled it as fast as he could, deflecting bullets that came in waves from the other guards. He backed up toward the window, deflecting and dodging. The riflemen refused to shoot as soon as Parisa got in the way, and her dagger flew so close to his head it cut hair.

With precision, Terran used his staff to pull guns from guard's hands and tossed them to the floor. He hit them in the jaw or stomach to knock them unconscious. They had not anticipated someone so well trained. Perseus gave him a little trouble. When Terran swung with his staff, Perseus blocked with his rifle. Perseus lost his footing when Terran's foot slid behind his and in one fluid motion, Terran's wooden staff knocked him to the ground.

As soon as he had a clear path to the window, he took it. Crashing through glass, he took a blind leap of faith. He grabbed the banner that hung below the window and rode it down until he landed on sand, Parisa hot on his trail. He bolted through the greenhouse courtyard, bullets whizzing by his head as he headed for the main gate.

"Close the gate!" Perseus shouted from the palace. Embassy guards scrambled to pull the leaver, bringing the gate down.

As the gate neared the ground, Terran threw the staff between the iron and the sand, rolling underneath the sharp spikes. After he cleared the gate, he heard Parisa do the same before the staff snapped and the gate came crashing to the ground. He could not believe that she had kept up with him thus far. She was far better trained than he had thought. He wondered how fast Perseus was and if he was lucky that she was chasing him instead. As they darted through Naa'a, Terran tried to shake her by turning into alleyways and jumping through buildings, but her course never faltered.

Finally, Terran spotted a thin alleyway, slid through it, and waited for her on the other side. Just as she came through, Terran threw his arm out and hit her hard on the head. She lay there, unconscious, and Terran looked down at her, his lips pursed in contemplation. "Great. This is just great."

Captive
Parisa

The Tavern, July of the Third Year

"Damn, she's not at all like I expected."

Parisa opened her eyes to a splitting headache and a gag in her mouth. She looked up at the man, or rather boy, who had said he was Rune Guildenhart, and the man she knew to be The King. She struggled to speak but could only mumble. The rag tasted dirty, and she did not understand where she was. The only way out was a small door above a short flight of stairs, and The King stood right in front of it. She wished that she had her dagger with her so she could cut the ropes, but it was nowhere to be found.

Rune laughed in amusement. It frustrated her to be in a position like this and his mockery did not help. He seemed without any worry at all. Rough rope chaffed her wrists as she attempted to wriggle away, her foot kicking a pile of books on the floor. She had never seen so much color, and the light in the room was too dim to discern her location.

Rune crouched to look her in the eyes. Even though he

did not look like Rune, it seemed he was of royal blood. He had a bright, cheery smile on his face, playful. The candlelight reflected in his blue eyes and she tried to read him but found it just as hard as it had been in the library. "Should we remove her gag?" he asked.

"Be my guest," The King replied.

As he reached up for her gag, she threw out her foot and kicked him in the stomach. He tumbled back and knocked his head against another pile of knickknacks. She began to rock the table, hoping to knock it over and slip out from under it. An inkwell tipped and began to fall, but The King caught it, not spilling a drop. He sat on the table and she soon found it too heavy for her to move. After a few moments of futile struggling, she was out of breath. Rune recovered and rubbed his head.

He ran his fingers through his long, unruly blond hair. He wore the colors of the Embassy, but Parisa was certain she had never seen him before. He scowled at her. "What'd you do that for?" he barked.

"She's feisty. I like her." The King crossed his legs and looked down at her. He looked familiar to Parisa as well. She was a little frightened of them, and she did not know what to expect. They held a power she did not understand.

"You were right when you said that they were teaching the Elite guards to combat us. She kept up with me the whole way here," the boy said.

"Impressive." The King slid off the table and waited to see if Parisa would struggle more. When she did not, he sat on the floor in front of her. "We don't want to hurt you and we're not the enemy," he assured. "If you stay calm, we'll get the gag out of your mouth. Trust me, I know how uncomfortable it is. That rag has also been lying in the corner for about a month, so I can't guarantee it's clean."

Parisa swallowed dust. The rag did taste rather awful, and she had nowhere to go. She did not know the layout of the building or where she could escape to. She did not even know if she was still inside the city. She nodded. There was nothing else she could do besides ask questions. The King removed the rag from her mouth, and she licked her lips, which were rather dry. "Why am I here? Where am I? What did you do with Rune Guildenhart?"

"Whoa, whoa, whoa, sweetheart," The King cooed. "One question at a time. You're here because you were chasing my Knight, and he managed to knock you out. He didn't want to leave you behind, so here you are. As to where you are... I can't tell you. You're not exactly on our side yet."

"On your side? Who said I was going to be on your side?"

"Exactly." Rune took his hand away from his head. "You have to be with us wholeheartedly. As for Rune Guildenhart, I *am* Rune Guildenhart."

"No, you're not," Parisa argued. "Rune Guildenhart is the son of Adriann Guildenhart. He's tall, a redhead, and old enough to be on the Council."

"Rune Guildenhart never existed. Adriann never had a son. That's why no one had ever heard of him. I used the excuse that I had grown up outside of Segeno to keep people off my scent. I'm surprised everyone bought everything I spoon fed them."

"Then who *are* you?"

"Terran La'Hall."

"You're the old Sovereign's son?"

Rune, or rather Terran, nodded. "Your father killed my parents."

"He's cruel and vicious sometimes... and he doesn't always have good judgement, but he's not a killer."

"He told it to me himself twice... in fact, he told me loads of secrets. He's done a lot of things to get into a position of power and none of them are good." Terran shot The King a warning glance. After a few moments, The King left the room. "It's hard... I can't even imagine being told my dad's a murderer."

"He's not nice, but he's done what's kept me safe. I'm the poster girl for women's rights now. I was the first woman in the guard. He did it so I could be strong."

"You don't really believe that do you?"

No. No she did not. Parisa bit her lip and Terran righted the stack of books he had knocked over. "He *told* me, Parisa. We played chess nearly weekly. During those games he revealed to me his plans, ambitions. There's a secret book he keeps locked in my parents' room, some sort of psychotic oppression manual, that he uses as his guide. It tells him to do things like tax the poor to feed his pockets, keep people of different skin shades apart. Lowborns, he calls them."

Everything started to make sense to Parisa, though she did not want it to. Was that the reason her father wanted to keep her from his sight? Of course it was. It always had been.

"He makes *loads* of money. Those expeditions under the city? Fake. Taxes on the rich? Nonexistent. He had a pack of dogs to do his bidding, but those forces are falling apart. He, along with

Wolff, intimidated Esmond and Vena into voting for horrible things. When he couldn't have his way, he threw a tantrum. He figured the easiest way out was to kill his biggest problems."

"Your parents?"

"My parents, Lexus, your mother... no one was safe. He first plotted to kill my mother, but realized my father held the same ideals. Then he conspired to kill him as well. It wasn't enough. I was last, but he didn't want to get his hands dirty. He went to Lexus, The King. Lexus had been close to my family. I don't remember him."

"My father didn't like when he said he was from the Embassy."

"No, he didn't. He was a part of the Council. He left shortly after Talbot asked him to erase my parents. Talbot then turned to Esmond; the person most easily intimidated. Wolff tried to get Vena to do it. They both never did the job. Talbot got so frustrated that he killed Elsa, Esmond's wife."

"No," Parisa choked through a tight throat. Tears were coming. She could feel them. "I'm sure that's not how she died."

"That's what Esmond told me. He didn't want you to fear your father, so he never told you. Talbot got sick of waiting and finally acquired Elite robes and a gun to shoot them himself. I saw him do it. I remember it clear as day."

Tears dripped over Parisa's eyelids and onto her cheeks. She cried not because she was hurt by what he said, but because she knew it was true.

"I came in from reading. I wanted to get lunch and when I came in to ask my mom when it would be ready, I saw a guard with the long barrel of a gun to my father's head."

"B-But why?"

"To put Segeno back together according to that damn book."

"He speaks the truth." The King returned with a few hot ciders. He handed Terran one, put his on the floor, and sat. "Can I untie you, or are you going to bolt?" he asked. "It would be a shame to spill this cider all over the place."

Parisa shook her head and The King sliced through her ropes. Once the hot cider was in her hand, she felt much better. The warmth radiated into her fingertips and she took a sip. The information overwhelmed her, but the cider helped a little. After a moment of thinking, she asked, "Everything you pretended to be was a lie?"

Terran laughed. "I played right into Talbot's hands."

Parisa said nothing and drank the cider. She was grateful for it. It reminded her of Perseus. He loved it to death. She ran her tongue over her lips and took a deep breath, thinking carefully on her next question. "Conspiracy. Explain that to me."

"When I was in the Embassy," The King began, "I watched Terran's mother make things right. There were loads of old, terrible laws that she sought to get rid of. For example, did you know that Segeno was founded with laws that made the guard more powerful than all laws? They could not be held accountable for their actions, as all of their actions were deemed just, even if they killed innocents in the streets."

"Is that really true?"

"On my honor. Sovereign La'Hall threw out that law.

257

The more I learned about the old laws of Segeno, the more I, and Sovereign La'Hall, saw the glaring issues. Fifty years ago, the residents of Naa'a never talked to the inhabitants of Dza'ya. Dza'ya was filled with problems that had been written into law, but no one in government positions knew or cared because no one listened. My theory is that whatever is in that book is the cause of all of this and may give us solutions as to how to fix this city."

"We have to stop your father from making things any worse," Terran added. He pulled from his pocket a deck of cards. "With these."

"Are those really magick, like everyone says?" Parisa asked.

"Yes."

Terran showed them to her but did not let her touch them. "It seems crazy, but they are. Every card is random. You can even get the same card twice in a row without even shuffling. The kicker is that you have to be chosen by them. If you're not, they're just normal cards. They can illuminate muddled lies... they did for me. I found purpose with these."

"So did I," The King added. The King unfolded a black velvet cloth to reveal cards that were as blue as a mountain lake.

Terran set down his deck and took the new cards in his hands. He fanned them before her, their edges glimmering in the dim light. The design on the back of the cards created an optical illusion, making the backs of the cards look as deep as a chasm. Terran pushed the cards back together into a neat stack. "These cards will show you that what I say is true. You may not like it. Trust me, I didn't like the truth either."

"I don't believe in magick tricks," Parisa said.

"Neither do I. It's not a magick trick. Just take them."

Parisa hovered her fingers over the cards. Energy pulsed into her fingertips. After a moment of deliberation, she took them. She watched Terran to make sure he was not thinking about doing anything suspicious. As soon as her hands touched the cards, everything changed. A blinding light blasted through Parisa's eyes and her head ached. Blood, a knife, a scream in the dark. A face, a loving face that looked like Parisa's pale with death. A pleased smile. The bang of a gunshot. Two dead, caught in an embrace. Her father.

When the vision ended, tears poured from Parisa's eyes. Her body began to tremble and shake, and the room spun. She gasped and shuddered as the cards fell to the ground, like startled birds. "I thought my mother left us," she sobbed.

"If your father is anything, he's a smooth talker." Terran's eyes tried to guess what she had seen.

"I don't remember my mother very well. My father told me she had betrayed our family by leaving us. He killed her, and he killed your parents, too. I... I won't stand by him anymore."

Terran stood and moved to the window. It was a fake, Parisa realized, and a candle danced behind its glass. The King's grey eyes searched for something as he watched everything unfold. He went to sit at his desk. Terran continued, "We're working to right the wrongs your father has committed. I can't say he will be spared. He could die... he could live. It all depends on the cards. It really does. If you joined our cause, we'd be really grateful. A few Embassy members are already on our side. Vena... and Esmond."

"Esmond is fighting with you?"

Terran nodded.

"I'll join, but we must get Perseus. He's all I have left. He's a good person, and a great fighter."

"If you can message him through the well, be my guest. The more the merrier," The King said. "I can use all the swords I can get."

"Do you want to use the cards?" Terran asked.

Parisa gazed down at the scattered blue cards on the ground. She recognized a few things. The first was that her father had an army of well-trained soldiers that were no match for ordinary citizens. The second was that her father was ruthless. Having an additional weapon on her side could be advantageous. The entire thing was crazy, anyway. Magick suddenly was very real.

"What's the catch?" Parisa's hands shook.

"Only that the truth hurts. We can practice the magick together, and we can use the cards to save Segeno from whatever blight this is."

"What do I have to do?" Parisa asked.

Terran laid out four cards from her deck in front of her as The King watched, and instructed, "Pick a card."

Clairvoyance
Terran

Atsa, August of the Third Year

Betrayal of loved ones is the sharpest sword.

"Like this?"

Terran looked up from the slip of paper at Parisa, who shuffled her cards in her hands.

"Yeah," he instructed. "You place it on the back of your hand. Watch."

He took a card and did a demonstration, watching the metal unfold. When the magick finished, he looked to the back of his hand to better understand the result. The silver loops formed a large beam and a noose that slipped down onto his wrist. His face scrunched and he tilted his head to the side, trying to understand the puzzle. "That's weird. I've never gotten The Hanged Man before."

"What does it do?"

Terran scoured his memory for the answer. He had read it in one of The King's books, but he could not recall the exact card.

261

"I don't remember. It had something to do with gravity."

He stood from the edge of the curb where they sat and jumped. Nothing. When he reached out to lean on the wall, scratching his head, a prickling sensation shot through his arm. His hand stuck a little, and he proceeded to walk up the wall, horizontal as if gravity no longer mattered. Once he reached the top, the card wore away, his skin returning to normal once more. "Well, cool!" he called down from the roof of the building to Parisa. "Good for climbing flat things."

"So, I draw one?" Parisa thumbed through her cards. "How long do they last?"

"Yup, you draw from the top. There are some cards that won't come at all, like face cards. Kings, Knights, Pages, and Queens. They're more for identification and for unlocking the magick. Oh, and you can't use suits that aren't yours."

"Suits?"

"For example... I'm the Knight of Wands. I can't use swords, or cups, or coins. I don't know how the cards know. They just... do. They won't draw out of my deck." Terran numbered off on his fingers and flicked a pebble down to where she sat below. "*You* can only use cups. I don't know how you're supposed to fight with those. As far as how long they last, it depends on the card and the situation. Sometimes they'll fade on their own, but you can halt its effect early if you need to. Once you shake it off, the card will return to the deck."

When Parisa drew a card, her face scrunched. "Hey, come down here for a second."

Terran jumped from the building and rolled down the

walk in the Atsa district, avoiding the street. Once he righted himself, he returned to his seat next to her. She flipped the card to show him the V of Cups. The corners of his mouth turned down in surprise, and he shrugged. "Give it a try."

The King had asked Terran to give Parisa a crash course in the cards. Now that she was missing from the palace, he was certain Talbot would make a move. It was only a matter of time. The guards were up in arms about what had happened, and patrol through the Naa'a district had doubled. Numbers had been pulled from the Atsa and Dza'ya districts, so Terran and The King were not worried about being spotted. Moving through Naa'a had now become much more difficult.

Perseus had reported to Talbot about Rune. The story among the guard was that the son of the old Sovereign had killed Rune Guildenhart and taken his place. Talbot was still thoroughly convinced that Rune Guildenhart *had* existed, and that he had not been tricked. Now, they hunted for a killer. It appalled Terran that Talbot could not see the snake in the grass. He would not know a traitor if it bit him in the leg.

Now, Parisa and Terran sat on a dirty street corner in Atsa and played with Parisa's new deck. Their plan moving forward was simple. Parisa was to try and get a message to Perseus through Esmond. Terran had dropped the letter off that morning. Once Esmond let him know what was going on, hopefully he would come knocking on the door, ready to help. Until that happened, The King wanted to play a waiting game. Talbot was scared. The King, as far as he was concerned, had infiltrated his walls three times. The paranoia had begun to set in.

Terran had not stopped thinking about the book Talbot had hidden from them. *The Old Way* was the key to understanding Talbot's thinking, and Terran wanted to return to claim it from its hiding spot. He only hoped Talbot had not moved it. It took a few days, but Parisa eventually came around and listened to everything Terran had to say. She was now more eager than ever to remove her father from the throne and return things to a stable place in order to make better change.

On that dirty street corner, Parisa placed the card onto the back of her hand as instructed. The card rippled into her skin, which took on a blue hue in the area around the card and created dark blue lines on her skin the shape of a single cup with a roman numeral V behind it. In a wiggling mirage, a single golden chalice appeared beside her. "Only one?" she asked. "Shouldn't there be five?"

She and Terran both stooped over the cup and peered inside. A clear liquid pooled in the gilded bowl, almost like water but thicker. In an instant, a watery, wavy image of a girl leaving an older man appeared. As she walked away, flowers grew in her stead and a boy joined beside her. Then, the cup disappeared just as quickly as it had come.

Terran looked to Parisa and muttered, "Maybe you're a prophet. The cards used to tell the future, so maybe Cups will give you that insight. Or, perhaps, they reveal hidden meaning in the present."

"Like what?"

"Like..." Terran pondered for a moment. "Like everything's going to be okay. You'll have to figure things out on your own, make new relationships. It's very personal, so you may be the only one who knows the answer."

"I'll let go of my father... I already have. You know—" Parisa looked around the Atsa district and added, "You're a lot nicer than I thought you'd be."

"It was an act. I told you."

"You did a really good job."

"What you did was very clever."

"Oh?"

"You really had to drug me?"

Parisa raised a skeptical eyebrow. "I did what it was my duty to do. I had to find you out."

"I understand." Terran was nervous. The play came to a close, and the final act approached. It made his stomach churn in knots.

"What now? I fear Perseus will get his letter too late."

"I put you to the test," someone stated behind them.

Parisa and Terran spun to find The King there, his arms crossed, and his face hidden by his hood.

"Your Majesty," Terran greeted. "What brings you to this part of town?"

"You still have more heirlooms to collect, and I want that book." The King took a seat beside the two of them. "Parisa, you're by no means an expert in the cards, but you're an adept fighter. Terran has been practicing for months, and I think the two of you together would be a force to be reckoned with. That book may tell us what secret garbage is running this city from behind closed doors and will shed some light on how we can fix it."

"Talbot hid it in a secret compartment in the Sovereign's room. If you move the bed away, it's in a secret space behind the wall," Terran explained.

"Do you think you two could retrieve it?"

Parisa and Terran slowly turned to look at each other. Parisa asked, "Just the two of us? Perseus has tripled security in the area. I'm a good fighter, but if I'm swarmed, I don't know if I can hold my own."

"But you are small. You and Terran both can use the cards to move in the cover of night to retrieve that book."

"I think I can handle it, Your Majesty." Terran turned a card over in his hand. "You can count on me."

"You also need to find the next parcel your parents left for you."

"Find what?" Parisa asked.

"I'm not sure what it is," Terran replied, "but my parents hid parcels and stashes for me all over the city. They were sure Talbot would destroy their family heirlooms and other gifts for me, so they hid it away. I have a set of armor that The King and I retrieved from Dza'ya, to protect my heart. They gave me riddles."

"What's the riddle?"

Terran showed Parisa the slip of paper. She glanced over the words, and then held up her deck of cards. "Maybe I can draw something to help?"

"Go for it."

Parisa pulled a card and showed the face to him, the X of Cups. When she flipped it onto her skin, a cup appeared with dark, murky water in it. The King raised his eyebrow in curiosity, and

266

the three of them leaned over to look in. In the watery reflection, a man held a ring. He set the ring onto the ground and sliced the metal in half with a sword, the swing precise and full of pain. He then sat alone in a dark room by himself. As the vision faded, Parisa nodded and whispered, "He broke a promise."

"What?" Terran had not understood at all.

"The man in the vision. He broke a ring, like a wedding ring, right? So, he broke a promise. I guarantee you that whatever it is that you're looking for is in a room of broken promises."

"Let's think about this," The King pondered. "What's the greatest promise Talbot has ever broken?"

"He is a destroyer of marriage," Parisa replied. "He ruined my mother and he ruined Terran's parents."

"Where do you think he would have poisoned your mother?" Terran asked.

"She worked in the Embassy palace, and she lived in the suite there with my father for a time. He refused to let me live there, so eventually my mother just moved into the house in Naa'a with me. The places that they would have private conversations was always the bedroom."

"It seems that, beyond all odds, my parents knew Talbot would kill them in the bedroom. They knew the strike was coming, and if he wanted to get them in a place where they were most vulnerable, it would have been in the Sovereign's suite."

"Let's hope your hunch is right," The King added.

"If we run into Perseus, we may be able to convince him to come with us," Parisa said.

"A fruitful trip. Tonight, then. You must be absolutely sure that you aren't seen. I couldn't stand to lose you, now that we're so close to our goal. I'll send you both off on your mission at eleven."

Loyalty
Parisa

The Tavern, August of the Third Year

When the three of them had returned to the tavern, The King sat himself down at the bar. Parisa watched him with eyes like a hawk. Her stomach churned as she looked about the space, taking in the faces of everyone present. Terran returned to his room in the back, presumably to prepare for the night, and she felt suddenly very alone.

All these people were traitors.

At least, that was how her father would have framed it. She tried as hard as she could to justify what she was going to do in her mind, and the guilt ate away at her still, though a month had passed. She had been stuffed into a back closet, a temporary place for her to stay until the fighting was done. Everything was wrong, very wrong.

The first Sovereign must have been a monster. He built the city with the intent of hurting everyone in it, but she did not yet know how deep the terrible truth went. She did know one thing for certain: her mother would not have stood for that. Her mother was a beautiful, peaceful person. She wanted equality for everyone and to have the best for her child. She wanted the best for Segeno. Parisa did not know what her father's motives were, or how he had come to be so hateful, but he had to be stopped.

After a while of standing in the doorway to the tavern, thinking on things that had been and things that would come, The King waved at her from the bar. She awkwardly shuffled to him, unsure if she wanted to talk. She had avoided him the last month. She avoided everyone, really. Everything felt like a betrayal, like she was the one at fault. She could not shake the feeling and had not wanted to make it worse by talking to anyone.

Parisa slid onto the stool beside The King and he passed her a glass of cider. He downed whatever it was he drank. "I got you a cider," he said. "Sorry. You're too young to drink yet, and I'm already wanted for literally everything else. Better not add underaged drinking to the crimes."

She could not help it, but she chuckled. "Thank you. I only really have a taste for fruit wines, anyway. That liquor made from agave is too strong."

"It'll kill you if you're not careful, that's for sure." The King passed his empty glass back to the bartender. "Are you holding out okay?"

"I'm... doing what I can." Parisa sipped at her cider, but it did not fill the hole in her heart.

"You've had a guilty look on your face all week. If you need someone to talk to, I'm a pretty good listening ear."

"You wouldn't understand."

"Would I not?"

Parisa swallowed a gulp of cider. It was rude of her to assume, but she did not care to share her secrets with stranger.

"I don't mean to pry. You don't have to say anything if you don't want to." The King ran his teeth over his bottom lip. "I felt guilty, too."

"What?"

"When I left the Embassy. I knew I was going to have to pull it apart at the seams, figure out why there was so much hate. For a long time, a year, at least, I felt like I was betraying my family. My brothers and my mother still live in Naa'a. I'm sure they've heard the news, that their son is a terrorist. It'll pass. You're doing the right thing."

Parisa watched the spices of her cider spin around in the cup. "Am I?"

"If it benefits other people more than it benefits yourself, then yes."

"It doesn't feel right."

"Your father needs to be brought to Justice. The people will bring the Embassy palace down eventually, with or without our help. Follow your heart and follow the cards. Decide for yourself where your loyalty lies."

Fanatic

Terran

The Tavern, August of the Third Year

In his little back room that he had lived in for longer than he would have imagined, Terran put on his new armor. The armor that his grandfather had made fit like a glove, and the little details caught the light of the candle in his room delicate, sparkling in the dark. Everything was almost over. The pain was almost gone. Terran could not wait to be free.

As he readied himself for the night, nerves making his fingertips tingle, he heard The King open the door to his office.

"It's... interesting for you to come at this time," Terran heard through the door. "What brings you to this place, and how did you learn of its existence?"

"My god sees all."

Terran's breath hitched. He recognized the voice of Widow Corine. She moved across the office and sat in Terran's usual chair. The King followed suit, and soon they were settled. Terran pressed his ear up against the door in hopes of hearing more.

"Is there something I can do for you?" The King asked.

"I want to help you."

"With what?"

"Your cause. The Embassy must fall."

"Now, I don't want to destroy our government."

"You and yours will break it down from the inside and build it up better. Every forest needs a fire to start new growth."

"How do you plan on helping us?"

"With numbers. My followers are willing to fight and die for the truth."

The King chuckled. "What is it that you know of truth?"

"What is it that you know of Justice?"

The King paused, intrigued by what she had said, and Terran heard him shift in his chair. "What does your god do for you?"

"She sees all that exists on this earth, and then blesses me with visions."

"Only you?"

"As of now, only me."

"Seems... sketchy."

"Do you want my men and women, or would you rather go into battle with your band of thieves alone?"

"I think you underestimate my numbers."

"I think you underestimate my magick."

The King said nothing for a time, thinking on his words. "How am I supposed to summon your god's soldiers?"

"We will come when my god sends us."

And with that, she stood and she left. Terran's hands shook.

He had been under the assumption that only The King's cards held magick, so who was this crazy woman to claim she wielded something just as powerful?

Infiltration
Parisa

Segeno, August of the Third Year

Parisa climbed to the top of the jeweler's with ease to find Terran there, shuffling his cards anxiously, and The King, who looked out over the Atsa district. The moon hung full and huge over the city and cast its silver light upon all it touched. The walls of the city rose to keep the terrors of the desert at bay. Parisa could not see the desert from the short rooftop, but she knew it was there. She could only imagine what sorts of creatures stalked the lands. If there were so many monsters in the walls, what kinds lay outside?

As soon as she approached, Terran put his cards into his pocket. He wore the robes he had worn at the masquerade, and brand new, glorious armor. His eyes met hers and she got goosebumps.

"Are you ready?" he asked.

She adjusted her Elite armor and replied, "As ready as I'll ever be."

"You two be careful," The King advised. "If it gets too dicey, just use cards and go. It's not worth it if you're going to die. Your number one priority is to make it back to me alive."

"Yes, Your Majesty." Terran saluted. Parisa watched the two of them look at each other for a long while until The King pulled Terran into a tight hug. They embraced there on the roof and Terran held still, stiff for a while, until he folded into the embrace. The King placed his hand on the back of Terran's head.

After a long moment, The King stepped back and wiped his eye quickly, hiding something, and coughed. "Go on."

Terran and Parisa began to run toward the palace, silent as thieves as they went. Parisa knew The King had good reason to be nervous. Every guard in the city was looking for her, but they were not looking for Terran La'Hall. Everyone thought Terran was dead.

"Hey... a question," Parisa dared to whisper as they stopped on a roof before the palace walls, which were intimidating and tall in the night. "How do you plan on getting through here?"

"I was hoping you'd know the way," he whispered back.

"There's a blind spot near the back that leads into the servant's quarters on the second floor. But... we'll have to scale the wall. There are no trees tall enough to—"

"There's always a way."

Parisa dropped from the Naa'a rooftop and ducked behind a tree as a guard passed. "Follow me," she commanded.

She dashed off and Terran followed close behind. A southern wall encased a small garden below the second floor of the palace. Two guards had their backs turned to the area and when Parisa and Terran got close enough to the spot, they were lost completely behind the wall. Parisa signaled to Terran to circle around, and before he could blink, she had crept into the garden. Terran turned a corner and the two of them grabbed the guards by the throat. Terran pressed down into his neck, covering his mouth to prevent screaming, until he fell still.

As soon as the guards fell silent, Parisa put her foot into the sill of one of the glass windows on the side of the tower. She was about to attempt to scale it when Terran held up his hand. "Wait. Don't forget you have the cards. There are easier ways up."

Parisa reached into her bag and pulled out a card with a woman surrounded by wheat on it. When the card melted into her skin, which turned crystalline blue like a star, she waited. Nothing seemed different save her hand. Hear heart jumped into her throat as the time passed. "What do I do?" she whispered.

"Which card did you draw?" he replied, keeping his eyes peeled for more guards.

"The Empress."

"Put your hand to the ground."

Parisa did as she was told, and the grass began to grow so violently that it created a pillar and pushed her up to the balcony on the second floor. As soon as she stepped onto solid ground, the blue of her skin faded, and the pillar withered. She looked down to see if Terran had followed, and he was already on his way up.

He held a single staff in his hand. This one was short in length and one large, beaming crystal jutted out of the top of it. With it, Terran created platforms of light that he used to scale the tower like stairs. When he stepped down onto the floor, he put his finger to his lips in silence.

The latched window opened much louder than either of them wanted, and it closed behind them with a resolute *click*. The palace kitchen was completely empty, devoid of servants at this hour and eerily quiet, the lights out. Parisa and Terran tiptoed toward the door that lead into the hall, listening for guards. Several sets of footsteps scurried down the hall, whether they were servants or guards, and Terran let out a heavy breath.

"What's the plan?" he whispered.

"Father's room is obviously on the top floor, but he doesn't sleep there anymore. The last couple of months he's been sleeping in the war room because he's paranoid, or not at all. It most likely will be empty, but we can always check beforehand. The elevator will be the fastest way up, but there are stairs at the back of the palace," she replied.

"The stairs are a pain, but will be much quieter. Where do the stairs connect to on your father's floor?"

"The hall where the elevator drops off."

"It sounds like there are dozens of people in the hall."

"Perseus tripled patrol."

Terran reached into his pocket and pulled a card from it. Temperance. "Great," he muttered under his breath. "That's hilarious."

"What?"

Terran looked to Parisa. "Do you feel comfortable using a card to get yourself through this or do you want to move with me?"

Parisa hesitated. She had barely had a month's practice with the cards, and the majority of that time had been spent reading a barrage of books given to her by The King. She did not feel versed in them and this entire situation made her nervous.

"Well?" Terran pressed.

"I'll go with you. I'm not ready yet."

Terran flipped the card and placed it on his hand, ready for it to take effect. Golden wings erupted out of his back as they had done for The King at the ball, and he turned back toward the balcony. He walked with Parisa back outside and looked upward, trying to gauge where the Sovereign's floor was. Parisa questioned everything that was happening. The goal was to move through the palace undetected and this was the flashiest thing the cards could have given them.

On the balcony, Terran put his arm around her waist. "Hold on tight. I've never done this."

Parisa clung to him as his wings beat and he launched them upward. His wings glistened in the moonlight and after a few swift beats they landed again on the topmost balcony. The view of the city from this high up was breathtaking, and the landscape beyond the walls looked less threatening and hot. As Terran landed, the wings evaporated into glitter and light. Parisa held a hand up to make sure they were not going to be found out, and she put her ear to the glass.

Inside, all was quiet. It was as she suspected. Her father had slept less and less in this room as he wanted to be closer to the guards below. He was less vulnerable that way. With her dagger she unlocked the window, and the two of them slunk inside.

They were, in fact, in Talbot's bedroom, even though Talbot

was gone. The room was dark and only the moon lit the way. Terran drew another card and in a moment a small ball of flame appeared in his hand. As he swept his hand around the room, hoping the light would point them in the right direction, Parisa took his hand. She was deathly afraid that they would get caught.

"Let's move to the bed," she whispered.

They hurried to Talbot's bed and Terran tossed his ball of flame into the air. It hovered about the room, taking on a life of its own, and the two of them pulled. The bed went screeching away from the wall and Terran fumbled around in the dark for the secret compartment. When he finally found it, he pushed the switch as Talbot had and the drawer popped out. When he reached inside to grab the book, he returned emptyhanded. His face paled, and Parisa nodded. "I bet he moved it," she said.

"We'll have to find it later. Let's focus on the riddle. Any insight?"

Parisa drew a card and her eyebrows furrowed when she looked at it. The Fool. She turned it around to Terran so he could see, and he grinned. He tapped the illustration and showed her. "Do you see that?"

Parisa looked to what he pointed at. The man on the card held a white rose in his hand. With gentle fingers, he lifted her chin, so her eyes trailed from the card to a vase of white roses in the room that had long since died. The two of them pushed the small side table away from the wall. Behind the legs of the furniture sat a small ventilation shaft.

Terran kneeled beside it and the ball of light that he had created vanished into nothing. He pried at the silver vent cover with his fingers. It was not big enough to fit an entire person into it, so Terran, holding his breath, reached his hands into the unknown once the cover popped off. He fumbled around for a few moments until his fingers touched something ice cold. With a loud thunk, a panel of wall moved away to reveal another hidden cubby containing a shining sword that matched the armor he wore.

Parisa's jaw dropped. "That's been in here this entire time?"

"My grandfather was one hell of a mechanical genius." Terran latched the scabbard of the sword to his belt. "Now, let's go find your boyfriend and get out of here."

"He is *not* my boyfriend. H-He's just a really good friend that I—"

"That you kiss? Let's go. We better not risk going back outside. Someone will see us for sure."

The two slunk from the bedroom to the front hall, and then to the stairs that led down to the lower floors when they heard the shouting.

"There's been a breach! Light coming from the Sovereign's room! Summon the captain!"

"I guess your boyfriend's coming to us," Terran chuckled. "We have to get down these stairs. Let's move!"

Terran began to jump down the stairs, two or three at a time, and Parisa followed as fast as the wind. As they darted down the stairs, a door slammed open a floor below. Half a dozen men poured through the opening, followed by Perseus, who looked up and down the stairwell to find the intruders. He raised his rifle to his shoulder and looked down the sights, only to see Parisa at the end. He faltered and lowered the gun again. "Parisa?"

"Get out of the way!" Terran shouted. He drew a card and slapped it onto his skin. Every nerve in his body tingled and granite and cracks rippled over his flesh, turning it to stone. With one solid step, Terran cracked the ground beneath the guards with his heel. A wave of earth rippled across the landing and a guard launched into the air, flying over the railing and down to the stories below. A shot fired in the small stairwell, and a bullet whizzed by Terran's head. With another *bang*, something sharp grazed his hand. He began to bleed, and he gripped his wrist as drops of red hit the marble.

"Parisa, what are you doing?" Perseus barked.

Parisa flipped another guard over her shoulder and slammed him into the stairs. She looked up at him with desperation in her eyes. "Perseus, call off your men for a moment!"

"Why did you come back to the palace, you traitor?" Perseus asked as he jumped over another moving wave of earth that Terran pushed with his feet. "What have you done to Parisa?"

"We came for you!" Parisa ducked around behind the group of guards and hit one on the back of the head, knocking him out.

"So, you brainwashed her, huh?" Perseus backed down the stairs a little and Terran dodged a bullet narrowly by leaping into one of the vacant Councilmember floors. Guards pursued and Terran pulled hunks of metal from the walls to hurl at them. Perseus lunged and nicked Terran's arm with his bayonet. "Maybe," he shouted, "if I kill you, the spell on her will break!"

Parisa took care of the remaining guards and turned to find that Perseus had kicked Terran to the ground and pinned him down. He had the bayonet to Terran's throat. "Why did The King kill Councilman Wolff?" he demanded.

"He was a monster who hit his wife," Terran spat back.

"And now you've done something to Parisa's head? You're the one siding with a killer. You killed Rune Guildenhart. It seems *you* are the monster, my friend."

Terran looked to Parisa with desperation. Parisa threw herself at Perseus, who dodged her artfully. The bayonet pressed into Terran's skin, drawing blood. Terran choked, "Use a card, Parisa! We have to get out of here!"

Parisa pulled a card from her pocket and laid it upon her hand. In only a moment, the ground beneath their feet trembled. Something massive rumbled and then an earth-shattering explosion boomed outside of the palace. Fire began to rain down outside the window and Perseus looked at Parisa like he had been shot.

Perseus ran to the balcony on the abandoned floor and looked upward. Whatever Parisa had drawn shook the whole building. Large pieces of debris fell from above and Terran took the opportunity to leap to his feet.

"What was *that*?" Parisa shouted and gripped the wall to prevent herself from falling in the earthquake.

"Grab Perseus if you wish. Let's get out of here." Terran moved to the door and looked down the stairs. "We need to move before more guards come."

Parisa grabbed Perseus by the hand and yanked him toward the stairs. He pulled his hand from her grip and looked at her with wild eyes. "I'm not coming with you."

"Perseus," Parisa demanded, "just stop being an idiot for a

moment."

"You *won't* take me alive!"

"Don't be a hero, Perseus. Do you want me to explain what's going on or not?"

Perseus deliberated for a few breaths, his eyes darting between Terran La'Hall and his best friend. After a moment, Parisa grabbed his hand again. Terran soon came barreling back toward them from the stairwell. "Not that way!"

A flood of guards dashed up the stairs and the three of them backed toward the abandoned balcony. Terran looked out to the ground below. They were still five stories up. Too high to jump. Terran drew a card and slapped it on his hand. "Parisa, draw a card. Now."

Parisa did as she was told, gripping Perseus' hand. The World. Terran took her by the arm and before she could think, he threw himself off the balcony, Perseus and Parisa in tow. They fell, headfirst toward the glass of the greenhouse, hurtling toward the ground. Guards piled onto the balcony to watch their fall. Parisa used her free hand to slap the card onto her arm. The three of them slowed as they neared the glass, and a swirling, circular portal opened beneath them. It swallowed them up and spat them out the other side in a burst of stars and light.

They emerged upright on the other side of the Embassy Palace wall. Perseus gasped, his head spinning, and Terran pointed to the buildings. He took only a moment to slam a new card onto his hand. "Quickly!" he shouted. "To the rooftops!"

"That was incredibly lucky," Parisa gasped as Terran clung to the wall, The Hanged Man helping him scale the wall with ease.

She pointed upward and glared at Perseus, who reeled from the fall. "Come on, Perseus. Let's *go*."

Perseus did as he was told and climbed, Parisa not far behind, and once they were safe on the rooftop the three of them turned back to the palace. The topmost floor came down in a shower of flames, burning as bright as a torch in the night, and it took out several of the other floors below it as it collapsed.

"What card did you use?" Terran gasped.

"The Tower." Parisa replied.

Trust
Terran

The Tavern, August of the Third Year

"You *blew* up the Embassy?"

"I-I didn't do it," Terran stammered. "Parisa was the one who drew the card."

"I said to lay *low!*" The King threw his arms up in frustration and yelled, "You blew up the entire Sovereign's floor! You've waged war!"

Terran said nothing for a while until he pulled the sword out from its sheath. "This is for you."

"What?" The King had turned his back on Terran, but when he spun around, he saw the sword resting in Terran's hands. "I thought that was for you."

"I don't know how to wield a sword. And you're a master swordsman, so take it. My mother would want you to have it."

The King snatched the sword from his hands and looked down the blade. "Well, I hope you're happy," he sneered. "Tomorrow we prepare for war."

"What's the plan?"

"I have my men. We're a hundred strong, but not strong enough to take down the guard. Widow Corine has offered reinforcements. I doubt she's got more than twenty men as well. While the guard is not trained well and they do not have the brightest commanding officers, bodies are bodies. Unless we're smart about it, we're going to lose."

"It'll be a bloodbath."

"Talbot wants a bloodbath, and we won't give it to him. The goal will be a flanking maneuver. We are going to circle around the palace and go in through the back."

"There's no back entra—"

"There is if you blow a hole in the wall."

Terran nodded. "Are you going to be okay?"

"We need to keep our heads level. Do you think Perseus is going to stab us in the back?"

"We're going to just have to find out."

Bewitched
Parisa

The Tavern, August of the Third Year

"Perseus, I'm not under a spell."

Terran had asked Parisa to blindfold her captain when they started to make their way to The King's hideout. He struggled, and Terran eventually resorted to knocking him out. He wanted to stay on the rooftops and argue all night, and Terran would not risk getting caught. They carried him the rest of the way and Parisa tied him to the table like she had been only a month ago.

Perseus smiled cynically and sneered, "How *else* could it be this way? You'd *never* work with The King. You were trained to do otherwise, and what about the blond one? He's a card user, too? You were supposed to *arrest* him, Parisa, not join him. I bet he made you do it."

"No. I joined them by my own free will," Parisa said. She pulled the blindfold from his eyes and showed him her tattoo. The card had stained her skin blue around the area where the tattoo danced across her neck, and the dark blue lines illustrated an image of a dove drinking from a chalice. "My father is a monster. I... I've known that my whole life. I just didn't want to believe it. We have to stop him. The blond boy is Terran La'Hall, the old Sovereign's son. He's not dead. He's been hiding out with The King all this time."

"You're insane. What did they put on your skin?"

"Listen to me. Terran is Rune. He was a spy, using a disguise. You're much safer here, Perseus. If—"

"*Safer?*" Perseus frowned. "I've never been safe in my entire life. Growing up, I wasn't *safe* from starving to death. In training, I wasn't *safe* from losing my family to disease. As an Elite, I'm not *safe* from Talbot's wrath. What makes you think I'll be safe here?"

"Lexus is a good man. We're going to get my father off the throne and *save* the poor, Perseus. Something horrible is going on and I'm almost to the bottom of it. We just need to get him out of the way so we'll—"

"We'll *what*, Parisa? The only way I can keep my family safe is to make sure I have pay in my pocket. Who's going to pay for their food while the government is in shambles? I can't just *abandon* them. And what? You want me to become a brainwashed zombie like *you?*"

Parisa hit him hard. She did not want to, but she did. It made him stop for a moment and she scowled at him. "How dare you. I'm *not* a zombie. Do you know how terrifying this is for me? I have nightmares that my father comes for me in the night to kill me. You know what I've learned? My father killed my mother. He fed her some sort of poison and put her into the wastes to dehydrate to death."

Perseus looked across Parisa's face, hoping to find truth there.

"He's killed dozens to get into a position of power. He probably didn't even love my mother. He wanted to marry her to get into the Embassy. He'll do whatever it takes. My father is going down, Perseus, and when Terran is Sovereign he'll give money to your family! He'll take money from Talbot's private reserves that he's been hoarding and give it to all the families in Atsa and Dza'ya. It will finally be all *right* here."

Perseus did not say anything for a long time and Parisa sighed, "I'm sorry I hit you."

He said nothing.

She hugged him tightly as if an earthquake could come at any moment and rip them apart. She whispered, "I don't want to fight you. I'm worried that if you stay with my father, I'll need to kill you, and I don't want that to happen. I just want this city to be fixed. It's humanity's last chance. We can't blow it." Perseus shook underneath her. She kissed him and sat up. "So, what do you say?"

"Parisa... if this doesn't work, I'll be executed. If I'm executed, my family won't eat. I'm the only one holding them up right now. I thought Terran La'Hall was dead. We stopped looking for him months ago."

"I know."

"Good on you for having faith in him, I guess, but Talbot is powerful. If there's even a slight chance that you'll lose, I'm off the team. Once Talbot gets the high ground, I will change sides."

"How could you?"

"I love you, but my family has to come first."

She nodded in response but said nothing.

"You're not bewitched?"

"No," Parisa laughed, sadness in her throat. "I just... woke up."

"What does... what does the tattoo mean?"

Parisa cut his ropes. "The Page of Cups represents me, or something. I don't really understand it all yet, myself. All I know is that magick is real and I blew up a tower. It's... a lot."

"Can everyone do magick? Could *I* do magick?"

"I could go get Terran to—"

"Already on it." Terran's voice trailed into the room as he opened the door. He jogged down the small flight of stairs holding a brand-new deck of cards. Parisa wondered how long he had been eavesdropping there.

"I don't want them," Perseus refused and put his hands up. "I'm not one of you. You may have convinced Parisa to change sides, but I won't. I'm good with a gun, thanks."

Terran nodded and returned the cards to his pocket. "Are you sure? One touch of these cards will reveal to you the truth if you believe in them."

"No. I don't want them. I won't have the mark of a traitor on my neck."

"Sure. That's fine. I'll go return them. The King's prepared you a room next to Parisa's. You may do as you like around the tavern except leave. The King will brief us tomorrow. Get some sleep."

"You can't order me around. As Captain of the Elite—"

"You're no captain here," Terran laughed. "It's okay. Let

your guard down a little. It'll help you clear your head."

"Good *night*, Terran," Parisa pressed. Terran raised his eyebrows and left the room. Parisa kissed Perseus on the cheek after Terran left. "I love you, Perseus."

Perseus' face turned bright red and he gazed at her, wide-eyed. "Y-You... you what?"

"I said I love you, you dummy."

"T-Thank you, I..."

"You have to trust me. Can you do that?"

"I'm terrified."

"Me too, but we'll get through this together."

"Am I *really* going to have to take orders from The King? He's weird and theatrical and I hate it."

"He's nice, I promise."

"And I'm a prisoner here?"

"I was for a little while, too. You'll be allowed more freedom as soon as The King feels like you won't betray him."

"I... should get to sleep." Perseus stood and stretched his legs, rubbing his wrists where the rope had restrained him. "I'll see you in the morning, then."

Parisa grabbed Perseus' hand and stopped him before he left the room. "Perseus?"

"Yes?"

She kissed him on the mouth and ran her fingers through his dark hair. When she pulled away, she locked him in a tight embrace. "I love you."

He hugged her as if time no longer mattered. "I love you, too."

Warfare
Terran

The Tavern, August of the Third Year

"At least *one* good thing came from this," The King muttered over a blueprint of the palace. "At least it's not winter yet. Fighting in the cold is the *worst*."

"Right," Terran laughed. "Are you solid on a plan?"

"It's as I said before. You, Perseus, Parisa and I will circle around the back and blow a hole in the throne room. From there, we hunt down Talbot. He won't dare try and walk through hundreds of my soldiers. We'll have him trapped like a rat."

"I still need to find the thing that's on the papers my parents left me."

"Well, read it. Let's hear it."

Terran pulled the paper from the envelope in his vest pocket and read it. "Truth lies with loyal friends. Loyalty comes from being true."

"Oh!" The King gasped like he had heard something obvious. "The people, Terran! Of course. If we overthrow Talbot, how do you know the people won't think you a tyrant as well? We need to get the people's support! A few extra hands with swords in them couldn't hurt either when we're storming the castle. My plan is to go to the Atsa park, make a statement and an announcement, and then strike."

"Lexus."

"Yes?"

"What happens if I don't want to be Sovereign?"

The King turned to look at Terran with shock in his eyes. "What do you mean, you don't want to be Sovereign?"

"I'm not the right person to do this. Talbot spent the better half of two years terrorizing anyone with skin a shade darker than an egg and I don't know if it's right for my pale face to be the one that leads the people. We need someone who's familiar with both worlds."

"Are you suggesting Parisa?"

"I'm suggesting Parisa."

"Hm." The King scratched at the bristle that had begun to grow on his jaw after days of unrest. "You'll have to do the convincing, Terran. Either way, they need to see you're alive and that you stand with her. Most of the people will recognize your face and with the cards in your hand they'll associate you with me, which is good. I've been good to them. I'll gather all the men I have, and we will go with you. Now, get out there. You, Perseus, me, and Parisa. They'll see that everyone is upset with Talbot and it will inspire a revolution."

Terran dashed out of The King's office into Parisa's temporary room. She had not yet woken up and Terran paused for a moment. He felt bad for deciding to wake her. After waiting for only a second longer, he knocked on the door. "Get up," he said. "We have some motivational work to do."

Parisa rubbed the sleep from her eyes and sat up. "What kind of work?"

"Get in your armor. We need to go have a conversation with some folks. I'll be back in ten minutes."

Terran stepped down the hall to Perseus' room, which had been a spare closet only hours ago. He was up and awake, already fastening his armor. Terran knocked on the door and said, "Good. You're up. We're going to the park in Atsa to try and gather more followers."

"I can't do that," the captain replied, curtly.

"What?"

"I can't be seen in public with you. If Talbot catches wind of that, I'm done for if you lose."

Terran leaned on the doorframe and let out a long sigh. "We won't lose."

"You're positive?"

Terran drew from his deck. The VI of Wands was what rested on the top. After looking at the card for a moment, he said, "We have reached an important milestone. We've harnessed our strengths and talents and have made it through chaos. Yes, things are... messy, but if we believe in who we are, we'll make it to the finish line."

"I don't believe that paper can tell the future."

"I didn't believe that paper could set me on fire, help me fly, and start revolutions, but here we are. Now, come on."

Terran stepped away from the room and fidgeted with his new armor. The King waited with him in the tavern until Perseus and Parisa appeared, ready for combat. They strode through Atsa with pride, heads high, bright colors showing. Perseus looked terrified, but Parisa gripped his hand as they moved down the streets. Even The King had his hood down. He wore emerald green, and his red hair caught in the morning sunlight.

When they got to the park, Terran came to a statue that Talbot had built of himself when he first became Sovereign and drew a card. He laid it on his hand and felt himself overwhelmed with power. The Strength card was perhaps the most straightforward in the entire deck. Terran grabbed the statue by its base, pulling it up from the ground, and crushing the silver it was made from in his bare hands. As it fell, the people around the area all stopped to look at what was being done. Terran swallowed hard and stood on the pedestal that remained.

"I... I don't really know how to start," he called to a now gathering crowd. "Gather around! I don't know if you know me, but I am Terran La'Hall, son of the last Sovereign." Terran paused as the crowd gasped and muttered, a now sizeable group milling in the center of the park. They all looked as though they had seen a ghost. "Many thought me dead, but I'm not! I survived the horrible fate which befell my parents. This means that Talbot is currently ruling in my place, which is against the law! If he knew I was here speaking out against him, he would surely kill me."

Terran read the crowd. Public speaking had always made him nervous, and his mouth felt dry in the hot desert sun. The King stepped up behind him and placed a hand on his shoulder.

"Go on," he whispered. "You're doing great."

"He is performing treacherous acts behind the backs of the people and I – we have come to stop it. I cannot do this alone! We have to do this together. We need to stand up to this tyrant! He killed my parents, has illegally taken the throne, and is choking out the voice of the people!" Terran jumped as the crowd roared. They had been waiting for this for a long time. "I cannot simply storm the castle and take him off the throne; otherwise, I am no better than he. I need *your* support, *your* trust!"

"Take up your arms!" The King raised his chin and shouted. The crowd cheered for a familiar face. "Help us end Talbot's schemes! No more ridiculous taxes! No more starving children! No more guards beating the innocent! No more seizing of crops! No more burning of houses! No more eviction! Stand up!"

"Talbot killed my parents," Terran continued. "He seized the throne by means of murder and must be punished."

"Even we stand up!" Parisa shouted to the large crowd that now gathered. Folks on errand runs from Naa'a milled about among the Atsa crowd, and a few guards stopped to listen. "The captain and I are sick of his games! Please, grab what weapons you can and follow us to the palace. We will make our voices heard."

Those who were already with The King stood silently in their white robes and waited. Terran froze where he stood, now the head of a mob. The King clasped Terran's shoulder and said, "It's us, Terran."

"Us?"

"You, me, Esmond, Vena, Parisa. We're revolutionaries. Now all that's left is to storm the walls."

Something brushed Terran's arm as a stranger stepped forward to gauge the crowd. "Good work, Your Majesty."

When Terran looked to his right, Widow Corine stood there, her hands tied and a blade on her hip. She smiled, the red stain on her face fresh. Behind her, two dozen people clad in blood red robes readied their weapons.

"Widow Corine," The King said. "You actually came."

"My god called, and I answered. The Truth will be uncovered on this day." She turned toward her group of religious zealots and raised her hands. "My doves! Today we fly to the palace walls to remove a lie-spreading tyrant from the throne. Today, The King is in charge. Our god's words of truth carry him on silver wings. Listen to his orders, and fight for our freedom!"

People cheered and Terran's heart pounded in his chest. Citizens would die today; he was sure of it. They would fall upon the swords of guards who knew no better. They could not afford to lose. Together, The King and Terran La'Hall stood in a milling crowd of unrest, ready to take down the man who had murdered his parents. Terran stammered, "We're really just going to waltz in?"

"Yep," The King replied. "Walk right in."

"No master plan?"

"Nope."

"No magickal words of wisdom?"

"Nope."

Terran swallowed thickly and looked down at his feet in the sand. "I—"

"Terran." The King placed his hands on Terran's shoulders,

the two of them a solid, unwavering thing among the flow of the crowd. "Don't be scared. Everything will work out in the end."

"I don't want this to become a bloodbath."

"We'll do our best to keep that from happening."

"What if... what if we fail?"

"We won't fail."

"But what if we do?"

Terran began to shake as he looked at the crowd, now armed with what weapons they had. Pitchforks and hoes were the main bludgeoning tool of choice. Terran feared for them. Perseus clung to Parisa so tightly he looked as though he feared Parisa would take flight, like a bird. The only one unphased by the unrest was Widow Corine.

"Then our success is not in the cards." The King clapped Terran hard on the back. "You know, you're the best responsibility I've ever had."

"I'm glad to have been such a burden." Terran turned to the crowd and raised his fist, shouting, "Let's take back Segeno! Give it back to the people!"

Retribution
Parisa

The Palace, August of the Third Year

Ink seeped into Parisa's skin, the blue puddle travelling across her hand in the shape of a wheel as the magick of the cards filled her veins. The world around her slowed to a crawl – Perseus, The King, everyone moving at a fraction of the speed that they had before. She had been given time. Her eyes darted upward to meet the face of her father, who screamed on a balcony above it all, hollering orders at his men. His face strained in the chaos and his skin reddened in the tension of the moment. For a second and only a second, she pitied him because she knew he was going to die.

In slow motion and screaming with all their might, the two mobs clashed with each other. A hundred guards came at a hundred citizens, weapons colliding and armor glinting. Parisa flew like a shooting star from soldier to soldier, using the back of her hand, her knees, her elbows, anything beside her knife to subdue her enemies. She disarmed them, grabbing as many weapons as she could and running them behind the front lines of the common folk. She knew because she had trained with them that the guards were useless without their precious training and their guns. One after another fell like flies as she flew, unsure of how long her card would last. She spun to duck under a sword that cut over her head, the King attacking with unrestrained rage at a guard behind her, six swords floating at his back. Terran screamed something at her father, though she could not make out what he said.

And then the card was done. The magick faded and she stood, exposed, in the middle of the battlefield.

"Your Majesty!" she cried. "I put weapons behind the front lines!"

"To arms!" The King cried. "Use their own weapons against them!"

Bullets flew from their side of the conflict, now. Everyday people dropped with holes in their chests and blood on the grass as they were cut down. The gaping hole that The King had blown into the throne room still burned as they fought. Parisa's hands trembled as she drew another card. IV of Cups. The King defended her as she recharged, his movements smooth and solid, filled with intention and purpose. He and Perseus cleared a path to the doors so they could get to Talbot before he had time to retreat.

"Don't worry!" Terran screamed. "We can take them!"

Parisa spun to find him defending a group of now unarmed civilians. He thrust a hand out, his palm glowing hot white with magick, a blast of scalding hot light blowing back a row of Talbot's men. Parisa's skin prickled with magick, and she looked to find her fingers glowing with mystery and an effect she did not know. She snapped and nothing happened, so she ignored what the cards had given her and fought her own military peers with her dagger. Someone grabbed at her collar, and she choked, dragged back by someone much larger than her. Whoever it was put the barrel of their gun against her head, and she twisted to get away from them. Perseus threw his fist into the guard's face and Parisa hit the grass. She jammed her metal-plated boot into the guard's shin, and he fell to his knees, stunned by everything that had happened.

And then another grappled Perseus. Parisa rose as fast as she was able and jammed her fingers into Commander Creven's eyes, hoping that something would happen, something to save Perseus. The commander froze, paralyzed by something that she could not see, and in an instant, he began to swat at himself. He panicked and slapped at his skin as though thousands of bugs that Parisa could not see crawled up and down his arms.

"Damned witch!" he screamed. "Get them off! Get them *off!*"

Guards and citizens alike fell in pools of blood that stained the white marble of the courtyard, splattered upon the green grass and blue flowers in the greenhouse. Friends screamed as people they had known their whole lives fell and Talbot watched from his balcony as Parisa and Terran helped clear the way. He paused for a moment, Parisa froze, trying to anticipate his next move, and then he retreated inside.

The tide turned. Parisa slammed her hands into every face she could find, and guards screamed and ran, left and right, with no care for their comrades. Widow Corine moved through the group like a shadow, her face expressionless and red smeared across her skin. Her followers walked through the fallen bodies like walking through flowers. They were surprisingly adept, using daggers and other religious objects to take care of the guards. They stood in front of citizens and protected them from blows, and Parisa watched one follower fall in defense of another. Loyal. She would give them that. In one large exhale, a Segenite resident stabbed a guard who collapsed into the grass. The King turned and pointed to the glass doors of the throne room.

"Go!" he shouted. "Before he can escape!"

The four of them bashed their way through the palace doors, blood smeared on Perseus' face and Terran's hands still hot. The glass shattered as they entered, followed by Widow Corine and her servants. Parisa expected a chase. Her father must have retreated to somewhere secret, his war room perhaps, and they would—

Talbot was there, sitting on his throne alone next to the rubble that The King had created. He gazed at a spot on the floor, eyes wide and red. Parisa did not even recognize him, with huge bags under his eyes and the way his hands gripped the armrests of the throne, so hard his knuckles whitened. The only other soldiers left alive followed them into the hall and Elite guards flanked Talbot, unwilling to let him die. They stood as a wall between the remaining surviving citizens. Parisa watched them run, returning to their families, not ready to take those odds.

"Well, look at you," Talbot sneered. "You and a bunch of pitchfork-wielding baboons. I knew you had been hiding in a rat's hole somewhere, La'Hall."

"I was *right* under your nose," Terran laughed. He bent

over in a slow, sarcastic bow and Parisa gripped her dagger as Elite guards twitched to stop him if necessary. "Can you keep a *secret*, Talbot? I *killed* my way to get here. Isn't that what you said?"

"*You!*" Talbot rose from his throne and cried, "*You* were Rune Guildenhart?"

"That crown is coming off," Terran rasped. "You're going to fall and you're going to fall hard."

The King turned to Perseus and Parisa and commanded, "Keep the Elites out of our way. We've got Talbot."

Perseus and Parisa flew into battle, against their own comrades, some boys that they had eaten lunches with. They had cut each other's hair, stitched each other's clothes. Parisa felt a hole form in her heart as they blindly attacked with full force. One man after another fell or ran, thanks to the power of Parisa's card. Talbot drew the sword he had at his side. "Why do you two never *die*?"

Talbot leapt at The King with fury, unexpected skill backing his blows. Parisa paused for a breath and watched her father fight. She had never seen him do anything of the sort, and his technique astonished her. His footwork solid and his strikes precise, he and The King danced across marble. Parisa reentered the fray as Perseus tapped out and Terran joined her but froze. She looked to his hands to find they had lost their light and that his card had put itself back in his deck. Frantically, he reached into his pocket for another card, but an Elite slashed at his hand and prevented him from doing so.

Someone lunged at Parisa, and she dove out of the way. One of the boys who had laughed at her on that first day of training, now a man, reached forward with a hand in an attempt to grapple her, but she slid out of the way just in time. Her fingertips still glowed, and she jammed her hands into his face, spots of glowing residue left behind on his skin when she jumped away. Immediately the soldier began to cry, and he screamed out, covering his head and ears, ducking away from something she could not see. It tortured her to watch someone suffer in that way, but it stopped him from doing something stupid.

"Parisa! Help!" Terran called.

A bullet whizzed past Parisa's head. One guard shot at her, and another drew his combat dagger, stabbing at her as they moved across the throne room. She went to touch him but found her card had faded as well. Her dagger flew with passion as she battled, and she frowned at him as a bullet grazed her arm. She looked to Terran to make sure he was still alive. He dodged blows, still breathing, and she called, "I'm a little busy!"

The next few moments happened quickly. Perseus' own soldiers ganged up on him and one took a large chunk out of his leg with a sword. Perseus fell to his knees as the other soldiers put their swords to his neck. Parisa ran to his side after she felled the soldiers that pursued her but was caught in a trap as two more ambushed her, pinning her to the floor. Most of the civilians had either died or fled, but Widow Corine stood tall among her followers, those who had been slain lying at her feet but those who still stood frozen like statues. An Elite put a gun to Widow Corine's head, and she smiled. It was over.

Chrysalis
Terran

The Palace, August of the Third Year

The King's card evaporated, his swords exploding into a burst of light and Talbot kicked him roughly in the stomach. In mere moments, Talbot knocked him to his knees and put the tip of his blade to The King's chest. The soldier that Terran faced raised his blade to kill him when Talbot held up his hand to signal his guard to stop. "Wait! Don't kill anyone! Not just yet."

The soldier sighed in disappointment.

"*You,*" Talbot spat at The King with such rage that Terran was sure he'd bore a hole right through The King's armor. "Lexus. I should have known you'd be back."

"You couldn't have killed me *that* easily, Talbot, and you should've guessed that I would have found some hole to crawl into," The King replied, playfulness on his tongue.

"You *ruined* my life," Talbot scowled. "I was *trying* to make a better Embassy, but you were *always* in the *way!*"

"Because what you're doing isn't *right!* You're choking

people like a snake!"

"So what? So what if I am? I lived in the *gutter* my whole life. I only got pulled out by chance."

"And you killed the woman who did it."

"Why?" Parisa demanded, tears in her eyes.

"Stuff it," Talbot replied. He looked as though she had just asked him about the weather. "I knew the moment that you were born that you'd be just as much of a problem as she was."

Terran looked to Parisa, who swallowed her tears and her disgust, her face pressed into the floor.

"I want to watch you *squirm*, Lexus." Talbot sliced The King's armor off by the straps, piece by piece. "*Squirm* like I squirmed my whole life. No armor. No *magick tricks*."

Talbot searched The King's coats until he found the hidden pocket, and he pulled the cards out, accidentally dropping them on the floor. He stooped, the tip of his sword still dangerously close to The King's heart, and picked up the cards. His eyes tore over the paper, curious, confused, but Talbot remained totally unaffected. He could not use them.

"This is *all*?" Talbot demanded. "This is what you've used to beat me back all of these years?" He set the cards down onto the ground and smiled at The King. "What are you without your cards?"

"No!" Widow Corine cried. "You know not what you do, destroying an ancient magick like that! The gods will come down on you, Talbot, and you will upset the balance of life and d—"

The Elite that guarded her pulled his trigger and a bullet went through her, ending Widow Corine faster than her heart could have beat. She slumped to the floor in a heap of red and lay still there.

"Widow," one of her servants whispered. "By the Goddess, go in peace and find Truth."

Talbot rolled his eyes and muttered, "Seems even gods can't protect you fools."

Talbot's sword shot down into the cards. A flash of light flooded the room but soon a blue substance the consistency of blood oozed out of the cards, turning orange as it seeped across the floor, melting into the cracks of the marble. Talbot ripped the sword from the deck and wiped the orange liquid off with The King's tunic, staining the fabric. The King smiled with a pang of sadness etched into the corners of his mouth and a tear twinkling in his eye as he raised his sword. "All right, Talbot. No more magick. Let's fight, man on man."

"It'll be my pleasure."

The King's silver, shining sword almost sparked as it clashed with Talbot's. They fought for what seemed like hours and Terran realized how good of a swordsman Talbot truly was. He must have trained for this day. As the battle drew on, The King began to gain the upper hand as Talbot tired. The two of them danced, like a snake and a hawk, across the floor, evenly matched. Terran's breath hitched, and his heart pounded. Lexus would win.

And then a soldier cocked his rifle.

The bullet whizzed past The King's head, and he turned to see where it had come from to defend himself. Talbot's fist hit his stomach. Blow after blow, Talbot bashed the King with his fist until, finally, he drove his sword through The King's heart.

The King looked up at Talbot in shock, then down at the sword in his body. He smiled at Terran and chuckled, "Huh. Go figure."

As The King fell to the ground, Terran kneed the soldier in front of him in the shin. He ripped the sword from the soldier's hands and stabbed him, running toward where The King lay. He knelt down at The King's side, where orange and red blood mixed on the white stone beneath him. Talbot began to approach but Terran raised his sword, hot tears in his eyes. "Don't you *touch* him! Don't you *dare* come near him!"

"Terran…" The King coughed and red stained his emerald robes, coming from him in waterfalls. Talbot heeded Terran's warning and moved away from them, smiling and waiting for a better moment. Salt in the wound. "Hey," The King choked. "It's okay…"

"No, it's not." Terran was not afraid to cry. He sobbed and tears bubbled down his face, causing dark splotches on Lexus' clothes. "It's n-not okay… you're one of my only friends. You're the only one I have left."

The King laughed, "I'm a part of the problem. I'm from the old world. You need to build up this place, Terran. Repair it. Living… living just wasn't in my cards today." He reached for his deck and pulled up a card, orange, magick blood dripping down his fingertips. The card was of a woman holding two scales; only she had a gaping hole in her chest from where the sword had punctured it. The King took Terran's hand and squeezed it, holding it as tightly as he could. "Justice."

Before Talbot could react, Terran drew a card and slapped

it onto the back of his hand. An immense power flowed into his body, as if he was open to the power of the cosmic universe filling him up from the inside, but this was not a righteous power. Terran felt a void open in his heart as if all love he had ever had, every empathetic fiber of his being, had been sucked into a sinkhole. This was a mean, cold, cruel power. Talbot rushed him with his sword, but Terran took the blade with his bare hands, slicing his skin, snapped the sword in half, and grabbed Talbot by the throat. His eyes burned hot in his skull; they glowed and crimson light reflected onto Talbot's skin. The other guards went to attack but Terran looked at them calmly as they approached. "Drop your weapons," he ordered.

They all froze. Every single guard in the room dropped their swords.

"What are you *doing*?" Talbot screamed. "You fools!"

"Leave the room."

All the soldiers obeyed.

Talbot wriggled in Terran's hands. "Please kill me... if you're going to do anything. I would rather die than live to see how you tear apart what I built."

"*Kill* you?" Terran gritted his teeth. Hot tears still streamed down his face. "*Kill* you? I will not *stoop* to your *level*. You *murderer*! No... do you know what it feels like to lose everything you have? Of course you don't... you don't have a heart. Allow me to educate you." Terran knocked the crown off Talbot's head. "What lies outside the walls of Segeno?"

"Nothing."

"Nothing... but what?"

"Settlements, mines."

"And?"

"Desert."

"That's right. A ruthless, scorching desert."

The room darkened as if Terran's rage ate the sun. Talbot had broken him. "I want you to leave the city," Terran barked. "You are never to speak to anyone again, not even a cry for help. You are to walk out into the desert and never stop walking. You are not to eat, you are not to sleep, and you will walk. You will let the desert consume you, and you will be constantly reminded of all the people you have hurt, all the wrongs you have done. The memories will haunt you like ghosts, ghosts that will make you scream in the middle of the night and make you wish you were never born. Now go."

Terran dropped Talbot and he began to walk in silence out into the streets of Naa'a, where Terran would never have to see him again. Widow Corine's servants parted for him like a split sea and Talbot stepped over the bodies of his fallen guards as he left until he was out of their sight. After Terran's card had worn off, and he returned to reality, he made his way over to The King, rested his head onto The King's chest, and cried.

Sovereign
Terran

The Palace, August of the Third Year

"He was the *true* king. Braver than any man I knew, Lexus was more to me than a friend. He was a father. He would always stop to help those in need and he saved me from falling into despair. I bless his journey and I hope the spirits are kind."

The royal tomb underneath the palace echoed Terran's words as if it had its own soul, beautiful and melancholy: sanctuary. Stone, tall, gothic arches crested the ceiling and torches lit the tombs of those in the Embassy who had passed on. Stone and marble mausoleums that marked where his parents lay had just been carved, but the coffins inside sat empty. Terran did not even know where their bodies had been discarded. The room made him somber, and he hated the place. His father, his father's father, and their fathers before them all lay there. Silence was a disease. Terran watched as The King was lowered into his stone prison where he would rest forever with sleeping warriors.

Terran threw in a white rose, as did others, and turned

away from the mausoleum. His heart ached with an indescribable sadness. He had no tears left. What he felt passed as pain but may have been some sort of sullen apathy. He didn't know. As he looked at the others, he could not comfort them. Vena wept silently, oceans and waterfalls of tears running down her face as if she threatened to cry away the entire water supply of Segeno. Occasionally, a loud sob would break forth from her mouth. Parisa and Perseus held each other and could not pull their eyes away from the coffin.

Esmond stood in front of the group and ushered them into the throne room after everyone had time to grieve. Days passed and people moved through the palace like ghosts. Terran stood for hours in Talbot's old bedroom, instructing his new servants to throw everything out. He would have artisans in Dza'ya make new furniture, sheets, everything. He didn't want any remnant of Talbot in his life. Until the bed was ready, he slept on the floor. After he had settled, Esmond encouraged him to make the next step in his transition to being the ruler of Segeno. It didn't feel right, but he had no choice. It was time.

"I don't want to be Sovereign," Terran had confided in Parisa before he stepped before the throne. "It doesn't feel right."

"You'll do great."

"What if... what if you did it?"

"I can't, Terran. I won't sit in the chair my father did."

Terran moved in front of his throne, the eyes of thousands of citizens of Segeno on him as he paused there. Widow Corine's servants rose at the front, heading the crowd of those who had helped take Segeno back from a tyrant. Sunlight streamed down through the windows and gave the room a heavenly air, but Terran did not feel enlightened. He was to be coronated that day. He spoke against it, but Esmond insisted. The sooner that Terran became the Sovereign, the sooner he could fix the messes that Talbot had made. The throne room fell silent as Terran stood there. Nausea bubbled up in his stomach, and he did not want to speak to or look at anyone. Esmond took the crown that had been worn by his parents' killer and placed it onto Terran's head. "Before you stands the true Sovereign of Segeno!" he proclaimed.

People clapped, and a few bowed. Terran bowed his head in response. He did not want to make it a spectacle. The King was more important than he was. The job he now undertook was more important.

Soon, people began to file out. The event was done and now the real work began. Esmond looked to Terran with empathy in his eyes. "So," he asked. "What are you going to do now?"

"I'm going to run this city the best I can... I know I'm young, but I'm aware of what I have to fix," Terran replied and turned to his throne. "Run it better. Clean it up."

"We're here for you. I'm sure your parents would be very proud of you. Lexus... Lexus *is* proud."

"Thank you."

Terran remained in the throne room even after Esmond left and, after all had gone, walked back to the tomb. Justice. Truth. What did it mean? What had it ever meant? This did not feel like Justice. When he arrived, he looked desolately at Lexus' coffin, a broken smile on his face. He pulled his cards from his pocket. There had to be something that he could do.

He shuffled and drew, pulling a card from the top. When he flipped it over, his jaw dropped. The King of Swords. Tears formed in his eyes, and he held the card to his chest. He sobbed, his cries echoing off the stone. What would he do with the card? He could not use it. His deck was not even supposed to allow him to draw such a card. He looked at the card again, the friendly face of the little king etched into its surface, and then to the stone on Lexus' grave. He was not alone. Terran would never be alone. He held the card close to him again and looked to where The King lay.

"I won't let you down. Rest in peace, friend. See you in a lifetime."

About the Author

I'm Tycho, and I love storytelling! I'm incredibly passionate about writing, art, and anything that allows me to create my own worlds. My goal is to write dreamy fiction for all ages that is unique, inspiring, and imaginative. I want my books to instill wonderment in the reader. I like to write about themes that include coming of age, magic realism, identity, relationships, and bullying. My books are intended for readers ages eight to twenty-five, and are meant to connect the world of the fantastical to everyday life.

I currently live in Colorado and work in publishing.

Visit TYCHODORIAN.COM to learn more.

Books by this Author

Braidy von Althuis and the Pesky Pest Controller
Braidy von Althuis and the Gullible Ghost Hunter
Braidy von Althuis and the Dastardly Djinn
Braidy von Althuis and the Changeling Children
Braidy von Althuis and the Final Fight
Court of Snakes: This Desert Cage
Heaven's Equal
One Pale Reflection
King of Dust

Special Thanks

Thank you to Kickstarter Backers:

Cynthia Dwelis

Marc Dwelis

Airic Fenn

Anna Margaret

James Owen Lowe and Mandy Wiswell

Kimberly Griego

Kelly Balding

Jase Kelly

Belle J.

Paul Kelly

Catherine Weir

Nate Coyle

Damion A Brown

Denis Graham

John Dwelis

Od Dwelis

Aunt Karen

Dr. Rebecca Ramirez-McKinley

@jaecobmusic

Jamie Frederick

Rhyknowscerious

Laine

An extra special thanks to my Patrons:

Cynthia Dwelis
Jamie Frederick
BluLibrarian
Catherine Thurston
SashPrime

Did you like this book? Please **review it on Amazon and Goodreads**! Your review is the best way for me to get exposure. I appreciate it, and I love you!

Want to help create more books and art?
Visit:
https://ko-fi.com/tycho_dorian

www.ingramcontent.com/pod-product-compliance
Lightning Source LLC
Chambersburg PA
CBHW031341260626
47153CB00022B/1826